"James Grethe is one of those rare people who is a critical thinker with the ability to think outside of the box. As a writer, he transfers those qualities to Michael and throws in a large dose of honor and "kick ass" to boot! Just when you think that you have everything figured out, you realize...you don't. Enjoy the ride!"

—*Jeff Foxworthy*

MICHAEL:
OPERATION LIBERTE'

by
James Grethe

Order this book online at www.trafford.com
or email orders@trafford.com

Most Trafford titles are also available at major online book retailers.

Note for Librarians: A cataloguing record for this book is available from Library
and Archives Canada at www.collectionscanada.ca/amicus/index-e.html

Printed in Victoria, BC, Canada.

isbn: 978-1-4269-1526-0 (sc)
isbn: 978-1-4269-1525-3 (dj)

Library of Congress Control Number: 2009935799

*Our mission is to efficiently provide the world's finest, most comprehensive book publishing
service, enabling every author to experience success. To find out how to publish your book, your
way, and have it available worldwide, visit us online at www.trafford.com*

Trafford rev. 09/17/2009

 www.trafford.com

North America & international
toll-free: 1 888 232 4444 (USA & Canada)
phone: 250 383 6864 ♦ fax: 812 355 4082

DEDICATION

To My Wondrous Wife Victoria, and
To My Equally Wondrous Daughters Pamela Gregg and Kathryn Glenn

Contents

CHAPTER ONE

Juantibes Cafe

A s he walked along the avenue Guy de Maupassant, he looked up at the azure blue sky. He rolled his shoulders back and stretched a little. The street was filled with tourists again, but this spring not so many Americans. The Americans were staying home because of the terrorist concerns about foreign travel. At the moment it seemed to please him that there were not so many US tourists. He stepped lively across the avenue, not hurrying too quickly and not tarrying too slowly. Either, he always felt, could be his undoing. Away from the beach, and along the avenue cafes, his gate was a little more relaxed and a little less tense. His exposure on the beach side was an element of which he was always aware. Over the years he had developed excellent peripheral awareness, and even in his 'retirement' he could never be too cautious.

A few yards ahead was the Juantibes Cafe. His afternoon delight in the sunshine watching people and traffic. It was a small thing, but it was 'his' ritual. He would read the Telegraph and the Herald, and occasionally the USA Today, with his Campari and soda crowned with a refreshing slice of French orange. A moment passed, then he moved forward again, examining the area, not telegraphing his intentions, just quietly viewing the scene before him. The closer he approached, the slower his gate, until he was on the front corner with the whole setting before him. Then, as usual, he turned slowly around and glanced about himself for any signs which might be unusual. Nothing caught his eye. He looked back across the outside tables. Still nothing. Then he stepped forward one more time.

At that moment, almost as the same ritual which takes place every afternoon, he was home in the Cap d'Antibes district. Misser Joe spied him and motioned toward the table in the outdoor area along the sidewalk. It was 'his' table saved by Misser Joe, everyday between two and three for this special person. He stood for a moment, acknowledging the Maitre'd. Then he proceeded through the other tables to 'his' table. This was a table not too close to the front walk and not too far to the rear against the back wall. It was his place to be near the rear, but with enough space in the front so as not to impede his quick departure if necessary.

"Bonjour, Monsieur Michael!"

"Bonjour, Misser Joe," he replied quietly.

In the beginning, when they first met, the Maitre'd had tried to be 'American' and introduced himself as Mr. Joe, which came out 'Misser Joe'. It stuck forever after that. They were friends. And although the language was always somewhat stilted in mixed pigeon English and pigeon French, they were able to communicate. The Apartment and the Juantibes Cafe were his homes when in the south of France.

'It was a good afternoon', Michael was thinking, 'one of those truly azure skies that the French Chamber of Commerce likes to take pictures of and post in brochures all over the world. It is that kind of day in the South of France.'

He looked up from his Campari and mused for the moment about the news in the papers and of the troubles everywhere. Nothing changes so much as it stays the same, and that is the only change, he thought. Once and awhile he had to come up just for the view, or in case there was something afoul on the beachfront along the street. If he kept his head in the newsprint too long, it made him uncomfortable.

This time, almost as his second nature, something caught his attention. He slowly put down the newspaper, a trained and controlled action. It was never his belief that anything should be done by reaction. Man must function by 'action' and never by 'reaction'. He felt that in reaction, the opposition has the advantage, while in action by his design, he has control of all the moves. He tried never to react quickly to any situation. Instead he would deliberately, even though sometimes it took conscious effort to talk to himself, take control of his moves.

As he looked across the cafe, there was Misser Joe talking with someone. Obviously they were discussing him. He shifted slightly. The Walther PPK lodged in his belt in the small of his back had over the years almost become part of his anatomy. Yet when these feelings arose, the gun was as bulky as a canon. He shifted to give his left hand the room it needed in case there was some sudden move that required his attention.

Misser Joe left the stranger and pushed his way through the tables. A half smile and half frown plastered the expression on the face of Maitre'd. He looked ahead, then away, then back again, as he pushed toward the table. It was time for some kind of explanation. Neither of the two men spoke much of the other's language, and that could be good, and it could be bad. They didn't bother each other with gossip, yet there were times when talk was necessary, like now.

"Um sorries, Sir. I am difficult now." Misser Joe paused and looked back over his shoulder at the stranger. His face turned back forward again. "Tat man," gesturing over his shoulder, "has look for you long time. He knew more tan me of you. He mus talk to you."

Misser Joe's eyes were wide with anxiety and concern. He wanted the whole thing not to have happened. Not with his friend who came everyday to the special table and read his English newspapers. He did not want to have to disturb him. But he did not know what to do. His eyes began to plead a little, as though he was explaining that he was caught in the middle and had to do this.

"Misser Joe," Michael said slowly and deliberately, not losing the stranger from his peripheral vision as he talked. He would not look at the person outside the cafe, that would consume his attention. Instead he lightly looked at Misser Joe, but knew every shift of the other person. "I come here almost every afternoon I am at the Apartment." Misser Joe nodded. "I come here for two reasons. The second reason," and he held up his index finger, "is because of the Campari and my newspaper and you." Misser Joe nodded again. "The first reason," and then he showed his thumb, "is because I like this location along the Juan les Pins beaches and the pretty girls who are topless." He sat even more upright, never losing the vision of the stranger. He rolled his shoulders back, as though stretching and flexing muscles, but only making certain his position was clear. "Now, what if," and he spoke slowly to try to make himself understood, "I don't like this person, and then I never come back to your cafe!"

"No, no, please don't say tat!" Misser Joe shifted and looked back over his shoulder at the stranger. "I um your friend, but" and he paused with difficulty, "please talk to this man." He turned his eyes down.

There was a long period of silence between the two men. It was an intrusion, and as always, perhaps a dangerous one. Misser Joe really did not know the extent of how dangerous it could be, except that there was a stranger and it was disturbing the afternoon tranquility.

It would be alright to speak to him, but Misser Joe should not ever do this again. Misser Joe nodded, half smiling with relief. He pushed his way through the tables toward the stranger.

The person standing out on the sidewalk of the avenue was stocky and light complexioned, and did not seem to be French, perhaps German or Dutch. Michael watched as the two men talked and gestured toward him. He shifted again, making certain that he had the advantage if necessary. A thought crossed his mind to stand up and move out toward the street. That would not be smart. If this was a setup, then the moment he stood up, he became a bigger target for someone else. That thought made him look slowly about the avenue and into the faces of many of the people standing and strolling. But he never lost the vision of the man with Misser Joe. The light complexioned man started across the cafe toward him.

Don't give him all your attention, he thought, stay alert and glance about yourself. He knew that if it was a setup, this stranger coming toward him would be to capture his primary interest and make him an available target for someone else.

"My name is Marcel, Marcel Akmed," the stranger said as he arrived at the table, extending his right hand in salutation.

Michael looked up at Marcel, then down at the hand. His eyes were now on the whole of Marcel, but his peripheral vision was conscious of as much as possible around the cafe. No handshake, and no full attention to whatever it was that he had to say. It would sound paranoid, but the years of his experience had proven otherwise. Cheap shots and cheap setups in too many locations over the years make any strange greeting seem suspicious.

"Sit down." he said firmly to Marcel. He did not like having to look up at the man. It did obstruct his view. "Now, why me?"

"I know who you are!" Marcel Akmed said in an authoritative comment. "I need your help. I have tried to find you." Then he paused. "I have been looking for an I5." He looked away, almost as though he realized that maybe he should not have said that. "What I mean is..."

"It's okay." Michael shrugged. "I don't know what you're talking about." Again he shifted his position to assure his clear advantage. "What kind of an accent is that?"

"Accent?" Marcel said. There was a raised eyebrow. His mind was obviously elsewhere and he was not ready for such a question.

"What kind of accent do you have?" He glanced past the man as he asked the question. It was now obvious to him that before Marcel could make a move on him, he could move faster. But there might be another somewhere about. He casually glanced, still keeping Marcel in his vision as he did. "What kind of accent is that? Where are you from?" He took a deep breath. "Where is your home originally?" Then he turned to directly face the man. "It's not that difficult! Who the hell are you, and what's your interest in me?"

Marcel brushed his light hair back from his forehead. "I am of an American parent and a North African parent. I was..."

"Which parent is from where?" he interrupted. Marcel looked with a frown.

"I asked which parent is from where?"

"My mother was American," he paused and swallowed, "and my father was North African. Akmed, do you know the name?"

Michael thought for a moment. The name now sounded familiar. "Why are you saying 'was' about both of them?"

"They are both dead." He looked away. This time it was Marcel who took the deep breath. "What is that supposed to be about?"

"It matters," he said. "Where in the U.S. was she from," and he looked more intently, "and where in the north of Africa was he from?"

"That's not important!"

"It might be. In any case, that's my decision." He motioned to Misser Joe for another Campari. "You come up to me, disturb my friend to find me, and then tell me that it does not matter when I ask you these questions." He folded the newspaper. "Perhaps we should not continue this talk. I really don't give a damn about you, about your problem, about who you are, and even less about your parents."

"No, please," Marcel said as he looked with open eyes. "My mother was a farm girl from the midwest. She was in an exchange program and met my father in Greece. He was from," and this time he was hesitating to form his words and watch for facial expression when he continued, "Libya." As he completed his statement, he sat back as though he had fulfilled the request, but even more important as though he had relieved himself of some deep dark burden.

"So she was corn fed and he had cous cous in his veins." He smiled a little. "Pretty much the same, if you ask me."

"They were killed." Marcel said. He seemed to want to talk about them now. "They were good people, and they were killed in Libya."

"That's all very interesting, but my afternoon is not complete until I have had three Camparis, two newspapers, and one good stroll down the topless beach to invigorate my hormones." He reached up to accept the third Campari from Misser Joe. Then he turned to look out across the avenue toward the beaches.

"I know who you are. You are an I5. I have to talk to you."

"I don't know what you're talking about. If you need to solve the death of your parents, go to the police. If you need an I5, go to the hospital. It sounds like that sort of thing to me."

Marcel grabbed his arm. The left arm. Michael looked down at Marcel's hand on his arm. Marcel moved his hand away and looked down at the table.

"My parents were killed recently. They knew about something from Libya. My father found out through some military friends. Not on purpose. He overheard it. He told my mother. Someone had them killed. But the information exists and we have to get to it."

"What are you talking about? Some information about how your parents were killed!" He looked around as he sipped the Campari. "And we have to get to it! What is this? I can't help you. I still don't know what you're talking about!"

"Please listen to me. A journalist who was captured and sent to Beirut has the information." Marcel brought both hands up and rested them on the table. "And he knows about the information that my father got."

"What does this have to do with me? I drink Campari, read English newspapers and look at the pretty girls on the beach. I think you need James Bond."

"You're better!"

"Excuse me?"

"I said you're better. I need you!"

"For what do you need me?" Now he was becoming suspicious that there must be someone else out there getting ready to make a move on him. There was no way this Marcel Akmed was real.

"I'll pay you ten thousand dollars to help me plan his escape." Marcel leaned forward. "If you only help me plan his escape, nothing more, I'll pay you."

"Why an escape?" He looked around once more. This whole thing did not make sense. "Why not go talk to him, and ask him for the information?"

"I did. He won't tell me anything unless I get him out. He's Egyptian. The Shiites don't want to kill him. But they don't know what to do with him."

"It's a bluff. He doesn't know anything. You get him out, then when he's safe, he says that he doesn't know anything. But in the meantime, he has escaped. And to help him escape, you could get killed. It wouldn't concern him, because even if you don't get him out, he's already there."

"No!"

"No what! What are you saying? I help you plan his escape, and I get ten thousand dollars. You don't make sense." He started to stand up. "I have finished my third Campari. I have not been able to read my newspapers. Now I am going to walk on the beaches for awhile."

"Please listen to me." He reached his hands upward. "There are two French officers in Marseille, at the garrison, who have recently been to Beirut. They have talked with him and they know the place." Now Marcel was standing. "If we can talk with them, they will help us. We can make a plan. That's all I want is a plan."

"Where do you get ten thousand dollars? Where do you get that I can plan this for you?" He turned slightly to look about. "It doesn't make any sense to me."

"My father worked for Mohammed Abba Dabbus." He said it like it would answer all the doubts. "My father had wealth. He sent to me a great deal of money. He was always trying to get money out of Libya.

It was his dream to one day leave Libya. His plan was to come to where I lived."

"And to you, as you say, is where?"

"I have lived in Paris and here along the Cote d'Azur."

"So what is it you want with me?" As he asked he stretched again and rubbed the handle of the Walther with his left hand as though only rubbing the small of his back as he flexed.

"Come with me to Marseille and listen to the French officers. I need someone to know if they are lying."

"How the hell am I supposed to know if they are telling the truth. What makes you think that I have ever been to Beirut?" He turned and looked at Marcel. "Take your money. Forget it. If your parents were killed in Libya, there is no sensible way for you to find out anything."

"It's not that they were killed, or how they died, or even who killed them." This time Marcel looked around as both men were standing. He gave the impression of not wanting to have any of the exposure either. "My concern is the information that my father had is very important."

"What kind of important?"

"Terrorist important!"

"Ugh, terrorists again. Look at the streets. The economy is off down here because of all that talk. But this is the first time in years I have been able to walk down the streets of Cannes, Nice, Monaco," and he gestured as he talked, "and not be hassled by a bunch of Americans in polyester doubleknit Bermuda shorts laughing and screaming and demanding." He started to move away from the table. "The idea of giving the coast a little breathing room doesn't seem so bad to me."

"Reagan bombed Libya!" Marcel said quickly. "And the information is about a meeting right after the bombing."

"Right." He turned back to the table, "So?"

"That's real! And that has to do with my concern."

He sat back down with Marcel. "Okay, I'll tell you what. You get a nice comfortable fast car, and you pay me ten thousand dollars in American cash," and then he grimaced, "and I'll take the ride to Marseille. I'll talk with your two French officers." He leaned forward on the table. "And I'll even suggest a plan. Then you're on your own. If it works out, that's fine, and if it doesn't" he raised his eyebrows, "tough shit!"

Marcel stood up with wide abandonment. "Agreed! I have the money here with me." He pulled a huge envelope from his breast pocket. "Take it now. I want to make sure you don't change your mind."

Michael looked at the envelope in Marcel's hand. He picked up the glass of watered ice and Campari, and sipped it a moment. Then he raised his eyebrows, and with his right hand he took the envelope. "So we go to Marseille for bouillabaisse, conversation and a plan for you to get yourself killed."

"Great!"

"Great?" He look around in amazement. No longer was he concerned about his safety with Marcel. He turned back to the stocky man. "One more thing," he said with a wry grin, "with all that cash, then as part of the deal I want to be in your will."

"My will?"

"Forget it. Sort of a little joke at this point." He thumbed through the envelope. Then he looked up at Marcel. "This whole damn thing doesn't make any sense. So, to be in a fool's will," the grin appeared again, "especially a rich fool's will, is smarter than anything you want to do!"

"You'll see." Marcel said. "I'll find out what he knows," he straightened as he spoke these words, "and then I will do something very important for the world."

"For the world?"

"For the world." His shoulders were back a little now, and his chin was tucked-in sort of military-like. "I will meet you here on Wednesday morning with the car. At eight o'clock. The officers will make themselves available. But I must speak to them first."

"How much do they get?"

"The same as I am giving you."

"Each?"

"Yes, but..."

"That's fine. Our bargain has been made. You come up to a total stranger in a cafe, ask him if he is an enema 5, and then offer to give him ten thousand dollars. The person with the ten thousand dollars leaves quietly, and never returns for the automobile ride to Marseille. Very nice touch."

"Oh you will be here. You will think about all of this. If only for the questions, you will be here." He gestured a little. "Besides this is your place in the afternoon when you are in town. When you are at the Apartment. You will be here." Marcel turned abruptly.

Michael stood for a few moments after Marcel had made his way through the rest of the Cafe and out onto the avenue. He did not like that last comment, knowing about the Apartment and the afternoon. He felt Misser Joe somewhere near watching and hoping for some sign of approval.

As Michael tucked the newspapers under his right arm, he looked over and saw the Maitre'd anxiously peering with eyebrows raised in hopes of that sign. It was slow in coming. The afternoons at the Juantibes Cafe were private and relaxed, and should never be disturbed by a stranger. Misser Joe must remember this. He turned toward his friend, nodded and smiled, and gave the sign to relieve the anxiety.

Misser Joe smiled broadly, waved slightly and nodded back. He looked at the Maitre'd a moment, shook his head as though showing a mild scolding. Then he turned and made his way through the tables.

'It is still such a beautiful azure afternoon.' He was smiling as he repeated his thoughts to himself. 'The kind that the French Chamber of Commerce liked to take pictures of and post in brochures all over the world.'

The Cote d'Azur, by French definition, is that area from the Italian border just east of Menton, along the coastal lands to just west of Toulon. This is where the Alps reach upward to breathe the air of the beautiful azure skies and then downward to drink of the beautiful waters of the blue Mediterranean. Marseille, on the other hand, is considered by many to be part of the French Riviera, or certainly to be an honored guest on the western limit. Being the largest port in France, and on the Mediterranean, it attracts hosts of people from all ports and countries bordering that great Sea. It is, like most huge port cities, a melting pot of various forms of humanity. To some French, this port city is a disgrace to the rest of the country. It embarrasses them in their true traditions of French heritage. As once did the Eiffel Tower. Nevertheless, Marseille is a very exciting place with good foods from all over the world. It is the place for French bouillabaisse and North African cous cous. A good French wine, some

French bread and bowl of bouillabaisse can render a smile in the heart and a warmth in the soul.

As he walked along the edge of the beaches he though about Marseille. It had been some time since last he was there. The memories were a bit painful, but the thought of the city itself was delightful. Circumstances had dictated the release of an English diplomat from Shiite Iranians who held him in a warehouse along the Corniches below the port. A shootout followed and most of the players were killed, including the English diplomat. Interpol did not have the authority to send him in directly. Too many agencies were involved. There were even questions about certain agents shooting each other.

But that was a few years ago, and today was a beautiful clear blue day on the French Riviera. The view of the topless girls was always a pleasant conclusion to his afternoon soiree, and it was not without its rewards. Often the girls would notice him as well and smile back, encouraging introductions. Some years had passed since Viet Nam, but he kept in excellent shape, firm body and usually with a full color of tan. He walked as though he wanted the top of his head to brush the ceiling or touch the clouds. It was important to him to be erect, straight back, and as a result, he seemed taller than he really was. Top siders, white shorts and a T-shirt were his usual attire. The topsiders were just right for the salt, sand and water along the beaches. He was never without an occasional turn to view the scenes about him, for anything unusual, anything different.

His direction was toward that triangle in front of the Avenue Guy de Maupassant. One of the three small apartment estates overlooking the beach front was his. The Cap d'Antibes was on one side and Juan les Pins on the other. The grounds surrounding his place boasted of a few shrubs, a couple of trees and a small rose garden area. The roses were his pride of workmanship.

It was at the roses where he stopped. He thought again about the comments Marcel made in knowing so much of his movements when he was at the Apartment here on the Cap. The feeling was one of disturbance. Yet the thought of changing such a pleasant routine annoyed him even more. How vulnerable was he?

CHAPTER TWO

The Apartment

T he Apartment was a free standing three story building. The middle
level was on the avenue. The driveway went directly from the
avenue down the side and around the back to the seaside into the
lower level. This was a basement, mostly underground, partially above
ground. A large metal door secured the basement. Although there were
windows in the basement, they were high, small and contained steel bars.
The basement itself had a large area for two cars to park, a work bench
and tools, and shovels and trowels for the garden. Almost one third
of the underground area was a wine cellar, in perfect temperature and
humidity. Although other amenities attracted him to this particular site, he
remembered that the wine cellar was a major contributing factor. Forward
in the basement, underground, there was a long narrow windowless room
he used for his target range.

The middle floor, or first floor, depending on whether you are French
or American, has an entrance on the street side, up a few steps, and a huge
balcony on the opposite side overlooking the Sea. The door and windows
were secure and the balcony, above the metal basement door, was too high
for any ordinary means of entrance. The basement and first floor, he felt,
were safe from intrusion.

On the middle floor was the living area, directly in from the avenue.
There was the kitchen, a small guest room and an enormous livingroom.
The livingroom, which was mostly an open area with couches and easy
chairs, focused on a large flagstone fireplace. To the right side was a
semi-formal dining corner, a wet bar and well stocked mirrored shelves of
worldwide liquors. To the left was a one meter TV screen. After moving

into the Apartment, he had TV cameras mounted for surveillance and antennas installed for television reception. A control panel enabled him to switch between areas of surveillance and television reception. The television reception included the U.S. Armed Forces network. Those programs were in English. Also, next to the screen on one side was a huge library of books, and on the other side was a collection of video tapes of movies and documentaries. He subscribed to the States and European clubs for English tapes. A bright young French technician from Grasse had wired his system for both U.S. and European technology. He paused a moment to insert a CD into the stereo system. The flat, melodious sounds of Chet Baker's trumpet and voice filled the apartment. It was the music of Baker's visit to the Cannes Film Festival the year before.

Above this entertainment level was the master bedroom suite, which shared the chimney from the fireplace below. A broad expanse of stairs rose to this upper level. Part of the floor seemed cantilevered out over the area below and part seemed well concealed toward the seaside. An open balcony upstairs gave the feeling of one huge upstairs/downstairs room. A person could lean against the brass railings and look down into the livingroom below. Off the master bedroom was his study. There he had a computer, files, and diskettes of information about Interpol projects. All access was locked out on both the computer and the diskettes. Large wooden cabinets held reams of pictures and information worldwide about Interpol agents and Interpol enemies.

The master bedroom, complete with fireplace, jacuzzi, and small wet bar, had a balcony the width of the house directly overlooking the Sea. This balcony, on a huge double chaise, was where he spent most all mornings. In the colder months, he wrapped in a huge terry cloth robe. In the warmer months, he was naked in briefs only. Whenever he could, he sat out on the balcony and watched the sky brighten from his left.

The Telegraph and Herald were delivered daily. In the mornings he might first reread a newspaper from the day before, then proceed with the current news. He had fresh fruit, cheese and a light French wine. When there was an occasional overnight female guest, he preferred to have her leave early and not share in his morning ritual. Sometimes they would come out and sit with him for awhile. But on the mornings when Monica was with him, which was often the case, she would either sleep in or be snuggled beside him on the chaise. She had become an integral part of his morning ritual. She had now become his only overnight female guest.

Putting aside those ideas for the moment, he picked a few roses and thought about the possibility of Monica being upstairs waiting. He looked up to the third floor balcony for her, but there was nothing. The front door was slightly ajar, so she must have arrived. She often left the door so in her haste to carry her bags and a few foreign gifts for him. The reflection of Marcel comments crossed his mind. He thought that her door routine might have to be changed.

"Hello, Luv," she said looking up from her unpacking as he sauntered up the broad stairs. "Ah, are those for me?"

"Of course they are, Luv," replying almost in a mimic of her 'Luv'. A smile crossed his face as he came around the bed with the flowers. "I've missed you."

"Ha," she responded, turning the roses around in her hands, "never could believe that. All those bloody young things out there on the beaches. It's good for you that I don't walk in on some of them."

They embraced a long moment. A full deep kiss made her feel as though maybe she had been missed. This was 'her' ritual to come to the South of France. He worked a lot. Even though he was supposed to be 'retired', he still worked a lot. She could not understand that. But she would never disturb that. There were times when they could be together. And that was her 'ritual' to come to him in the South of France.

"You look fantastic," he said, pushing her gently back for a view. "What a great body! The gals on the beach couldn't touch this body."

She stood for a moment, still holding the roses in one hand and a slip from the suitcase in the other. Near the bed, on his side, was a small liquor cabinet. He poured two short shots of Remy Martin.

"How many have you made love with while I was gone?" she asked, turning back to her unpacking, and not really wanting to know, but a sort of tease and question.

On the lounge, he laid his head back, sipping on the Remy with his dirty topsiders on the cushion. She was of good build, he thought. Full breasts, nice waist and nice round hips. Her legs were full without being heavy and muscular, but certainly not skinny. How many miles does a flight attendant walk in the duration of a trip?

Her uniform was laying mussed across the bed where she tossed it when she arrived. The first thing she always did was to take off the uniform and parade around the place in her slip. She would take her underwear off from under the slip. The slip gave her comfort and freedom after being cooped up for so long, and yet it still gave her modesty. He was watching her while she went about her chores. The silk slip clung to every curve and shape. Her long red hair hung casually about her shoulders. Occasionally she had to brush it aside with her hand to see him.

"I never make love 'with' someone under thirty," he finally replied, as he held the Remy up to the light. "I only make love 'to' someone under thirty." She stopped her unpacking to straighten up and look at him. "Over thirty, then I make love 'with' someone. It takes the twenties for you gals to learn to make love 'with'.

Monica looked over at him for a moment. She smiled. How the hell had she ever gotten involved with a person like this? There were so many guys. So how did she get involved with him? She picked up the roses again and looked at them. She was always trying to catch up to him.

"How long do we have together?" he said, eyeing her over his glass. His sound was soft and interested, but not altogether convincing.

"You bastard!" she said softly in her heavy English accent. "Are you asking, hoping I'll leave soon or hoping I'll stay long?"

"Hey, why don't we order in tonight? What is it? Feel fishy...," he sounded like he was musing, "...or do you want to beef?" He looked at her as he spoke, almost with a grin.

"I want to go out," she said, acting a bit annoyed. "I don't want to be here with you tonight!"

"Good, then I'll order up for us."

He got up from the lounge and headed over to the phone.

"Wait a minute!" she almost yelled. "I bloody, bloody said I want to go out tonight! I only have till Wednesday morning! So I want to go out tonight."

He paused at the phone, which was near his bedroom liquor supply. The bottle of Remy was almost empty. It was time to bring up another bottle from below. Before pouring the next drink, he held up the bottle, turned it slowly, and looked at her through the dark glass of the bottle. He then moved it to one side, and winked an eye at her.

"I'll order up some lobster and muscles, and cold champagne." He put the Remy back in the cabinet. "...and if you still want to go out, the Cap is yours." All this he said with a smile. That twinkle was in his eyes. "Besides I have an envelope full of money that's burning a hole in my pocket."

You bastard, she thought to herself, of course I don't want to go out tonight. But don't be so smart about it! One more sip of the Remy and she came over to him to sit in his lap. This was why she was here. To be with him in the Apartment. She did not want to go out on the Cap.

"Pierre, this is the Apartment." He paused.

His eyes were on Monica. She was in his lap, with her Remy looking right into his eyes. "My lady is here, and we would like lobsters and steamed muscles and champagne for the evening." He listened. "Merci." A little of his only French.

Michael was probably the only person in the entire South of France, she felt, who got home delivery of meals. While she showered, another bottle of Remy was brought up and opened ceremoniously. It was so good to have her here again. She was wrapped in one of the huge terrycloth robes, hair still wet. They drank and kissed and while they waited, they climbed into the huge brass bed, and they made love 'with' each other. She felt good to be back with him, and he felt very happy to have her there.

The meal was exactly as any Maitre'd on the coast would have prepared and presented. They laughed and talked and drank and ate. Then shortly before midnight, when the eating and drinking was complete, they got back into the huge brass bed. It was a very comfortable evening, he thought, without tension, and without being concerned about the view of his surroundings. With Remy glasses on both sides of the bed, they both fell to sleep, smiling and snuggled.

Suddenly, a couple of hours after they fell asleep, all hell broke loose! Lights were on as Michael came to, blinking and squinting. Voices were everywhere in the room.

"Sprechen Sie Deutsch? Sprechen Sie Deutsch?" some masculine voice was yelling at him. Michael tried to focus. "Don't move! I got the girl and I'll cut her if you move!" The same voice now spoke a broken English with a heavy German accent.

The images were gradually becoming clearer. There were two men in the room. Lights were bright all about him. The overhead light was shining down on everyone, and they held flashlights on him. He could barely make out the room. There was one male directly across the bed from him holding a gun aimed at Michael's face. The other male was over toward the broad staircase holding Monica in his arms.

"Monica!" he shouted, sitting upright in the bed, looking about the room.

"Don't move!" the same someone said in broken English. "I vant an I5 for my trophy! You move and she gets cut in the teets!" The man holding Monica shifted his stance. "Make another move and I'll break her heart."

Their voices were guttural, broken English. He still tried to see the scene around him. Never let the primary person out of eye contact, but keep the other in peripheral vision. He watched the man with Monica. She squirmed as he held her tight against his chest and a knife against her breasts. The other man was leaning across the bed with the gun pointed at him. He would not look at that man. His attention must be directly before him, letting the other relax a little. Plans by action, never by reaction. He was talking to himself as he went through the scenario before him.

Suddenly Michael spun to his left, dropped below the bed and grabbed his old issue 45 which he kept mounted in a holster on the bed frame. Voices screamed and a shot rang out from the man aiming the gun at him on the bed. He came up quickly to the left of his drop and fired once into the face of the gun holder. The impact knocked the assailant back against the chest of drawers in the corner. Silence! Then there was noise from another person on the level below. The voice was German and loud. Michael did not understand the words, but he knew the questions.

The man with Monica stood before him. They stared at each other.

"Don't move!" the captor said, shifting from one foot to the other. "I'll kill her. You put the gun down!"

The captor hesitated, now holding the knife close to Monica's throat. The voice from the level below was louder, and it was obvious that someone yelling out in German was coming up the stairs. The captor yelled back in German.

Patiently Michael raised the 45 slowly up to an even angle. The gun was in his left hand, braced by the cup of his right hand, making a firm, steady aim at his target. This was what they were taught in basic. This was how you fired at targets. Bring the firing hand up slowly, brace it with the other hand to make it a rifle, then slowly squeeze the trigger. Don't pull! Don't jerk the trigger! Just gently squeeze the trigger until the gun goes off. A perfect score.

BALAM! was the sound that resounded through the room. The captor's head lurched back with a perfectly round hole above the bridge of his nose right between his eyebrows. His arms flailed out about him as he bounced against the wall. Seconds passed, then he staggered forward and fell at Monica's feet. She jumped back, hands on her face screaming. Michael turned to the stairs, left hand still poised with the aim of the 45 braced by the right hand. A figure appeared in the doorway, calling out in German. Another moment passed as the new person looked down at the body on the floor. He looked up into the sight of the 45. BALAM! Again the old Air Force issue rang out, and again a person reeled backwards. This time down the stairs, tumbling and finally coming to rest some twenty feet below on the next landing.

The silence seemed to hurt his ears for awhile. Monica was safe in the corner. Huddled down now in a crouched position, face buried in her hands. Still there was silence. Michael was listening for any other sounds in the Apartment. He moved carefully toward the door and looked down at the man below on the landing. Nothing moved. He looked at the two other men. Both were still. There was blood about the room, he finally noticed. Blood where they had been hit and where they had fallen. His eyes came to rest on Monica.

"Be still." he whispered. Then he turned and cautiously checked the landing on his level before descending to the man below. After checking the man below, he continued on down to the storage area on the ground floor.

"Body Bags!" she yelled at him. Monica was finally sitting on the side of the bed. She was drinking a Remy. His arm was around her. "Why do you have body bags in your house? I don't even know what body bags are!"

He gave her a squeeze, downing another gulp of brandy. There was work to be done. Those were body bags alright, and exactly for this purpose. Methodically he rolled one body to one side, slipped the bag underneath, then rolled the body back zipping him up. Each person was searched for identification and information. Finally, when he finished, he went over to the phone next to the bed and made a call.

"Bonsour," he said. "This is the Apartment." There was a pause. "I have three bodies for you." Monica looked up at the scene before her eyes. Then she looked over at him on the telephone. "I found a green plastic card on each of them. On one side is what looks like a bird above what looks like fire or flames. On the other side is a number. I found number two, number seven, and number ten." Now he looked at Monica to check her condition.

"It means," the Voice on the other end of the telephone line said, "that you are it for the Baader-Meinof group." There was a moment of quiet. Then the Voice, which was French in origin but with clear English tones, continued. "The number of members in each group varies. But be advised, Amerigo, that the number three is the leader. The last if you get that far." Again, a moment of silence. "The club is Phoenix, part of the Baader-Meinof group!"

"What are you telling me! The Baader-Meinof group has me as their target! I mean is that what you are saying? They have more important things to do than worry about me."

The Voice on the phone seemed to ignore Michael's comments and continued. "Phoenix is the training unit of the Baader group. They are learning to kill. You have been selected as their target!"

"Why didn't they kill me sleeping?"

"Their plan is to capture their victim and video tape the torture. The tapes are used to show the suffering and the breakdown." The Voice paused, sounding almost amused by it all. "It is to make us all feel vulnerable. If you live to kill a few of them, then they will try to murder you and take some photographs." There was the silence. "I wonder why they picked you. Have you ever met Andreas Baader or Ulrike Meinof?"

"No!" Michael replied emphatically. "I've never had anything to do with the Baader people!" Michael's voice was beginning to sound annoyed.

"Hmmm." was the response. "Why did you say Baader and not Meinof. Ulrike was really not bad looking. Maybe you fancied her somewhere."

Michael took a deep breath. "Another thing! How the hell did they get in here without me hearing the alarm? I want the system checked!" Again he took a deep breath as he looked over at the bodies. "Okay, so whoever they are, I've got them in bags. The place is a mess. I'm going to check into the Eden Roc. I'll get back in a day or so. Have the place spotless...and have the alarm system checked!"

"Eden Roc!" the Voice said, amused. "You'll never get into the Eden Roc tonight." It almost sounded like a threat or a bet! The Voice now seemed less concerned about the bodies and more amused about the Eden Roc.

"You get the place clean," again he looked over at Monica who was now standing and looking around the room, "and then check the Eden Roc to see if I'm there." He hung up the phone.

"Hey kid, of all the gin joints in all the towns in all the world, you gotta pick my gin joint to come into on a night like this!"

Monica allowed a small smile to work its way across her lips. She was looking at him as he spoke.

"What is this? Who the hell are you? You told me you were independently wealthy, that you were an international consultant..." She put her head onto his shoulder. "Who the hell are you?"

"Tomorrow, Luv, I'll tell you all about it when the sun comes up! Tomorrow is another day."

CHAPTER THREE

Interpol Five

T he next couple of days were somewhat tense. Not like the usual 'bloody' fights they had, with the great 'bloody' makeups which followed. Monica had been suspicious of his 'business' involvements for quite sometime. She convinced herself that they were not illegal, so she stayed out of it. And she really did not want to know anyway. But with a knife at her throat and dead bodies in the Apartment, she now felt that she had a right to know more. She tried to be subtle with her questions, but as always in the past, it seemed that only when she was direct would he even attempt to answer her questions.

It was his feeling that she should not know too much. It was important to protect her. The less she knew, the less exposure to danger. Yet he knew that she would have to know something more about him. Something more about his `business'.

Michael sat out on the balcony most of the next couple of days, while Monica busied herself with usual chores about the Apartment. On the surface there was no apparent tension between them. But they were both smart enough to know that the other was thinking about the night of the Phoenix.

Once sometime ago, Michael remembered, he was dating a croupier from Monte Carlo. And she got caught in crossfire. He pushed back the chair and put his feet up on the railing. It had happened on a drizzly spring evening when he was called into a project-in-progress by the Voice. The croupier and he had spent the afternoon in St. Tropez, and on their way to Grasse for dinner, he was called. Like Monica, he reflected, she had known very little about his personal life. Like Monica, she had chosen not to mention it.

When they reached the site at a little airstrip outside of Vence, she was to stay in the car. The car, hidden in a clump of shrubs, was out of sight of the airstrip. She would be safe, he felt. According to the Voice, an abduction was in progress. Two North Africans had kidnapped an official of Monaco and were on their way to a waiting airplane outside of Vence. The police of Monaco, without manpower or training, were helpless to pursue. The French were called in, and when the Voice over heard the transmission he intercepted and volunteered Michael. The French police out of Nice would of course back him up.

When all the shooting started, the croupier left the car and tried to sneak up to see the action. Michael paused in his reflection to try to remember her name. She was caught in the crossfire and took a number of rounds from an Uzi in the belly. So, he thought, it is best if Monica stays out of it.

Shopping day was always on Tuesday. And this Tuesday, even with the strain, would not be an exception. They travelled around old Antibes, meandering in and out of all the familiar shops, nodding, smiling and buying. Especially they liked to shop in the open markets for groceries for the Apartment. They both consciously avoided any comments about the Phoenix affair. But inside of Monica, she was becoming more and more upset over the lack of explanation. She did not want to have to bring up the subject. But certainly, she thought, he could.

The weather was pleasant for a late springtime in the south of France. The final stop, after the sun had set and many of the shops were closed, with bags mostly of fresh produce and fresh fruit, was always to cap off the evening with a couple of cognacs at the Juantibes Cafe. This Tuesday evening Misser Joe was attempting to be his attentive yet casual French self. Monica seemed to sense nothing. But Michael did not believe it. He knew that Misser Joe was still uncomfortable about the introduction to Marcel. With all else that had happened, Michael felt that it was like focusing additional tension right on Monica. Surely she must sense Misser Joe's discomfort.

The progress of time at the Cafe went very slowly. Michael glanced at the clock more often then usual, and Monica noticed that he did. Tomorrow was Wednesday, if he could make it that long, he thought, chances were that she would begin to dismiss the event by the time she returned from her trip. During their separation, she would gradually mellow and pass off the intensity of the event. At least that was what he was hoping. His thoughts were interrupted by Monica suggesting that they head for home. After a nod toward Misser Joe, they were on the Guy de Maupassant, meandering through the people just like anyone else on the avenue.

Back at the Apartment they sat on the bedroom balcony looking at the moon lay silvery streaks across the Mediterranean. He knew she was dealing with a number of deep questions. But he had to wait it out. He had to see if it would pass. She might choose to let it go.

And she watched him closely, wanting him to open up and volunteer. But he did not. Instead he projected his usual well controlled self. Yet she knew that he must be wondering what she was wondering. She baited him a couple of times, giving him the opportunity to open up. But each time his demeanor was casual and into some other subject. It appeared obvious to her that they were both tuned to the same subject.

So many times in his life, he had to wait out the pressure with controlled patience. He wanted her to know enough to release her anxiety, but not so much as she could be in jeopardy for her information. Their conversations were short, abrupt and to the point. He tracked her emotions carefully.

Then finally, as she was beginning to pack for her trip on Wednesday morning, she could hold back no more. Tuesday night had been a sleepless one, and now she was tired and anxious even before her trip.

"I met you on that trip to Cairo," she said leaning forward on the chaise lounge.

It was time for that frontal attack. She took a deep breath and let out a long sigh. She was now determined not to leave on her trip without getting into his guts. Not to fly from Nice to Paris, then on to Helsinki, two days in Moscow, return to Paris and finally back in Nice, almost a week later. She had to relieve the inner pressures she felt. There was not going to be any 'mellowing' during that period.

"You told me you were independently wealthy. You told me that you were retired. You damn well told me you dabbled in international affairs." She sat back upright. "Then all this bloody crap hits the fan. People try to kill us. You come up shooting with that big gun!" Her head was shaking with dismay. "And those damn body bags. Who the hell has body bags in their homes?"

He was sitting across from her, watching her pack. All he had on was a pair of brief walking shorts. No undershorts, just the walking shorts. It was his way of sleeping without any clothes, then putting on his brief walking shorts first thing in the morning. That way he would go downstairs to fix the coffee and their fresh fruit for their bedroom 'petit de'jeuner'. No sweet rolls, and no cold cuts and bread. Instead it was coffee and a huge bowl of 'le fruit de la saison'.

"I am independently wealthy." he replied softly. "I am suppose to be retired."

Michael wanted Monica to relax a little before her departure. He too had been awake some of the night and knew that she had had a restless go of it. There was no reason, he felt, for her to be uptight all during the flight and back again to the Apartment. Apparently he could no longer wait out the time hoping for her to leave without broaching the subject. When he spoke he tried to speak softly with a calm demeanor.

"That doesn't make any sense." She said, getting up from her seat. "I need a drink. I really need a drink." She looked directly at Michael. "I can't have a drink. But I want a drink!"

"It's like the old gunfighter in the American west. Someone is trying to take you out or someone is trying to get you to help them." Michael shrugged as he spoke. "So what can I tell you. I don't want you involved. We've been doing okay. You haven't even been aware of any of this. So it's not so important. Is it!" Not a question, but instead more like a statement.

"You're damn right it is!" she said reeling back around to face him. "I want it all right now! I've got to leave. I'm bloody well pissed. And I'm afraid." Her voice began to soften. "I don't want anything to happen to you. You know what it means to be away. I used to think about those young birdies on the beach," and she looked into his eyes, "but now I'll really worry about you. So get laid, but don't get shot!"

"I'm okay." he tried to say softly. "I've got plenty of protection. I've got Interpol protection."

There, he said it. He didn't have to worry about working a flight. He could have a drink. Even if she could not, he could have a drink, and so he did. He had a beer.

"Talk to me, you bloody Yank!" There were tears in her eyes.

His explanation started slowly. "When I left Viet Nam, I started for the U.S." He took a breath. "My plans changed and I ended up in the middle of the Middle East. I enlisted with the Israeli Mossad." He checked her expressions for a reaction. There was none. "That's the equivalent to the CIA and the KGB. It's their undercover group." Again he paused. This time he sipped on the beer. "Maybe a little tougher. It's sort of a covert operation developed to end the terrorism directed at Israel." He was still watching her expressions. "I served in Palestine. Then I spent some time in Lebanon, especially in Beirut. It was still a beautiful city then." His eyes reflected memories. "The Paris of the Middle East."

In a very melodious, nonalarming tone, he continued his story. Monica was dressing for her flight, pausing occasionally at any portion of the story which caught her attention.

He explained how the French had been very active as colonials in Viet Nam. Then the communists decided that the French should leave. In fact it was their fight until Dien Bien Phu. The communists kicked them out. That was in May of 1954.

"Like the Brits," and he glanced with a smile toward Monica, "the French have always had colonies in the Middle East and in the Far East."

Her reaction was to shrug, turn down the corners of her mouth and raise her eyebrows.

"So," he said casually, "in my time when I got to Viet Nam, my actions had not gone unnoticed by the French. They decided to honor 'heroes' with decorations. Some alternative to their vacating the area years before when the fight was just beginning. They would never want to recognize the U.S. But they could do that for individuals, even if they were Americans." He sipped the beer again, deliberately keeping the pace casual. "So at that point I expatriated to France, becoming an active member of their Interpol force. It has not really been very exciting." he commented, again in a casual off-the-cuff manner, watching her reactions. "Today I have the rank of a French Interpol Five. An I5!"

"What's an I5? What does that mean?"

"It's almost like a management job. That's why I retired. According to my files, I am retired. If I had gotten another promotion, I would have had to go inside."

"Go inside...?"

"A desk job." he said with a slight curl to his lip. "I have," he looked directly at her and smiled a little, "been an international marshall presiding against the evils of the Empire." His last comment was almost sarcastic, but she didn't feel that way. She only looked at him, almost with a blank stare.

"Where do you come from? Where is your family?" Now she was feeling stronger about getting to the truth. "That's enough about the French. I don't have much time. Tell me who you are!" She was sitting on the bed with her uniform skirt on, no blouse yet, only her bra. "I want to know who you were before all this happened."

"Monica." He said her name firmly with no tone modulation. She looked up when he spoke her name. "That's enough. I have to leave for Marseille. You have to leave for your trip. I'll be here when you get back." He got out of his chair and came over to her, pulling her close against him, holding her tightly.

That was the end of it. She knew that she would get nothing more. He was still holding her close to him. That was the same feeling she had felt so many times in the past and never really understood until this moment. It was that feeling she had sensed sometimes before when she left. It was feeling that there was something pending that she should know about. But he had never told her and she never asked. Now she understood this feeling she had had so many times. She almost nodded as she thought about it.

So there was no more talk of backgrounds or personal identities. Instead for the next hour they both attempted to return to the small talk about the Apartment and about groceries and about what he would eat while she was gone. They planned their next outing, dinner in Nice at their favorite place. Strangely, she was feeling better. Just finally breaking into the subject seemed to release the pressure like a steam valve. Methodically she packed, and then she was ready to leave.

"Take care of yourself." she said. "I'll be thinking about you."

Michael smiled and once more held her close to him. "You won't even have time to miss me. Helsinki and Moscow. You probably have a Finnish boyfriend over there." The matter of Phoenix was closed.

After he helped her to the taxi, he went up to the upstairs balcony and looked out across the Mediterranean. Somewhere deep inside was a wall. Often he told himself that it was there to protect those who tried to get too close. But every now and then he would question that motive. The truth might be that he was afraid to get close to anyone. Over the years there had been many girls of many ethnic and national backgrounds. And in each case he found some reason to move on. He was officially retired, he reminded himself, and things were suppose to get better. His activity in the force was suppose to dwindle away and soon he would be forgotten. When was all that going to happen! With one last look across the Sea, he turned and started to prepare himself for the ordeal ahead. Marcel Akmed was to be along shortly.

CHAPTER FOUR

Marseille

The hour and a half drive to Marseille was uneventful. The men talked some about France, about North Africa and about politics in general. They never really got into the matter at hand. Marcel was a person of quiet, nonargumentative demeanor. Although they broached many controversial subjects, and Marcel would make his own position, if Michael disagreed or took another point of view, he would quickly turn his point to be agreeable and pleasant. It was not as though he was being subservient, Michael thought, he just seemed to have an agreeable personality. He wanted no conflict. Such a strange type of man Michael felt that he was. One who wanted pay a great deal of money to find some secret information, and yet what would this person do with the knowledge once he had it. How was this man going to do something courageous enough to save the world, he thought as he looked over at the driver. And for a fleeting moment he remembered his own circumstances being shotdown over North Viet Nam. He had never thought of himself as an aggressive man. It started out as survival for Michael, but what was it for Marcel.

While Marcel staring ahead looking down the highway, Michael looked about, and his mind turned to thinking of Monica. How could he correct the situation? There was no place for her in all of this. And he wondered about his self-imposed wall, protecting himself from emotional intrusion. At best they had had much time together without having a disaster. If anything, this 'Phoenix' training program had to be handled immediately. But then, he thought to himself, there will be other problems. Monica made him feel so good when she was around.

His thoughts meandered ahead to the situation before them, then back to the situation which he had left behind. He was rambling inside of his head. What he felt he really wanted now was to turn the car around, go back to the apartment, find Monica waiting there, and spend the next few days alone with her. Cowardly and retreating maybe, but it gave him a comfortable feeling.

I am financially independent, he thought. There was so much money banked away. But where could they go? Then he wondered if he was fantasizing again.

Michael's mind wandered in and out of ideas about getting away. Sometimes Marcel would break the silence with comments of the countryside, or ask penetrating questions about Michael's experience. He always answered directly, without adding any flavor to the subject. The conversation during the trip went from political attitudes to small, noncontroversial subjects, and to finally silence.

It was midmorning when they cruised into the city, picked up the Avenue de Toulon, passed through the Place Castellane, and headed toward the Vieux Port.

Fort S. Nicolas was on the east entrance to the harbor, with Fort Saint Jean on the west side, these were the protectors keeping the enemies of France out of the port. Modern soldiers occupied the grounds of Fort S. Nicolas, and that was Marcel's destination.

At the Fort entrance, Marcel spoke to the guards, and soon they were driving inside, across the parade grounds headed for the officers quarters. Michael looked about as they crossed the open parade ground, remembering the place from many years before. He had visited the Fort before, but now he was remembering another parade ground. A smile crossed his lips and he breathed a deep sigh. On just such grounds, at Fontainebleau, Marshall Gaston Perez had decorated him, kissed him and congratulated him on his efforts in Viet Nam. With no place to go, the invitation as a selected member of the Interpol elite corps appealed to him. Fighting, killing and survival had become second nature - why not apply it to the civilian sector, he thought. Besides, the Interpol elite were both inside Interpol and independent contract agents.

As they walked through the courtyard, he looked back once more at the parade grounds behind him. Inside, they entered a plain, austere wooden room. There were wooden floors, wooden chairs, a wooden counter; everything wooden, even the soldier guarding the inner office seemed wooden. There were pictures of French heroes and officers. On the wall near the wooden soldier, he spied a group photo which included Marshall Perez. He was looking at it when two officers entered the room.

"Bonjour" the Captain said, looking from one man to the other. "Who is Marcel?" he asked in French.

"I am," spoke Marcel in English, "and this is my agent. He is the man I told you about. He is here to help me." There was an awkward pause, then Marcel continued. "As I told you, I want him to be part of our meeting. He knows all about the Egyptian journalist. He has agreed to help with the plan to get information out of Girod Said."

Without leaving the photo, Michael looked at the Captain. He thought, this is a man much too old to be a Captain. The other officer was much younger, perhaps a little old for his rank of Lieutenant, but then again, maybe not.

"Yes, of course." the Captain replied with a nod and a forced smile. The Captain was now speaking in English. "I am Captain DuVall," still offering the forced smile and with a slight gesture of the head, "and this is Lieutenant Bornier. We both know of Girod. We know where they are holding him."

The two officers stood for a moment while Michael looked back at the photo. Marcel was standing awkwardly, and the wooden soldier was rigid.

"Please," the Captain spoke, "come with me to my office. We can have privacy." Again the forced smile.

As they entered the small office, all Michael could think of was how wooden everything was. Another wooden chair was brought into the room, and the conversation began.

The Captain, being the senior officer present, began about himself. He explained how he had spent much of his career in the North African campaigns, from Morocco to Cairo and finally in Beirut. He had friends, and some enemies he added, forcing the smile again. He seemed to bask in the ramblings of his own story. He insisted that he was so competent that he could obtain information about anything from most anywhere. It was as though he was taking advantage of talking to refresh himself and to further impress his Lieutenant. Patience once again seemed to finally have a certain reward. In all of his talking he arrived at the period of his career in Viet Nam.

He had reached the rank of Field Colonel during the early battles. Because of stupidity and politics, he explained, his rank was held over his head, dangled before him, and finally when he had served long enough to be considered for a star, he was reduced, not to Major, but to company grade Captain.

At that point in his story, he paused for awhile. He looked at the two men, then at the Lieutenant. All three seemed to shift simultaneously on the hard wooden chairs.

"And I know who you are!" he said looking back at the person sitting between the Lieutenant and Marcel. The person who seemed the most uncomfortable on the wooden chair, and the most disinterested in his long story. "Marcel told me you were coming. You are the American. Amerigo." There was a pause. "I remember when you were issued an invitation to join the Interpol corp."

The story continued about how he remembered the decorations at Fontainebleau. It was while he was still an acting Colonel, just before he almost got his star, but instead lost his rank. He recalled newspaper articles. He was present when the decision was made to make selections for the Interpol Elite. It was beginning to sound as though he was either trying to take credit for the invitation to Michael, or that he was resenting the invitation to the American. To Michael it seemed obvious that it was the latter.

"I am impressed with your career, Captain." Michael said firmly. "We are all impressed with your career. How can you help my friend Marcel?"

"Hah, I can help in many ways" he mused. "But how I choose to help is my decision. Why should I help you, Amerigo. Marcel Akmed said that he needed my help. But he has you now!"

There was an air of contempt in the Captain's speech. His chin was raised slightly in an air of arrogance. Michael had seen that air of resentment before in the French toward the Americans, especially when he received his commission in the French Interpol. The Parisians, he was thinking, are even more blatantly arrogant than even the New Yorkers. But who cannot love the New Yorkers, or the French either. A smile had crept across his lips as he thought of the Captain.

"Captain!" Michael looked up at the Lieutenant, then back to the Captain. "We are here for information to help us free the man Marcel needs. He said you could help. Marcel needs to get information out of him."

"I can help, but perhaps, now that I know who you are, I should think about it! I am recalling how no one recognized me for my courageous deeds in Viet Nam. No one offered me a reward for the dangers I had taken." He stood up straighter, pushing out his chest. "Then years later you come along. In the fifties, it was hell in Viet Nam. Not in the sixties, with the whole American army." He looked directly at Michael. "It will take a great deal more money for me to help!"

Michael turned slowly to Marcel. "What does he mean by 'more money'? Have you paid this asshole frog yet?"

Marcel nodded yes.

The Captain jumped up, leaning across his small wooden desk. "Don't insult me!" he yelled. "You have no authority in my office!"

"So you have already paid him!" Michael looked at the Captain then back at Marcel.

Again Marcel nodded yes.

He turned to the Lieutenant. "What do you know?"

The Lieutenant shifted uneasily and looked over at the Captain.

"Holy shit, Marcel," Michael said, "you paid the asshole frog and his dummy friend. Dwiddledee and dwiddledum!" He sat back and looked at the Captain, who was still leaning across the small desk. "I told you they couldn't help you." He sat up slowly, as though planning to leave. The PPK in the small of his back had grown uncomfortable from the long ride, more uncomfortable from the hard wooden back chairs, and now completely uncomfortable because of the Captain.

The Captain reached toward the phone. "I'll call for the Officer of the Day. I'll have you arrested!" he shouted.

Marcel's eyes widened, looking from one to the other. The Lieutenant stood up with his back against the small wooden window frame.

As the Captain started to lift the phone receiver from its cradle, Michael came up off of his chair, and all in one motion his right hand pushed the receiver back down while the PPK suddenly appeared in his left with the barrel shoved into the Captain's still open mouth.

"Now," he said quietly, "everybody sit down and don't make a sound." His eyes were directly on the Captain, but he knew the moves of both of the other men. They had obediently resumed their sitting positions. "Since my decorations, Captain, I have not only accepted the invitation, but I have become an I5." He released his grip on the phone receiver and slowly pulled the PPK out of the Captain's mouth. "You do know what that means, don't you!"

Michael's manner was relaxed and softly spoken. A moment of silence passed as the two men, on opposing sides of the small wooden desk, eyed each other.

"Show me proof." mumbled the Captain, wide-eyed and shaken. He was trying to be firm, but was still quite shaken. He could not lose face before his Lieutenant.

"Test me!" Michael said as he backed off a little. "I'll kill you. As an I5 I need no explanation. The French government accepts that. The Lieutenant will get to see my proof." Now he looked at the other two, one on each side of him. He felt he could release his pressure on the Captain. It was time for patience again. "Tell Marcel how you can help him. And show him what information you have. Tell him how you are going to do more than you originally planned."

This time his story had substance. The Captain pulled a large brown envelope out of a desk drawer. It contained drawings of Beirut, of the inner city where Girod Said was being held captive, and finally drawings of the prison rooms. DuVall told of his involvements in Beirut, and how he had gotten involved with the Jihad. Once before he had actually negotiated the release of certain hostages from the Shiite Moslem terrorists. Over the years he had gotten even closer to them, sometimes acting to handle ransom monies for all parties involved. At that point he made a feeble attempt to explain that it was his honor which caused him to get so involved. Unnoticed by the other two, the presence of the PPK made him admit that he had done so for a fee as part of the ransom. The Lieutenant had become his courier, and now was as deeply involved as he was.

Details of a plan began to unfold. Marcel began to ask questions and take notes. He wrote down names, locations and amounts of money. The Captain, motivated by noticing the occasional slight pat of the PPK, explained how he would make the contacts and told Marcel what had to be done for each date and location.

"Marcel, I think that the Captain and his friend should be with you when you go to Beirut. It is best for the plan that he accompany you." The smile was back as Michael looked at the Captain. "Don't you think that it would be better for Marcel, since you already have his money, to help him in Beirut?" Although it sounded like it might be a question, everyone in the room knew that it was not a question.

"Of course," DuVall said, looking at the PPK, "my plan was already to be in Beirut when Marcel is there. That way I can assure him of success."

"I am so glad that you saved that part of the plan for last." Michael said. "Marcel told me on the way here today that he hoped you would go with him."

"The only thing is," the Captain said almost inaudibly, and he glanced at Michael when he spoke, "there may be more money necessary to pay certain people in Beirut."

"It's interesting," Michael said, "that you mention more money for certain people in Beirut after you told Marcel that you would go with him. I hope that you were not planning to let him go alone without knowing who to pay."

"No!" the Captain insisted. "It has always been my plan to go with him. I was going to explain these additional complications to him."

"What do you think, Marcel?" Michael asked.

"It's okay. I have the money. But I would like it if you went with us." Marcel spoke almost apologetically. It was like he was saying that he was sorry to bring it up, please excuse me. But at the same time, he had to at least say it.

Michael ignored the comment. Instead he reached across the wooden desk and shook the hand of the Captain.

"Good, Captain DuVall, I feel much better that you are in the thick of the action again. A man of your experience can safely help Marcel accomplish his mission."

Almost three hours had passed since they first crossed the courtyard entering the wooden ante room to await the officers. Slowly the PPK returned to its resting place in the small of Michael's back.

"I am most sorry Captain," he said as all four were standing in the courtyard, "for the inconveniences which we have caused today."

The Captain shifted a moment, looking about the courtyard. He was not sure how to take the comment. But then in this best `lassaire faire' attitude and gesture, assured all concerned that there was never any danger and he was not the least bit serious about his attempt to make the phone call. His intentions were to be helpful all along and were only misread at that critical moment.

Michael and Marcel strode out of the courtyard toward the parking area. Marcel was walking and mumbling, and trying to review his notes, totally absorbed in his thoughts.

"Marcel," Michael said when they reached the car, "I'm hungry. I remember a place along the Corniches called 'LazyAndre's'. Oysters, bouillabaisse and wine." He smiled as he spoke. "A fitting place for you to read, learn and inwardly digest your notes."

Without any further comments on the afternoon, Michael got behind the wheel of the car and drove out of the Fort toward the harbor. Once on the Corniches, he located one of his old eating place, `LazyAndre's'.

Unfortunately, it was midafternoon now, the regular waiters were away until evening. Only some young new waiters were about the restaurant. Marcel and Michael had to sit near the street because the rest of the tables were closed until six.

There were other restaurants along the way, some completely open. Elsewhere they could sit where they pleased. He did not like the idea of sitting so close to the street. But he did want to have the bouillabaisse of `LazyAndre's'. Sadly, even taking the orders seemed like an intrusion on these young waiters.

The aggravation was worth it. The food was as good as he remembered. Unfortunately his old waiter friends were either gone from the restaurant or would not be returning until late.

The two men sat, eating, sipping wine and now reviewing the afternoon. He told Marcel explicitly that he would have to destroy the notes before they left for Antibes. Everything had to be memorized. Anything written down and left about could act against him. Marcel worked at trying to memorize his notes. Finally, Marcel could contain himself no longer. He was studying the notes, but his thoughts kept going back to the Captain and certain things he had said about Viet Nam and decorations.

"Are you really the Viet Fox?" he asked, looking timidly over the rim of his wine glass while he sipped. "I heard that you are the Viet Fox."

"There were many who could have been the Viet Fox." Michael shifted slightly and looked directly at Marcel. "The French felt very good about me, they felt a need to cleanse their own guilt. And there was some controversy over me and all that Viet Fox publicity." He smiled. "So they decorated me, honored me, and I stayed in France."

"But who are you?" Marcel asked. "Other people have told me about you. And the Captain said he knew you." His accent would seem to get a little heavier at times when he got excited. "And zat is veree confusing to me. You must be the Viet Fox!" He closed with deliberation. He was satisfied that he had chosen the right person to help him.

"More important to me, Marcel, is how did you find me?"

"A friend in the French police connected me with an agent inside the Bandit Repression Brigade. The agent discussed my problem with me and then gave me the name of a contact in Antibes." Marcel was obviously feeling relieved as he told his story. "In the South of France this other agent listened to my story and recommended that I speak with you. But," and Marcel grinned a little, "he warned me to approach you cautiously and in a public place. So I watched you a while and finally got up enough nerve to speak to you."

Michael sat back, having listened to Marcel for those few moments. A better feeling of well being came back. The Bandit Regression Brigade was a group of independent agents working like private detectives do in the U.S. It could have come from a worse source, he thought.

"Tell me about Viet Nam and what you did!" Marcel insisted. "I mean, if you are the Viet Fox, it's incredible that I am sitting here talking to you." Marcel put the glass down. "I mean, you're like the legend of Viet Nam!"

One of the young waiters came over to the table and poured more wine. Michael was uncomfortable sitting that close to the street. It was a vulnerable feeling, a feeling ordinary people would probably not feel. But his life was not something anyone would call ordinary.

"You know," Michael said, leaning forward. It was as though he wanted to talk a little. "I used to spend hours in the jungle developing better sensors, especially the vision. It's amazing what one can do with eye muscles and brain concentration. I would focus near and focus far, and repeat the exercise a hundred times without interruption. I would try to focus one eye near and one eye far. I would stare straight ahead and count the leaves on the trees on both sides of me."

At this point he paused for a moment. Inside he was reflecting and remembering. Marcel was eager to listen.

"It got so that my eyesight actually improved and imperfections would stand out. Colors, even shades of color, movement, motion, all stood out so strongly that my eyes reacted quickly and precisely." He took a deep breath, sighed and sat back. "Peripheral vision and awareness was so important to my survival. As a kid," and he grinned a little, "I would sit in a room, open my eyes wide, try to see every object while staring straight ahead. I would count to ten slowly, close my eyes and reconstruct the room in detail. Like anything, training leads to perfection. I got extremely good at it." He held up his glass a moment, turned it slowly and looked at the amber color of the wine. "But peripheral vision for survival became my most important sense. My hearing was developed well in the jungle, but the peripheral scene saved my life many times. All the senses come together to create that sixth sense of danger."

Marcel was very pleased to be there listening to the story. He was very pleased that he had chosen such a person to be here with him during his visit. The money was worth the payment. If only there was someway to convince him to go to Beirut.

"Marcel," he said quietly, "you have paid a great deal of money." He spoke as though he knew what Marcel was thinking. "From what Captain DuVall has planned, there is more that you'll have to spend. Tell me about your father."

Marcel sat upright, showing a little pride in the interest being shown in him. Besides, it was his turn to tell some of his story.

"The oil in Libya is sold openly on the world market with OPEC." He leaned forward a little. "But Abba Dabbus sells a great deal on the black market without OPEC knowledge. What is sold openly goes to Libya and to maintain OPEC. The people of Libya do see some of that, and there is some show of progress."

A pause seemed appropriate for Marcel at this point. The next few statements were to be so secretive and revealing, that he had to set the mood. "The rest of the oil, the black market oil, has to be paid in gold bullion." He looked across the table. "Abba does not trust the currency of any nation. Besides, Abba always claimed that any currency of a nation would make that nation a partner in his scheme. Gold, on the other hand, could not be traced and could be used anywhere."

"But Marcel, gold is an impractical commodity. You can't travel with it. You can't try to spend it without being notice..." He sat back for a moment thinking that he would like a Campari. The wine was finally getting to his taste buds. "...and there are banks where money cannot be traced. There are many ways besides gold!"

"Not for Abba." Marcel replied. "In his Compound home, the Bab Azizya, there is probably a billion dollars worth of gold bullion. Unknown by the Libyan people and unknown by OPEC, all hidden away in Bab Azizya. But you are right, so what does he do with it?" Marcel sipped wine. "My father was paid well from two sources of income. Abba occasionally paid my father extra with his gold for certain projects. These projects became more and more terrorist projects. My father felt that it was Abba's plan to cause confusion elsewhere. It was to take interest away from Libya and the gold."

"Paranoia" Michael said. "He's protecting a huge amount of personal wealth that is in an unrealistic form and it's become his fear of the rest of the world. So much oil is turning into so much more gold bullion!"

"Exactly," Marcel said, "Abba does not fear any country as much as the U.S. He feels they are smarter than anyone. And it is American companies who are involved in pumping the oil. Suppose they begin to report his secret sales to OPEC. He needs America, he thrives on America and in some self destructive way, he wants to destroy America."

"Is that like biting the hand that feeds you?"

"Yes!" Marcel sat back a moment, his eyes rolled upward and he looked at the late afternoon sky. "In April all of his paranoia came to one immense focus when the U.S. bombed Libya. He was being scolded and attacked by that entity which he loves and hates the most. Furthermore," and Marcel brought his eyes down, "he was panicked over the possibility that the bombing of his Bab Azizya compound would have opened the walls to his underground vaults and everyone could have found the gold." Marcel looked directly across the table. "Maybe the people would have started rioting and the gold would be stolen. Abba has been sick with grief and fear. He thought that his headquarters compound was completely protected, and no one would dare to violate it! That is the substance of my need to know!"

"The man in Beirut! Girod Said."

"He grew up with me. His father was a journalist. Now he's a journalist. He knows what my father knew." Marcel narrowed his eyes as he continued. "Abba intends to retaliate with an immense act of terrorism to show the world." He paused a moment. "Even if it means his own destruction! He is a madman!"

"Excuse Moi, Monsieur," a waiter was leaning toward Marcel, "telephone."

Marcel frowned and looked across the table. Michael raised his eyebrows and then gestured with his head to follow the waiter. Marcel got up slowly, looking around the cafe and up and down the street. The waiter was waiting. He turned and followed the young man to the inside of the cafe.

Suddenly quiet seemed to be everywhere. Even the sounds of traffic on the streets had become muted. Michael sat alone, sipping on the Campari and soda. His head was upright, as he brought the drink up to his lips. With what seemed as though no eye blinks, he stared straight ahead, again as he had done so many times, seeing everything on both sides around him. All sensing systems were turned on and turned up.

Then, without turning or looking back, he knew that whatever it was, it was coming from behind him. As he sprang from the chair throwing himself away from the streetside, he pulled the PPK with his left hand, sprawling and knocking tables and chairs as he went.

In his place at the table, one of those old sardine shaped Citroens jumped the curb and smashed into the tables and umbrellas. The engine was revved very high and the wheels squealed as the tires crossed the curb and skidded on the walkway. Chairs and tables bounced about in all directions. The impact had missed him by a moment and a few feet. The bristling hair on the back of his neck had saved him.

As the Citroen came to rest over tables and chairs, wedged against a huge flower pot, the driver began frantically trying to back the car out. The PPK was up, leveled and fired twice, once taking out the front right tire and once taking out the back right tire. Michael wanted the driver alive. He could shoot and cripple him, but he wanted to take him alive.

The driver, frustrated, jumped out of the car waving an Uzi in his right hand and shouting in German. He fired a few rounds aimlessly at the tables about him. Then there was silence.

The PPK, held firmly in the left hand and braced by the palm of the right, was aimed directly at that spot above the bridge of the nose and between the eyes of the driver. The driver stood motionless a moment, looking at the PPK. The Uzi slipped from his hand, and then suddenly the other hand came up and put something into his mouth.

"No!" Michael yelled. The PPK fired, not at the head, but at the left shoulder, knocking the driver backwards and rotating him to the left. "No, damn it!"

By the time he pushed away chairs and tables and got to the driver, the man was near death. He grabbed the man's throat and tried to choke out whatever he had taken. The driver's eyes closed and his head fell limply to one side.

"What was it?"

Marcel had come out from inside. He was standing back a few feet, but close enough to see it all.

"Cyanide!" he said as he stood up, putting the PPK back into the belt in the small of his back. "I wanted the bastard to talk to me."

Then he bent down and began searching through the man's clothes. Again he stood up, this time with something in his hand. It was hard for Marcel to see, but it was some kind of green card with the number nine on it. There was also some kind of bird, but before he could see more, Michael put the card in a back pocket near the PPK.

"Let's talk to that waiter!" he said, still stooping over the man, not turning his head as he spoke.

The waiter was of no help. Someone called on the telephone, described the two men and said to call the one described as Marcel to the telephone. That was the full story. By the way the waiter looked at Michael, and the expressions of the other waiters, it seemed most reasonable that the story was the truth.

Michael pushed back to the inside bar and ordered a Remy for the road. Marcel followed him in, shaken somewhat, not as excited as he had been by all the intrigue. He looked back at the tables and the street outside. Those screeching European police sirens could be heard in the distance. A shake of the head, a sigh and a look at the man at the bar with the Remy made him feel somewhat better.

"Let's go!" Michael said, taking Marcel by the arm and walking out between the tables just as the police cars pulled up. "Bonjour, officer." he said, politely nodding, keeping a firm grip on Marcel and marching them right through the gathering crowd. He held tightly, looking straight ahead, walking upright and firmly all the way to the car.

"Now, Marcel," he said one they were settled in the car, "my job is complete, I have my pay and you, my friend," he looked at Marcel, "have your enema 5." With that he laughed and threw his head back.

Marcel had picked him up at the Cafe and Marcel dropped him back in front of the Juantibes Cafe. It was always a little better to show some caution and not expose one's self too much. The less Marcel knew of his detailed life, he felt, the better for all concerned.

Misser Joe approached him hesitantly as he stood on the street curb watching Marcel drive way. A Campari and soda was offered by the Maitre'd, with eyebrows raised, hoping that all had gone well between the two.

Michael made the man wonder for a while. But then he assured Misser Joe that all was well and that there would be no blame for the introduction. Relief crossed the Maitre'd's forehead and he relaxed the raised brows.

Returning to the apartment, he entered carefully as he always did. The security system was in force. Certain precautions had to be taken, precautions which only he knew. Not true, he thought, as he paused for a moment; Monica also knew the entrance and exit codes. In light of what had been happening, that might not be such a good idea. It certainly compromised her in the event she was caught between him and the Baader-Meinhof trainees. The Phoenix Gang!

Once inside, he poured a short shot of Remy and went to the telephone. "This is the Apartment." he said, holding the brandy glass up to the light. "I had a run in with number nine today in Marseille."

"I know," the Voice responded. "We had a report before the police arrived."

"Oh, that's great," he said with irritation. "If you guys move so fast, why the hell didn't you report to me what was going to happen before it did!"

"Our people are aware of you," the Voice said firmly, "but we don't babysit you."

"What about the pictures? You said that they would want pictures."

"The camera was probably nearby." There was a pause while the Voice spoke with someone else on the other end. "Nobody got a glimpse of anything. But I would suggest that a camera was there."

"I've got four of them now. Will they back off?"

"No, the stronger you get, the greater their challenge. Last month a chapter of the Red Brigade followed their target into a maximum security wing of an asylum. He was put there for protection. The Italian Interpol felt it was best." The Voice paused, as though taking a puff on a cigarette or sipping a drink. He could not hear any ice, so he decided that the Voice was smoking. "They stripped him of his weapon because of their concern for the inmates. Two o'clock in the morning the Brigade got him. They strangled him with piano wire, almost cut his head off. They took pictures."

"Aw, shit!" Michael said, gulping the last of the Remy to feel his own throat swallow.

"Pictures were sent everywhere. Before he was killed, he had gotten ten of the chapter." Then that light amused sound returned to the Voice as he continued. "But he was only an 19!" Silence. "We do expect more from you."

"Thanks." he said, lowering the phone back onto the cradle. When cave men had stone axes, he thought, they could cause little damage in any given time. But today, the terrorists have modern weapons and nuclear power at their disposal. He shook his head as he sat reflecting. They could destroy whole communities and hold entire nations hostage. He shook his head again, then flipped off the lamp and stretched out across the bed. He would consider all those things tomorrow, but now he was very tired, and he wished, as he closed his eyes, that Monica was there.

CHAPTER FIVE

Revelations

T he next few days found Michael restless and lonesome. He checked and restocked the wine cellar and his food stuffs. Music throughout the apartment seemed to be a little louder than usual, perhaps it would drowned out some of the thoughts which he tried to resist. His mind wandered back and forth between Monica and Marcel. Occasionally he would frown. How could he have gotten so caught up in such difficult situations with these two? Obviously he was feeling guilty about the Phoenix affair with Monica, but then he was also thinking a great deal about Marcel. If Marcel went to Beirut with those two French officers, especially that DuVall, chances were that he would not come back. It made him uncomfortable. That was his considerate, concerned way of getting involved. The good Lord always takes care of drunks and stupids, and where he doesn't have time, then if Michael has met the man, he would take care of him. His head shook slowly from side to side as he thought about that. A wry grin was winding its way across his lips.

His walks were brisk, body upright and straight with head erect. The glances and flirtatious eye contacts were still present along the beaches. That too, like the music, caused him to dismiss some of the thoughts which he tried to resist. Always his walks ended with a newspaper and a cocktail at the Juantibes Cafe, either a Campari and soda or a Glenlivet on the rocks. Misser Joe, ever practicing his pigeon English, was satisfied that he had not caused a lasting discomfort between himself and his friend.

Early on the evening when he knew that it was time for Monica to return, he sat sipping and reading and catching the views of the cute bodies of the strutting 'birdies'. Then slowly a large shadow crossed over him, and his senses sent out signals. Not like the response necessary in Marseille, but signals just the same. He very methodically put down the newspaper, leaning forward just a bit to clear an angle for the left hand to reach the PPK.

As he looked up, there stood a tall, square shouldered man, wearing an overcoat. An overcoat in this warm temperature, he thought. Then it was obvious why. In the right pocket was his hand holding what appeared, by the outline, to be a large weapon. A sidearm perhaps, he thought, but maybe an Uzi. As he looked directly into the eyes of the man before him, he connected with the movement of yet another man out on the curb, facing toward both of them. The man near the street also had a large overcoat and his right hand in the pocket.

"Move!" the voice said with a guttural accent, gesturing the right hand in the pocket. "Move or you die here!"

It was another German accent, he thought, as he looked from one overcoated man to the other. This was his first direct look at the man on the curb. That man was younger, and seemed a bit nervous about the whole activity. He was shifting and looking about, not keeping his attention on Michael. It would be to Michael's advantage with the backup person covering the street to be so nervous. As he looked to the street, and started to slowly rise out of his seat, he still had the man in front of him in his full vision, and now he could see Misser Joe coming across the Cafe.

Misser Joe came slowly with a large iron skillet. He knew that the Maitre'd had probably not spotted the backup man. Whatever happened from this point on, he knew that his first move would have to be at the backup, the man on the street. Misser Joe was vulnerable on his left side.

Suddenly Misser Joe swung the skillet up in the air and down on the overcoated man's head. The impact made a loud metal resounding sound, almost like a huge bell being rung.

Quickly Michael was out of the seat trying to get a clear shot to the curbside. But as the impact of the iron skillet connected with the man's head, he pulled out his 9mm German sidearm and fell against Michael. The nervous backup man pulled his gun free and aimed in toward the trio.

The crowd screamed and shouted and pushed in all directions. By reflex action, Michael pushed Misser Joe down and turned the unconscious man in front of him as a shield. The PPK seemed to leap from the small of his back to his left hand.

But before there was anything further happened, the backup man solved the first of the two problems. From out near the street, he fired repeatedly, each time hitting his own comrade with 9mm bullets. The gun clicked empty and he stood for a moment, wide-eyed, looking at the Baader-Meinhof prize target very much alive, holding up his dead comrade as a shield. Suddenly in a burst of fear, he dropped the empty gun and darted out into the traffic of the busy Guy de Mauppasant.

First he was struck from the left as he ran in front of a truck, then stumbling forward he was hit from the opposite side. Tires squealed and horns blared as cars screeched to a halt, all turned and sideways. There was silence on the Avenue and silence in the Cafe. The backup man had come to rest under the front wheel of a new Mercedes.

The crowd was very quiet, almost as though the aftermath of a sudden shock. The vehicles on the avenue were stopped. There was some shouting, but not a great deal. It was as though everyone in the immediate area had taken part in this murderous drama, and now they were trying to recover. Everything seemed to be happening very slowly. It was like slow motion.

Misser Joe got up from the ground and began straightening tables and chairs. Some of the people standing around started helping.

The American French 15 settled the dead overcoated man down into one of the chairs Misser Joe had turned up. He rummaged through the pockets, looking for what he knew would be there, a green Phoenix card. In the top shirt pocket was the card, number eight. He walked carefully and with even steps, maintaining a well poised balance as he moved out to the street. There could be more backups about, he thought, maybe with cameras. Maybe they would now try their luck. He pushed aside the truck driver and knelt down beside the man in the street. Another search and another green card. Number four!

Michael looked up and around at the crowd gathered about the dead man. He smiled, reflecting on his childhood.

"This is like collecting baseball cards!" he said in loud clear English.

Those around him glanced at each other. Even if they understood English, they did not understand 'baseball cards'.

As he stood up, he remembered the comment from the voice on the phone, 'We do expect more from you!' He look around carefully, trying to find any additional disturbance.

Satisfied that all was calm, and also hearing the police sirens screech as they approached, he pushed through a heavier crowd back to the cafe. Here he found Misser Joe. They looked at each other a moment, then they sealed the trauma with an embrace. Misser Joe was shaking a little, and his smile was nervous, but inside he felt good about helping 'his friend'.

"Thanks, ole buddy." Michael said. His hands held Misser Joe's shoulders.

As the police pushed through the Avenue and in through the Cafe, Michael decided he would have to come back for his cocktail and newspaper, but for now he really should leave.

As he meandered along the Guy de Maupassant at the edge of the beach, he could see ahead to the apartment. His mood was down and he felt alone. Spring was behaving very nicely, and these first weeks of June were warm with clear evenings. It was nice being in Antibes, since everyone, he thought, had to be somewhere.

Up ahead he spied a taxi stop in front of his place, and Monica, in uniform, get out of the cab with her luggage. She paused to pay the driver then headed for the front door. That sight certainly helped his mood. She disengaged the alarm and went inside. Again, he knew she was being careless, even after their last incident.

"Of all the gin joints in all the towns in all the world," he was saying as he came in the open door behind her, "you have to pick my gin joint to come to on a night like this."

"Oh I missed you!" she said hugging him. It was long 'welcome home' kiss. "I always worry about you." She backed a little to look at him. "What was all that commotion down the street? The taxi almost didn't get through."

"Nothing serious. It looked like some North African and frogs got into a fist fight on the Avenue."

"I just knew," she said looking directly into his eyes, "that you would be in the middle, right the bloody middle of it."

"Not me," he said, "I don't bother with someone else's mess." Then so as to change the subject, he kissed her again, holding her close to him. He proceeded to set the apartment in a romantic mood, music and champagne.

Monica was just in from a trip and she wanted to shower and relax. As she dragged the 'wimp wheels' up the stairs with her luggage strapped on, he went over to the entertainment center to program the stereo selections. Right behind her up the stairs to the master suite he came bringing a bottle of champagne and two long tuliped glasses. He lounged across the bed watching her undress while she rambled on about her trip and about her concern for the growing terrorist threats.

It made him feel good to watch her take off her clothes. Very seductive, he thought, as she opened her bra and then pulled down the brief panties she wore. She was standing in front of him, naked with a glass of champagne in one hand and gesturing about terrorists with the other. He only smiled and stared at the firm well formed body.

"You don't listen to me." Monica said, in her disgusted sounding voice. "This whole terrorist thing!"

Michael looked up at her face. He was listening, and he understood how keyed-up she was. Coming down after a trip was bad enough, time zones crossed, serving people on the plane, walking constantly, and now the added dimension of terrorism could certainly make anyone even more anxious. He looked at her eyes. He knew that she wanted eye contact to feel as though he was listening.

"Thirty thousand feet up is no place to have to deal with a bunch of crazy people who might blowup the plane." She wrapped herself in one of the large white robes as she continued. "I'm a woman! That makes it even harder!"

"Monica," he started, "tell me what the airline is doing." He was focused on her subject now. "Tell me about the training."

"I mean," she said as though she did not hear him, "women are always concerned even walking the streets. Some crazy man could grab me anytime. He could rape me, and then bludgeon me to death after he's finished." She was pouring another champagne as she spoke. "And now, at thirty thousand feet in the air, during a hijacking when everyone is scared to death, we are supposed to cooperate."

Michael got up and held her a moment. She nuzzled her chin into his chest. He wasn't sure if it was the subject of the terrorists, or her tension during the past few days thinking about the Phoenix thing.

"I'm sorry." she said softly.

"Tell me," he said again, "what is Air France doing."

Monica reached over to the dresser and flipped open her wallet. There were pictures of two little girls and a very young boy.

"My nieces and a nephew." She looked at the pictures. "The terrorists in the Middle East are supposed to be sentimental. Especially since they're Arabs, and Arabs are very family oriented."

Michael backed off a little. She was beginning to relax. She was beginning to talk about it, and she needed some space.

"I'm supposed to tell them that these are my children. I love them. I'm supposed to cry because I miss them. Then they'll relax. I can help them and keep them from getting violent. Maybe it will keep them from hurting anyone."

She was still looking at the pictures as she sat down across from him, leaning forward with her elbows on her knees, the wallet in one hand and her glass in the other.

"All the toilets are locked before takeoff. That's supposed to keep anyone from hiding in there. If anyone has to leave the plane after boarding, we have to have an escort go with them. If they get away from the escort, then we have to deplane everyone and search the plane."

Monica got up from the seat across from Michael.

"I'm tired. This champagne is going to my head." She gestured with a hand to her forehead.

"What else?"

"Baggage." she replied.

"Baggage?"

"If you check your baggage, but," she looked up again, "you don't show up at the plane, then we hold the flight to get the baggage off."

"Does it happen often?"

"No. Only once that I know. It was out of Athens." She turned away and walked a little as she continued. "Then when transit passengers change planes, their baggage is put on the tarmac, in a holding area, and the passengers identify their luggage."

"What if luggage is not identified?"

"It's bloody well destroyed!"

Michael shook his head lightly. He did not want to broadcast concern. He was beginning to understand what she was talking about, and what she was feeling.

"The flight attendants are all checked as well. They check our baggage, and use the electronic probe on us. Once I brought back a set of stag handled carving knives from Germany. The Germans are very efficient. Security took the knives." She was almost smiling now. "It took me three months to get them delivered to the Air France base in Paris. I got a severe reprimand from the company."

Michael got up and poured each of them another champagne.

"You'll sleep well. After a hot shower you'll relax and sleep well."

"We're supposed to talk with the terrorists." She was going back to the beginning. "We're supposed to talk about family, parents, children, where we live, school, anything sort of domestic. It helps the terrorists feel less tense. If they're calm, they might not hurt anyone."

Michael nodded as he looked at Monica. Not some of the terrorist groups he had had to deal with, he thought. They are so fanatical that no conversation works with them. He felt she was going a little beyond the point of having just talked it all out.

Michael shifted a little.

"That's enough, Monica." He got up and held her close to him.

She stepped back a way, took a deep breath and turned and entered the huge tiled shower, still carrying her champagne.

The shower stall was very large with tiled benches on the far side. It had been built as a steam closet. Through the glass door he watched her shape move about, bathing herself, stopping to sip champagne. Again he smiled as he watched.

It was time for another bottle, and to join her in the steam closet, but before doing so, he thought about the front door and the security system.

The alarm panel next to the bed headboard would not clear through. It indicated intrusion. He sat for a moment, listening beyond the sound of the hot shower water. There was nothing. He got up, PPK in hand and went downstairs to the living area. His gait was casual and his appearance was relaxed. It was the image he wanted to give an intruder. Someone would think him unconcerned and they might make the first mistake. But he found nothing. All was quiet except for the soft sounds of Sarah Vaughn's voice with the Oscar Peterson trio.

The intrusion signal came from the front door. Not Monica's fault, he thought, because he had followed her inside. He closed and locked the door. Once the area was checked and secured, he grabbed up another cold champagne and bolted two steps at a time up to the master suite.

"Well," she said, as he got into the steam room with her, naked as she and carrying a fresh cold champagne bottle, "look at what I see." She spoke gesturing down at his medium erection.

"Ah ha," he replied. "All you want is to screw my body. I'm more than just a pretty face, you know." She had reached down to fondle him.

For the next few minutes they kissed, hugged and caressed each other. It was more obvious that he was excited. His medium erection had turned into a full 'hard on'. They continued to kiss and he patiently covered her whole body with kisses, pausing occasionally where he knew she felt the touch of this mouth against her would arouse her as well.

After the champagne and enough time for them to be boiled red from the heat, they stepped out of the steamroom. Still wet, they embraced and fell across the huge oversized bed.

The evening was cool with a light Mediterranean breeze as later they sat out on the balcony looking across the Sea toward the lights of Cannes. Michael had opened a new bottle of Remy Martin.

"Tell me about you." she said, snuggled up into a fetal position in the chaise lounge, covered warmly with one of those large thick Hotel Muerice bathrobes. "I don't want to start another argument, but after the other night, I want to know who you are. You don't work, you don't talk about investments." She shifted slightly on the lounge. She was smiling to try to keep him relaxed. "Just who the hell are you?"

He looked at her for a moment, over the edge of the brandy snifter. "I am a French military pensioner. The French government takes very good care of me."

"This is some nice way for the French to take care of you. This is no pension income."

She shifted again, trying to find that comfortable spot. "After the other night..." she hesitated, "and that phone call to someone to come clean up, and then the night at the Eden Roc..." she was watching him while she spoke, looking for some kind of sign, "...everything was paid for. Everyone there knew you." Then she stopped.

"Why don't we go back to bed for a while?"

"No!" she replied.

"A walk on the beach?"

"No, be serious!" Her voice was deeper and more direct. "Talk to me. Tell me something. I have been worrying about it."

"I am commissioned by the French government as a consultant to certain police matter." He stopped.

"What happened in Marseille?" She did not want to attack a specific subject, but he continued to resist her. She was not sure if it was fear or curiosity or concern that pushed on her questioning.

"Nothing of interest happened. We drove to Marseille, had a nice visit at the military post, ate bouillabaisse, and then we drove back."

"That's all! Then why did you have to go with him!" It was a question made as a statement. "You saved my life. You didn't even hesitate. You knew what you were doing." Now she showed anger in her voice.

"It's not that important." He gave her a disgusted look, hoping to discourage the line of conversation. "I am commissioned by the French government to act with Interpol."

He paused. If only she had gotten through all of this while away on her trip. He realized that he was wrong when he thought that she would have been over the Phoenix affair.

"That's it. That's all there is!" he continued. "I am trained to handle situations like the other night. It might sound strange, but it's like driving a car. After a while you act instinctively, without conscious thought. Thought slows the reflexes."

She picked up the cognac bottle and came back over to him on his chaise. They were both warm in their bathrobes along with the cognac ambiance.

"This stuff bloody well slows the reflexes." she said holding up the bottle. "What happened before the French?"

"I was in the U.S. Air Force in the 60's. I got caught behind the lines and they kept me there."

"The Vietnamese?"

"No, the U.S. Air Force." He sipped some cognac, not looking at her, more like looking up the Juan les Pin beaches and not focusing on anything. "They called me an MIA." This is a lot like thinking out loud, he thought. Then he repeated himself. "They called me an MIA!"

She was watching his face closely. She had no idea what an MIA was, but she did not want to interrupt him.

"Missing in action..." he mumbled, almost thoughtlessly, "...and they kept it that way." Now he looked at her. "They notified my family that I was missing. They used me behind the lines. I was used to rescue downed pilots and to help kidnapped diplomats get out of the Viet Cong control in the north." He shook his head a little. "They kept my identity a secret for years." He looked at her. "My wife remarried!" Then he stopped. The light from the moon glistened across the Sea and reflected in his eyes.

Monica leaned closer and kissed his cheek. His gaze was off somewhere else again.

"Do you know what that means?" He looked at her again. "I spent years back and forth behind the lines. They brought me out from time to time to take my pulse, get a physical, and then sent me back. At first there was talk about how popular I was. That unknown jungle guerilla was a hero for the American people, in a war not doing so well for them." He paused, reflecting a moment. "Then later, the war got more unpopular and I became unpopular. First they treated me like a hero, and then they treated me like a criminal!"

He got up from the chaise, downed the rest of what cognac was in the glass. Again he filled the glass, higher than socially acceptable. It was obvious that his aggravation was increasing, both from the cognac and from the talk about Viet Nam.

"Those bastards used me, burned me out and threw me away. I had the enemy trying to kill me in the beginning. They came after me in Seoul on my rest tours, and even in Tokyo. They had spies trying to kill me everywhere, even in the hospital. But then suddenly I had other people trying to get rid of me, and they were supposed to be on the same side I am. Finally," he paused to take a deep breath, "they gave me a huge supply of money, a new identity, and then proceeded to tell me that I couldn't go home. They didn't even want me anywhere in the United States. If I went back without permission, I would be considered an 'alien with the intent to do harm'. I would be deported or imprisoned."

He paused long enough for another deep swallow of cognac. "They put me on an airplane out of Tokyo for Tel Aviv."

"Tel Aviv!"

Slowly his level of anger began to come down. He leaned against the balcony railing a moment, reflecting deep inside, thinking quickly of specific moments which he hated, but had lived and relived over the years.

"So along came a French Interpol contact. Viet Nam had been a disaster for the French. They were looking for a way to save face. They commissioned me to work with them. But from then on I did everything on my terms. I was in the Interpol elite group where only a few select people are trained to work. I became a French Interpol Five. I don't know how many there are, but I don't think there are very many. Today," and now he was turned back toward Monica, "I am considered inactive."

Monica shifted uneasily. Michael was beginning to ramble. He was getting anxious and angry.

"I've got money put away. I can enjoy any of the beastly comforts I choose, especially in the Interpol countries. So!"

"What happened in Berlin?" she asked cautiously. He was back in her presence. She was being cautious, but she wanted to find out a little more. After the other night, during her flight she had remembered the incident they had about his Berlin trip.

"Berlin?" he asked.

"Berlin!" she replied. "That's the only other time I can remember such a bloody fight over your personal business."

Now he remembered that it was the Berlin trip when he told her that he was off for a brief visit on business, and she did not hear from him for two weeks. He had never explained the truth. At this moment he couldn't remember what story he had manufactured about his absence, but he never did tell her the truth.

When he got there, he now told her, he had to enter East Berlin and connect with a hostage. The hostage was a setup. He was captured by the Volpo. He was embarrassed, he continued, because they traded him back to the West for one of their people. He spent two weeks cramped in a four by four concrete cell. Gruel was shoved into him through a narrow opening, and all the while he sat in his own waste.

Some of his story to Monica was true. The part about the cell was mostly true. He had gone in after the brothers of Nezer Hindawi. The bombing in Berlin was done by Nezer's brothers. He got them, and on the way out, one of the Interpol operatives was a double agent. Just like always, enemies on both sides.

It was as though he were alone on the balcony overlooking the Mediterranean. He had drifted away from her again. He was saying the words aloud, and Monica could hear, but it was more like he was at a confession, or more like saying words so he could hear the story from himself for the first time.

Then he stopped again, this time ending the commentary. Finally he came over to her, took her by the hand and led her back into the bedroom. They embraced on the bed. He was holding her very still. As tired as she was, she was wide awake thinking about all he had said. She felt the deep, steady breathing as he began to sleep in the crook of her arm.

CHAPTER SIX

Target Practice

T he next few days were somewhat relaxing on the surface. They enjoyed the days on the beaches, walking and picnicking, and the evenings of casual dinners usually finishing with cognacs at the Juantibes Cafe. Monica tried to relax, and she tried hard to relax Michael, but there was a change now. Maybe it was something he was into or maybe it was because he had opened himself up to her. She wanted a number of times to approach the issues straight on, but was not strong enough to deal with the possibility of total rejection. Usually he understood her proddings. In the past she always quizzed him about the 'birdies' on the beach. But that was different. This was more serious. She wanted to know everything, but maybe she had gone too far. Her mind was vacillating. She thought that she should probably apologize.

On their third night back together, as they came up from the far side of the beach on their way back to the Apartment, he sensed the presence of someone in the shadows at the front of the building. Gently he held Monica back a little, gesturing for her to wait, then quietly he altered his route and crept up behind the darkened figure.

"Wait! Stop!" the voice yelled out in English with a French accent.

Monica came running up to the front of the Apartment. There was Michael. He had someone shoved back against the doorway, and his PPK was in the man's face.

"I'm Marcel." the voice mumbled, still in French English, with the sounds of fear. "I'm Marcel. I need to talk with you."

Monica stood off a few feet watching the bizarre drama take place. Michael looked at Marcel a moment, still in the dark shadows of the building. He stepped back, replaced the PPK and walked off a few paces.

"I'm sorry." Marcel said. "I rang the bell. I have been waiting right here. I didn't want to disturb you."

"It's okay. Let's go inside," he said gesturing with one arm and reaching out to Monica with the other.

"I didn't know how to call you." Marcel said once they were inside. "You told me that story in Marseille, but I didn't know how you wanted me to call you. I am so sorry!"

"I didn't want you to call me!" he replied with a slight grin. "This is Monica." She nodded at Marcel. "I think you should leave us." Michael said to her. "Marcel has something to tell me. It won't take long." She nodded toward Marcel, then she headed up the wide stairs which led to the master suite.

After she disappeared beyond the top landing, the two men settled back in easy chairs. Marcel was anxious to talk. He was having serious problems with contacts in Beirut. The French officers were still planning to meet him and to get him inside to find Girod Said. But he felt that they were not to be trusted. It was the Captain's attitude when he called him. They talked a number of times, trying to make arrangements. But he felt something was wrong. His worse fear, other than not connecting with Girod, was that he would be kidnapped and locked away. He had to go but he was so afraid for his life.

"Here!" Marcel said handing Michael a large brown envelope. "Here's five hundred thousand francs. Take it! If we get back I will give you another five hundred thousand."

Marcel shifted and looked at Michael, while still holding out the envelope. Michael leaned forward and took the envelope, opening it and flipping through the bills.

"It's all there." Marcel said.

"I know." Michael replied. "Give me a couple of days. Girod will keep!"

Marcel shrugged. He had no idea what might be happening in Beirut or what the messages from his father were. They talked a short time longer, with Marcel making most of the time that he had. He was very nervous talking about Michael going with him to Beirut. He was trying to establish a plan for the trip. At least Michael said that he would think about it. He did not know that Michael was already concerned about Marcel going to Beirut with the French officers.

Soon they parted, and Marcel seemed very pleased. After securing the premises, Michael stood for a moment thinking about Monica's safety. She was very vulnerable around him. Something should be done to help her protect herself. He went upstairs to find her. She looked lovely, he thought, standing out on the balcony in the warm June evening.

"You look fantastic." he said as he slipped his arms around her waist. "Tomorrow morning," he continued softly in her ear, "I'm going to teach you how to shoot."

She turned her face toward him. "You tell me I look bloody great, then you tell me you'll teach me to shoot!"

"If you look that 'bloody' great, you have to protect yourself," he answered with a grin and raised eyebrows. "It's like so many things we reject. We don't understand them. Once you get the hang of a piece, then you'll feel very comfortable." He took her hand. "Tonight we'll knock off our own kind of piece, get a good night's sleep, and tomorrow you'll shake hands with a firearm piece."

Although it was something she seemed to dread, the thought of learning to shoot began to excite her a little. The idea of actually holding a gun and firing it made her blood pressure rise. She felt turned on.

"You know," he said in the darkened room as they climbed into bed, "I think all this terrorism is Abba Dabbus' psychotic loss of identity. Poor Colonel Mohammed Abba Dabbus' problems go back to his childhood. When he was growing up he didn't know if his name was to be spoken to cast a magic spell. Abbra Cadabra, Abba Dabbus. Or maybe he thought that his name was the phrase old Fred Flintstone used to cry out when he was happy. Abba Dabba Du, Abba Dabbus!"

She could not see his face in the darkness as she snuggled into his arms, but she was grinning a little, and she knew that he probably had a broad smile, pleased with himself over such a discovery.

In the morning he brought up fried eggs, french sausage, toasted bagels and a couple of bullshots. Not their usual 'petit de' jeuner'. It was something to give her strength and to relax the tenseness during her shooting lessons. She ate well. A bloody better U.K. breakfast than I usually get, she thought. Later, downstairs he unlocked the door off the workshop area, a doorway through which she had never gone.

"This," he announced as he led her inside and closed the door, "is my targeting room. I sound proofed it!"

It was also obvious, she thought, that he was pleased to have the room and to be showing it to her. It was a long narrow room with targets at the other end. Where they stood were stools and shelves and guns and shooting equipment.

Over the next few hours, he carefully and meticulously showed her how to load and how to shoot. They started with a single action revolver where the hammer had to be cocked first before the gun would fire. It had the easiest trigger pull. Then they went to double action revolvers, starting with a 22 caliber and ending with the 44 magnum. Her moods changed from excitement to anxiety and then back to excitement. She was thankful for the ear plugs. Next she went on to automatic pistols. Finally she fired Michael's PPK.

For a while she was tense, but gradually throughout the morning she began to relax. Soon she began to feel accomplishment in just hitting the target. Then each time she got closer to the bull's-eye, she felt better.

"Bring the right arm up, extend, use the arm long and steady, almost like a rifle. Hold the heel of your right hand in the palm of your left. Approach the target straight on, facing it directly." She heard those instructions over and over again. "Now squeeze the trigger. Don't pull it! Don't jerk it! Just a firm steady squeeze."

When finally she succeeded in the squeeze routine, sometimes the gun would go off and startle her. It pleased him. That meant she was not pulling the trigger expecting the gun to fire.

They took a break for lunch, and she soon found herself wanting to hurry with food so that she could get back to her lessons.

In the afternoon he gave her an electronic pistol. It had every identical feature as a real gun; weight, trigger firmness, and even sound and recoil when it fired. Only now he programmed the long room before her to gradually change in brightness and darkness, and for targets of human and animal forms to suddenly appear at various locations and distances. Each firing was recorded both in speed and accuracy by an electronic beam from the barrel of the gun. At first she shot at everything, killing a harmless grandmother and even shooting Bambi, but then after awhile she used judgement and her score improved.

"Let me show you some old tricks of the wild American west." he said as he buckled on an old western rig and tied the holster to his thigh. His left hand was open flat, palm down, just above the butt of the six shooter in its holster. On the back of his hand was a French franc. As she watched, almost in the speed of a blink, he dropped his hand to the gun, drew it out of the holster, cocked the hammer as it came up and fired a bull's-eye at the target ten meters away. The action had been so swift and so well time, that by the time gravity pulled the franc down, the holster was empty, the gun fired and the franc fell into the empty holster.

Monica looked at him a moment, then over at the bull's-eye. She stepped closer and looked down into the holster to see the franc in the cavity where the gun had been.

"Now, this time I need you to help me." he said handing her a six shooter. "Pull the hammer back and point the gun in that direction." He pointed toward a large target. "My gun is holstered. When you see me start to move to draw the gun, you just squeeze your trigger and shoot the target." She looked at him a moment. "I will draw and fire before you can shoot your gun."

They stood near each other, bodies facing the targets. She had her gun cocked and ready to fire, pointing down the room, but she was looking at his left hand. He started to move, and she reacted as fast as she could, simply squeezing the trigger. But her gun was the second sound heard in the room.

He laughed as he twirled the six shooter about, spinning from one hand to the other, and then flipping it back onto the holster. "Good old western movies always show the good guy waiting for the bad guy to draw first." As he unbuckled the western rig he looked at her with a smile. "He who draws first, lives!"

CHAPTER SEVEN
Beirut

I n the airport terminal in Nice, Marcel and Michael were separated for quite sometime. They only met again when they settled into their first class seats just before takeoff. Marcel was worried that maybe Michael would not board the plane. He had needed a few days to think about it, as he said. But then, he told Marcel he would go with him to Beirut. There was no explanation, and Marcel was beginning to learn. If Michael would go along on the trip, best leave whatever reasons unsaid. Marcel was glad to have his 'agent' with him on such a journey.

After a few moments in their seats, and still no words had been spoken, Marcel wanted to ask about the PPK. He knew it was there. It was always there. But what he really wanted to know was how Michael got through the security checkpoint. Did he identify himself as an I5! Did they recognize him? Did all the security people, especially in Nice, know him? He would not ask. If Michael wanted to talk about, he would.

The flight was uneventful, both men occupied in their own thoughts. Marcel sat by the window, looking out across the clouds and not wanting anything to drink. While Michael out on the aisle, had a couple of brandies and although his attention was sometime on the flight attendants, his peripheral surveillance kept watch on the entire first class cabin. He was uncomfortable being cooped in an airplane without any means of escape. For some strange reason he reflected on Monica's comment about 'the brandy dulling the senses, if anything would'. But that was the way he always worked!

It was afternoon when the plane landed and began its taxi toward the Beirut terminal. The fighting devastation was less than anticipated, Marcel was thinking to himself. He had expected to see everything bombed and destroyed with fighting everywhere. He thought the airport would be overrun with soldiers. Actually, it appeared quite normal.

Michael looked past him out through the window, remembering his last visit to Beirut. There were changes even here at the airport which he could sense. The old hustle seemed to be gone and instead, although not obvious, there was a sense of tense awareness in everyone. The deplaning was a bit more confusing than before.

"Bon jour, Comrades!"

Marcel looked up as he was coming into the gatehouse. There were the two French officers.

"I see," said Captain DuVall, "that you have brought your friend along." Marcel glanced over at Michael who seemed to be ignoring them. "Too bad," continuing to speak in French said the Captain, "I had hoped that we could enjoy this visit as close friends ourselves," glancing toward Michael, "and without him."

Marcel fit the mood of his surroundings as he too became tense. This was not the time to antagonize the Captain and certainly this was not the time to aggravate Michael. He looked away for the moment, pretending to look at the airport sights.

Michael came over to the Captain, and in his best French said, "You do your job," he paused, "just like you're told." He looked at Marcel who was now looking wide-eyed at the two. "Marcel has the extra money you said that he would need. Do your job," he continued in French, "and keep your ass and your Lieutenant's ass out of my way! In all this fighting around here, you just might earn those decorations you want, and with a hole in the middle of your forehead!"

The Captain stood motionless for a moment. It was obvious by the set jaw and the anger in his eyes that he wanted to cold-cock Michael right in the terminal. Seconds past, the two backed off and Marcel could begin to feel a little less tenseness from both. The Lieutenant was a few feet behind the Captain and appeared to present no threat whatsoever.

"George Habash has made it possible for us to meet your man." the Captain said breaking the silence, now speaking in English. "Do you know him?" As he asked he looked from one to the other.

Marcel shook his head negatively, while Michael gave no reaction.

"Habash will have to be paid. He is the head of the Popular Front for Liberation of Palestine. At first, when I arrived, there was resistance from Emile Abdallah himself." He looked one to the other, and again Marcel shook his head negatively. "He is the head of the Lebanese Armed

Revolutionary Factions. He is to be paid through Habash. His friends are Salim el-Khoury and the wild man Abu Akram."

Michael reacted. He looked more intently at the Captain. These were ruthless killers. Leaders of their people, they say, and terrorism is only a definition used by the Westerners. They are heroes to their people. Habash was a reasonable man, or so he seemed, Michael remembered, but Abu Akram, the code name for the wild terrorist of the Middle East knew no allegiance and held no regard for any nationalities or religions, power was his only master.

"Your man is being held in the old Muslim jail, quartered where drunks and rapists are locked. Now, it's also a fortification for captured enemies of the People's Lebanese Revolution." He paused deliberately for a moment, glancing at Michael but focusing his next comments on Marcel. "We will take you to the building, get you inside, and you pay me and we leave."

"No!" It was Marcel who spoke. Michael had started to speak, but was cutoff by Marcel. "No!" he repeated. "You take us to the building, you take us inside, you make sure we get to Girod," and now he glanced at Michael for support, "and then you stay with us until we get back here. You'll get paid when I have Girod out of there!"

"But if something should happen to you, I won't get my money. I have been here for over a week making preparations for you. If you die I don't get paid. If I don't get the money, then Habash and the others will see to it that I don't leave Beirut."

"Exactly." mumbled Marcel.

"If he dies," and this time it was Michael, much to the relief of Marcel, "then you die. You won't need the money. The chances of him dying with you along to help us are much less than if you were paid now." Michael smiled his warmest and friendliest smile. "Do I make myself clear?"

The Captain nodded affirmatively.

"Exactly!" Marcel mumbled again.

"Good, now you and your Lieutenant lead the way."

The foursome meandered through the streets for almost an hour, as the area became more and more battle torn. Marcel had become quite uncomfortable, glancing about frequently. His calming factor was Michael, relaxed and appearing rather confident. To Michael the region was not unfamiliar. There were more battle scars, but certain landmarks remained. He was satisfied that at least they were headed toward the old Muslim jail.

Finally inside the old building, Michael looked around, and although he had never been inside, it did appear as he had imagined it. Dark, poorly lit corridors lead off into blackness where rows of jail doors lined both sides of the walkways.

The Captain spoke in Arabic to a tired, crusty uniformed Arab who was leaning against the doorjamb of what appeared to be the entrance to the jail office. Michael could catch enough of the conversation to know that the Captain was being straight, and he knew that Marcel was getting it all. He would react quickly if he heard something wrong.

The Captain would certainly think that Marcel had the money with him, Michael was thinking. To kill them and take the money would be easier than going through this charade.

Soon they were ushered into a small dirty room where there was a wooden kitchen table and a few straight back wooden chairs. A man was being led into the room from another doorway, and although the light was dim, he squinted from the brightness.

"Girod?" Marcel muttered as he rose from the chair.

"Marcel" was the response, "you have come. My good friend, you have come."

As they embraced, the dirty uniformed guard sauntered back out through one of the doorways, seemingly very unconcerned.

"Out Captain!" Michael said. His voice was firm and authoritative. "You and your Lieutenant get outside and stay there."

"Pay us first!"

"If we pay you, there's no chance of us getting out. With you," again he smiled, "we'll probably get back out."

"I don't have much time, Marcel." the tired figure of Girod spoke. He mixed French, English and some street Egyptian in the language. "They want to make an example of me to other journalists." He looked around the room, finally adjusting to the light and realizing that there were three alone together.

"This is Michael," Marcel said in a whisper, "he is a French Interpol Five. He is here to help us!"

Girod looked at Michael, only as if trying to focus. Marcel was not sure that he had understood.

"The bombing has upset Abba more than ever." Girod continued in a raspy, sore voice. "He plans to get his gold out of Tripoli. I think your father said to the Jofrah region, maybe even into northern Chad. Abba wants Chad." There was silence for a moment as Girod seemed to try to catch his breath. "I have two Libyan passes for us, signed by Abba himself."

Marcel sat upright. "Two passes. Why two passes?" Then like suddenly hearing the rest of what Girod said. "Signed by Abba!"

"I do not know why. I received two Libyan Elite-passes signed by Abba. They came to me after your father was dead. I don't know why."

He looked at Marcel. "Maybe someone wanted us to come back to Libya!" Then he looked at Michael through half closed eyelids. "Maybe someone wanted you to bring your French Interpol Five friend to Libya."

"What did my father tell you?"

"Two dates are most important. The first is 1986 April and the other is 1986 July."

"What does it mean?" Marcel asked whispering and leaning closer to Girod.

"He said it was Abba's revenge, and that he was using the phrase 'Remember 1986 April' to rally the Libyans." Girod sat back. "That was the month of the bombing. But I think it is some kind of code to remove the gold from Bab Azizya! Right under the noses of the Libyan people."

Michael leaned forward, and mimicking to the best of his ability the mixture of languages he asked about the details of the conversation with Marcel's father, any other contacts, and finally where the passes were located.

Girod talked along in a quiet, tired voice, trying to remember events to answer Michael. It was obvious to the other two that he had suffered while in the old Muslim jail. He knew nothing else of any importance.

"Room 212, Hotel Meridian, taped under the dresser drawer." he answered when finally he got to that question. He looked at Michael. "Something is going to happen soon at the Bab Azizya Compound. Marcel's father felt sure that Abba is planning to move the gold and maybe destroy the Compound. Maybe he will blame it on the Americans. Maybe it will be so destroyed that the world will not find him. If America is blamed, maybe he will have the gold and no one will know."

Michael looked at Girod for a moment. How naive this person must be. Abba might blow up the Compound and blame America, but he is not clever enough to take that large bulk of gold and disappear. Abba's ego is such that he will surface, and surface often. No, Michael thought, there must be more to this. He looked at Marcel.

"Do you suppose that one of those passes was meant for me?" Michael asked, his comment triggered by Girod's earlier comment. That wry grin appeared again.

"I don't know." replied Marcel, not sure what to say.

"I think it might be. It does seem to be for me to use." Girod said, looking at Michael as he spoke. "If not for you to use, then maybe for someone else."

"But why any passes at all?" Marcel interrupted. "I have no plans to go to Libya."

Suddenly the sound of gun shots filled the outside corridor, sounding loud and very close. Without hesitation Michael was out of his seat, the PPK materialized into his grasp. He was out of the door.

Marcel and Girod sat motionless for a few moments as voices called out and the sound of shots continued. In the doorway again was Michael.

"The Captain and his Lieutenant are dead!" The PPK was part of his hand. "We'll head south to the Christian region." His thoughts were for the Jordan or Israel countries, out of Lebanon. He had strong support in both places.

As he reached to help Girod up, a figure appeared in the doorway behind him and fired directly into Girod's chest. Michael spun around and fired, but the man was gone. Outside in the corridor the light was too dim to see. Voices were still calling out and gun shots could be heard in both directions.

"Hold it, Monsieur!"

From the other doorway into the room had come three dirty uniformed guards. They had automatic weapons pointed at him and Marcel. Girod was on the floor.

"Put them in separate cells. They have killed the prisoner!" one of the guards said as he took the PPK from Michael.

They grabbed Marcel and Michael and dragged them from the room. Marcel was looking back at the motionless figure of Girod on the floor, but Michael was looking ahead and sizing his captors.

Once the guards had left him in the musty, dirt floored cell, he checked the room. Something was making him feel uncomfortable. The hairs on the back of his neck were straight as porcupine quills. Not because of being in Beirut, or being in a cell, but that the events which had just occurred seemed so contrived, so preplanned. It was an old feeling he felt. The man in the doorway could have shot him as well. But he didn't. It was an old feeling. It was as though he was being preserved for the moment, for a higher plan at some later time. It reminded him of some of the days in Nam when someone was looking out for him. Not to protect him, only to save him for another assignment. And he remembered other cells he had occupied. In Australia, Indonesia, and even East Berlin.

"Excuse me, Monsieur." It was a dirty uniformed guard standing at the cell door. He was speaking in French. "You have a roommate." As Michael looked over, the figure of another man entered the cell. The guard pushed the cell door closed and disappeared down the corridor.

All those earlier uncomfortable feelings left Michael quickly. Now he had signals of warning. It did not fit the pattern of his survival. This was an additional intrusion. It did not fit the pattern.

The man acted casual and disinterested. Too disinterested, thought Michael. This person is making a point to relax him. It seemed obvious that Michael was supposed to feel relaxed in his presence.

"Haben Sie eine zigarette, bitte?" Michael asked.

"Nein, Ich habe keine!"

Suddenly the stranger stiffened and turned around. The question to him for a cigarette was in German. His negative response was an automatic reaction. The two men stared at each other.

"What now, asshole!" Michael stated in English.

The stranger stood before him, blocking the closed doorway. Michael's instincts were fast at work, reflecting over the objects and locations of items in the cell. His adrenalin was pumping. In spite of the situation, it always felt good when he reached his adrenal high. Afterall, he was always better in war than in peace.

Suddenly, the German produced a knife from nowhere. He crouched slightly, knife in right hand and left arm extended for balance. Michael stared at his opponent, feeling the vacancy in the small of his back.

Then, with a quick whirling karate kick he missed the knife and caught the man in the chin, knocking him back against the doorway. A gunshot sounded outside the cell. Michael lunged at the man against the door, grabbing the hand with the knife, twisting the wrist, and thrusting the blade into his chest. The man stood for a moment, staring back at Michael, then he slowly slid down the door. The knife was so deep into his chest that only the handle was visible. Even in the dimly lit cell, Michael could see the blood spreading across the front of the man's shirt.

As he slid down, the door opened slowly from his weight, and he fell backwards out into the corridor. Michael pulled the knife out and stood very still, waiting for the next action. Why had the door opened? Nothing happened. There was no movement and no sound. All was very quiet.

Then very carefully Michael stepped over the body and checked the corridor. There was no one. No one except another man on the floor of the corridor outside the cell. The gunshot had taken care of the outside person.

Michael bent over the German in the cell doorway and searched the body until he found what he expected. A card was in his upper pocket with the number 1. He looked at it a moment, then put it in his pocket. He reached over to the other body. The man in the corridor had been shot in the back of the head. The dead man still held a gun in his hand. Michael put the knife down and took the gun from the tight dead grasp. He studied the face for a moment, then began to search again. Number 6 was in his back pocket.

Sounds from one end of the corridor brought him back from his thoughts. The time was now, and now he had to find Marcel and get out of the Muslim jail.

Two cells down he found Marcel sitting on the cot, head down in the palms of his hands, staring at the dirt floor. The cell door was unlocked. Another interesting ploy, he thought. He signaled to Marcel.

Before he would leave, Michael made his way through the empty corridor until he found the jail office. The vacancy in the small of his back left him wanting his PPK. Again without resistance, he found the automatic laying on the desk. There was no one anywhere in the area. It's all too easy, he was thinking.

"Michael!" Marcel whispered as they made their way through the back alleys. "I'm afraid of this. We might get killed. They killed Girod. How can we get out!"

"First we get the passes!"

"No! Let's leave now. Maybe they can't find us at night like this."

"They know exactly where we are. Someone wants us to get those passes." He stopped for a moment and looked at Marcel in the yellow street light. "And I intend to get the passes and find out what that someone wants."

"No!" mumbled Marcel. "It is not what I thought. These people are not like us. They don't care. Human life doesn't matter."

"Which people? Where?" Michael stood for a moment, reflecting on other people and other places. "Let me tell you something, Marcel," and he grasped Marcel's shirt firmly. "When you know your enemies, you know who you are up against, but when you think you know your friends, you never know who to trust!" He looked into Marcel's eyes. "Ten enemies I can handle, but one traitor friend is disastrous!"

Once into the Meridian Hotel, they boldly walked through the lobby and took the stairs to the second floor. Everyone in the lobby ignored them. Marcel was scared, but by now Michael knew that they were suppose to be ignored. Room 212 was locked, but easily opened. One dresser drawer was half opened. It was obvious that the passes would be taped under that drawer. It was all too easy!

As the Air France jumbo jet lifted smoothly from the runway and was airborne, Michael sat back a little more relaxed. He looked at the man sitting next to him. Marcel was tense, staring straight ahead at the back of the seat in front of them. His eyes seemed not to blink. Michael watched for a moment, then touched his forearm.

"We're being used, Marcel." Marcel nodded, but continued to look ahead. "Girod was setup, captured and dangled in front of you." He corrected his observation. "In front of us!" He tightened his grip on Marcel. "How did you know about me? How did you know where to find me?"

Marcel felt the strength in the hand on his arm. He broke off the stare and turned to Michael.

"I don't remember. As I told you before, I knew I needed experienced help. I knew I needed someone to help me." He looked away. "I remember. My father's friend told me to get help in France. He told me who to see. He knew I lived on the Cote d'Azur." He looked back at Michael. "But not this. This is too bizarre. My mother must have been killed to make my father seek revenge. Then he was killed." He looked again at Michael, as though searching for a reaction. "And now Girod is dead! If what you say is true, are we to die when we complete our task?"

"Probably!" smiled Michael. "But not this task. I expect my tasks to take me well into the next century, and myself well past the century mark. As the Georgian Russians attest to yogurt for centurion life, I attest to Campari, champagne, caviar, a beautiful setting, and a beautiful woman to share it with."

His smile turned into a grin. "But," he continued, "is there anything else about locating me. Think!"

Marcel took a deep breath and sat back for a moment. "No, I can't think of anything important. I made contact with the name I was given. That person had a friend who had a friend, and when I explained that I needed an expert, then your name came up."

"What about DuVall and Bornier?"

"Who?" Marcel turned.

"Those two French officers! How did you find out about them?"

"I don't remember." He looked ahead, pensive. "Somewhere along the way I found out that they could get me into Beirut. That was before you. They could get me to Girod who had something to tell me about my father."

"It must be Hassad." Michael said.

"You mean Hafez Hassad?"

"Could be. He wants a greater Syria. One that includes Syria, Jordan, Israel, and Lebanon." Michael sat back, somewhat pleased with what might be the truth behind the events. "In 1976 he had Kemal Jumblatt killed when he was getting too big for his britches. Then in 1982, he killed Bashir Gemayel, the Christian leader because of his ties to King Hussein and to Israel. It might be that he wants Abba Dabbus out of the way. It might be that he has planned this whole thing for us to get into Libya. Even though the Iranian terrorists use Beirut as their headquarters, his Syrian army is in charge. He encourages the Jihad to stay in Beirut." Michael looked at Marcel. "He's got you mad because of the death of your parents, and now Girod. He's got me concerned because the subject is international terrorism and blaming the U.S. for destroying Bab Azizya. Maybe he knows about the gold Abba has, and wants to take it away from him..." He looked ahead again, "...with our help."

Michael lifted his glass and examined the amber color of his cognac. Maybe Monica is right, he thought. Maybe the spirits on the flight into Beirut dulled his senses. Maybe they wouldn't have gotten Girod.

Michael sat back, handling the Libyan pass in his hands, looking at Abba's signature, and trying to read the Arabic. He felt, during the rest of the trip back to Nice, that whoever was behind this, must have a long carefully planned program. In Arabic stamped across the back of the pass were the words "Remember 1986 April Remember". Occasionally, he would try to read Arabic words from left to right as in English. He remembered Girod saying '1986 April'. The signature of Colonel Mohammed Abba Dabbus fascinated him even more. To actually have in his hand, with his left thumb lightly rubbing the name, this original signature by Abba.

Finally he looked over at Marcel, who by this time had relaxed enough to be napping. He looked over at two stewardesses deep in French conversation, and then he let the lids of his eyes close and he too napped.

CHAPTER EIGHT

Traitor

I n old Antibes, Michael stood on the ramparts with the Chateau
Grimaldi behind him, looking out across the Mediterranean. His
thoughts were on Marcel and the jumbled confusion of Beirut and
the 'Remember' messages. It was not so long ago, he felt, that he had still
been in the jungle of Viet Nam. Yet, if he counted the years, a long time
had past.

He shook his head a little as he jumped down from the stone wall
into the walkway of the courtyard garden. The years have past so quickly.
Sometimes he could actually allow himself to feel as though he were
somewhere else, in a time long past, living at that moment as he had lived.
Even so, he reflected, he could go back before Viet Nam and remember
and feel what it was like when he was first married, and when they were
being sent overseas to Tokyo. As a child he was told that he had a vivid
imagination. That imagination might even play tricks on him, he often
thought, sometime not being able to absolutely separate the real past
from what he felt it should have been. But then again, he would console
himself with the comfort of knowing that a strong healthy imagination had
probably saved his sanity on more than one lone and gruelling situation,
especially in the jungle.

As he meandered through the Picasso museum housed in the Chateau,
avoiding tourists, he smiled a little feeling that in spite of it all, many folks
would think that it really could not get any better than this. Maybe if he
had it all to do over again, he wouldn't change anything.

Just down from the museum, still inside the walls of the old city of
Antibes, is an area of outdoor flea markets and fresh vegetables and fruit

stands. At night the food market, which is in the open air covered high above by a corrugated roof, becomes outdoor restaurants and cafes.

Beyond the shopping area is a maze of narrow streets and alleys lined with more shops, cafes, food stands and restaurants, all comprising the makeup of the old inner city. The entire old city is within the huge stone wall. For the protection of the city, a fortress was built to ward off the Mediterranean pirates, especially the Moors from North Africa.

A harbor separates old Antibes from the fort itself. In the late 1700's, a young Lieutenant Napoleon Bonaparte in the French Army was assigned to the fort, Fort Carre. Napoleon had grown to love this coast so well, that years later upon his escape from Saint Helena Island, it was to this region he returned to rally his supporters and begin his triumphant march back to Paris.

Below the ancient City of Antibes is a broad piece of land which juts out into the Mediterranean forming a significant peninsula, recognized as the world renowned Cap Antibes. It is the place of resorts, homes, hotels, and playground for the world's rich and famous. It is along the upper west beaches of this peninsula, which is called Juan les Pins, where a not so famous, unassuming supposedly retired Interpol agent has his beach Apartment overlooking the Mediterranean. To the west is the Sea and to the east are the activities of the Guy de Maupassant Avenue. Westward from Cap Antibes is Cannes, a young, exciting area which has become very active and wild, particularly during the month of May. Somewhat beyond Cannes are the bikini beaches of St. Tropez.

In the opposite direction from Cap Antibes, only some twenty minutes to the east is Nice, a city more sedate and sophisticated, established with residents of maturity and wealth. Another half an hour drive is Monaco and the gambling casinos of Monte Carlo. Then there is the Italian Riviera and a few hours inland is Milano.

Michael finally seated himself at a small table outside a cafe in one of the narrow streets. As he sipped on the Stella Artois beer, he doodled on a napkin. His thoughts seemed to be again focusing on Marcel and Tripoli.

It would be exciting, he was thinking as he wrote out 'Remember 1986 April Remember', to sneak into Tripoli with Abba's own signature on the pass, get inside the Bab Azizya Compound and destroy the madman's headquarters. A much simpler way than bombing the whole city, he thought. He turned the napkin over and drew a crude map of Tripoli streets as he remembered them, depicting the center with a large rectangle representing the Compound. As he studied the drawing, he meticulously searched his memory banks in an attempt to reconstruct everything he could remember about the actual setting. Soon he realized that he was confusing what he thought he remembered with newscasts, pictures and probably that old standby, his imagination.

The sun was just setting when he ambled into the Socca Restaurant on the Rue Thuret. It was his favorite place for bouillabaisse. The owners had gotten to recognize him, and to seat him in his favorite area in the rear, away from the doorway, and facing the open windows. It was not odd to them, many people had comfortable locations in the restaurant. To them Michael was just another familiar person who came in often for beer and bouillabaisse. Another expatriated American. They had gotten to know a little more about the way he liked his bouillabaisse. By now it was no chore to quickly add certain 'specialties' and serve him a hot, spicy meal. He would sometimes sit for hours, slowly sampling the variety of flavors in such a dish, sipping on one beer after another. Often the owner would insist upon reheating the food as it was probably too cool to enjoy. Then upon the owner's return from the kitchen, Michael would be served another piping hot full dinner course. This was just such an evening of comfortable relaxation, allowing himself to only reflect upon thoughts which brought him pleasure and nothing of those which brought him pain.

"Excuse me."

Michael looked up to see a man standing next to the table.

"May I sit with you?"

Michael looked around the restaurant. There were a number of empty tables. There was no reason for this person to ask to sit at this table.

"May I?"

Michael looked at the man. He was medium height, with a small pencil like mustache, dressed European, not American or even English, and probably not a tourist. Then he realized the man spoke to him in English. There was an accent, but it was almost perfect English.

Why, Michael thought, does he need to sit here? Why did he speak to me in English?

"I know who you are," the man said. "You are Amerigo, an I5 agent. It is important that I speak to you. I need to talk to you."

The man was leaning forward very close to Michael. His hands were on the table as he leaned across the plate of bouillabaisse.

Again Michael looked at the man. Rarely did he hear his Interpol code name used. The PPK in his back belt began to feel as though it was moving. It always seemed to come to life during situations like these. He leaned forward slightly and dropped his left arm.

"My code name is Friedriche," he said as he sat down. "I'm from Berlin. I'm a German agent." He sat looking at Michael. "Please relax, I need your help!"

The man seemed to be sincere, almost pleading for Michael to listen to him. As the two stared at each other for that moment, the tranquil realization which had engulfed Michael earlier was gone. His senses were turned up and as their eyes were still connected, his ears listened about the room and he expanded his peripheral vision to see from wall to wall, including the open windows, the doorway and even the tables close on each side.

"I am an I10. Mostly I have been 'inside' in the office. My division was for investigation, to interrogate enemy agents."

Friedriche sat down. He sat back against the hard straight back of the chair. Michael motioned for a waitress, holding up a beer bottle and gesturing to Friedriche.

"They shouldn't have promoted me. I was an I12 for years. I was really a clerk. Then they made me an I11 and I went to work for the head of the division." He looked about the room slowly. "I was very happy in the division. I am not an 'outside' man. I am not a physical person!"

"So what do you want with me?" He was appearing to relax a little, keeping an eye on the stranger from Berlin. "If you need to complain, write a letter to Europe Central. If you need advice, write to Tante Emily in Der Spiegel. She'll tell you how to handle your problems."

"Nein!" he responded.

"I mention a German newspaper and you reply in German!"

Friedriche frowned.

"What do you know about the Baader-Meinhof?"

It was Michael who now took the initiative. As the waitress placed the beers on the table, Michael smiled and motioned that he was finally finished with his meal. She grinned, picked up the plates, and backed off toward the kitchen.

"You worked 'inside'. You worked inside in German Central. You should know all about the Baader-Meinhof."

Friedriche looked at Michael. His brow was slightly wrinkled, and the expression on his face was like he had tasted something sour. Then he continued, almost ignoring Michael's questions and comments.

"...then they felt I was so smart about the business that I should go 'outside'. They promoted me to I10 and sent me out to do undercover work. At first it wasn't so bad. I liked the intrigue. I learned to use disguises, sneak around back alleys,...break into enemy offices."

Friedriche was very nervous as he sipped on the beer and glanced around the room. Michael followed his eyes, just in case there was contact with someone else in the room. Everything was in order, nothing seemed to be out of place. But Friedriche was acting very anxious.

"After a while I started to get scared. I wanted to come back inside, but they wouldn't let me." His head started to slump down a little. "Then I got involved in 'consulting'. Opportunities aside from the agency started to come to me. People seemed to know who I am. They knew about my inside work and the information I had. That's why I need to talk to you."

There was a long pause. Michael was acting sort of interested. But more concerned about the possibility of a setup, and even more irritated by having his evening disturbed. He was listening, but more important, he thought, this could be a source for some information about the Baader-Meinhof.

"I know you have been consulting outside of the company. Your 'projects' have been approved by France Central and even Europe Central. But they keep a monitor on you." Friedriche looked directly at Michael. "I know a lot about you. I learned more before I came to find you. The highest ranked 'outside' agent in France, and the first I5 foreigner ever appointed."

Michael caught the last phrase. It interested him. The first I5 foreigner ever appointed.

"The first I5 from a foreign country?" Michael mumbled. "And a foreign country like America!"

"And they sometimes have arguments about you being an American, Amerigo. Your next promotion is to go inside as a French regional director of outside agents."

"I wouldn't do that!"

"I said I wouldn't go out, either, but I had to!"

"I have already resigned. I haven't had an official assignment in years."

"Some were not so official, but still you get involved in Interpol work." Friedriche smiled a little. "Sometimes your 'consulting' is setup by the service."

Michael thought for a moment, reflecting quickly over a number of activities since he had resigned. Which were really just 'consulting', and which were setups from Interpol France?

"What about my recent consulting?" Michael asked, a little anger in his voice, but still in control. "What about the trip I just took?"

Friedriche looked puzzled. His brows wrinkled again.

"I don't know what you're doing right now, or about you going to Beirut!"

"I said that I went on a trip, but I didn't say where!"

The uneasiness of the man was increasing. He looked away, not like before when he was looking around, more now like he was averting the gaze from Michael. Even on his consulting jobs, he still had access to any Central files. If Central was monitoring Michael, then Friedriche would know.

"Tell me about your trip." The question was strained. The expression on Friedriche's face showed that he was feeling stupid. "I did hear about Beirut...but it was from another source."

"What source?" Michael asked. That was a feeble attempt to coverup, he thought.

"My consulting source!" He shifted slightly as he spoke, looking at Michael again. "That's what I am trying to explain. I started doing consulting, mostly with Germany Central approval. Then more and more I drifted away from the agency. Finally I was acting out my part as an agent, and working for other groups. I could still get inside and check the files. It was of good use to my contractors. They used my talents and they paid me well." He looked directly at Michael. "They used me for my names and locations. They paid me well, and they didn't send me out to get killed!"

"Don't bullshit me, you Kraut, tell me about this thing with me and my trip to Beirut!" Michael sat up straight, clearing his left side. "What the hell do you really want with me?"

Friedriche looked at Michael's eyes. Michael was now showing anger. It might work to his advantage, he thought. He studied Michael for that moment.

"Whatever you're doing, it doesn't sound official. As far as I know, it's not official, but," and he leaned forward a little, "if it's official or not, don't bullshit me. IEC knows what you're doing."

Michael sat back and took a deep swallow of beer. "What about the Baader-Meinhof?" His thoughts moved on to Germany. "You know those people. You must have names and locations on them. I want to know the headquarters. Why are they bothering me?"

"Amerigo, let's go for a walk. Maybe I can explain. I need some fresh air." He stood up as he was talking. "We'll have a beer up the street. I will explain the Phoenix training plan."

Michael looked around the room a moment, checking for anything unusual. Then he pulled out a fold of francs. After so many times at

Socca's, he knew what he should leave to pay the bill and what to leave to-insure-promptness for the next time.

As they stepped out onto the Rue Thuret, the sudden rush of cool air coming down the street from the Sea felt refreshing. Michael started to turn toward Friedriche when he felt the hard, dull pain of the barrel of a gun being shoved into his ribs. Then, as he froze for a moment, he felt Friedriche slowly remove the PPK from his back belt.

"You did that very well," Michael muttered.

"I learned more from consulting than I ever did in the service."

Michael looked down at the P38 automatic pistol being held against him.

"Don't try anything, Amerigo, you are being watched!" He nudged the weapon against the ribs. "Start walking down to the corner, then turn right and go into the alley."

Michael started walking, but very slowly. He felt he knew this type of person. Friedriche was really an 'inside' man and was very scared about now. Someone might be setting up both of them.

"I was the agent in Berlin. It was my consulting that got you caught by the Volpo police." Friedriche was talking as they walked. It was as though it might make him feel stronger if he talked about how tough he was in setting up Michael in Berlin. "I used the German Central files the nights that you were in the East Berlin jail and I made certain no one could trace my involvement. There are advantages to being an Interpol clerk." He nudged Michael with the barrel of the gun. "That was before the coming of the Phoenix."

Michael stopped at the corner. His arms were not raised, but he held them upward from the elbows with the palms turned out. He looked at Friedriche and started to slowly lower his hands. Friedriche pulled the P38 back and stepped away a few feet. Michael stared at him.

"Halt!"

Michael and Friedriche both turned toward the alley. A tall man was standing in the shadows. Although his face was hidden, the 44 Magnum automatic could be seen by the light of the street.

"Baader-Meinhof." Michael mumbled as he looked back at Friedriche.

"The Phoenix training group."

Friedriche looked relieved as he turned back to Michael and nodded the affirmative. "My clients didn't get you in Berlin, but this client pays more, and I'll get you this time. These people take very good care of me." He was tucking the PPK and his own P38 into his pants belt as he backed farther away. The two Interpol agents faced each other for a moment.

Then Friedriche turned and headed down the rue toward the old town Place Nationale.

"Kommt!" the man in the shadows said. He waved the gun at Michael, beckoning him into the alley. "Sie sind tot!" he said, smiling as Michael entered the alleyway, his eyes adjusting to the dark shadows.

There before him stood the German, the next killer sent out by the Baader-Meinhof for his Phoenix training. The man stood directly in front of him, both feet set equally from his body. The gun was in his right hand, held squarely before him.

"Your friend has deserted you," Michael said in German.

"He is no friend," was the thick Prussian dialect reply. "We use him as we need him. He is a coward."

"...and you?"

"I am here to kill you."

"What about pictures?"

"I can take pictures, or I get the coward to take pictures."

"What about Beirut? Why were your people in Beirut? That's a dangerous place, even for the Baader-Meinhof."

Michael was stalling, waiting for the right move. The German had enough talk. It was obvious to Michael, as so many he had met in his life already, that to kill one on one is difficult for most people. The killing in war is impersonal, and done at some distance. Even assassinations are usually done over distance. Michael contemplated the man's face as he thought about what must be going on in the man's mind.

The German shifted his weight slightly and that was the moment Michael needed.

Suddenly, as a whirling dervish, he planted his right foot, and brought a quick well placed knee up into the man's groin. The German moaned, hobbled back a step and bent over cupping his testicles in his hands. He had dropped the automatic pistol.

Without hesitation, Michael moved forward again. He grabbed the assassin by the hair on the back of his head and pulled it back, causing the face to come up, chin high. Then, with as much force as he could impart, Michael slammed the palm of his left hand upward against the tip of the nose that separates the nostrils. He drove the cartilage of the man's nose straight up into the assassin's brain.

Michael had performed a 'frontal lobotomy'!

The German stood upright, at first. There was no longer any pain from his testicles. There was no longer any pain from the cut on his face. There was no longer any pain. As he just stood there, eyes glassy and staring ahead. Slight traces of blood droplets began to appear on his lower lids, then trickles ran slowly down his cheeks. Heavier streams of blood oozed out of this ears and out of his nostrils. Michael stepped away carefully, watching the man closely. Sometimes this operation did not work perfectly, and the patient became hysterical and violent.

As Michael picked up the 44 Magnum, he watched the German drop to his knees, back erect and chin still held upward. The man simply appeared to be praying and staring. Another moment passed while Michael watched from the shadows where the gun had come to rest. Everything seemed so quiet. He was listening beyond the street sounds for other noises to be heard. But there were none. No one had witnessed the event. At the end of the alley, people passed along the street chatting in various languages, some glancing about but not able to see anything because of the darkness.

As he had now learned, Michael came back to the kneeling man, and reached inside the man's shirt pocket for the green identification card. Here was number five. Michael looked at it again in the light to make certain that the 5 was not a 3. The game was getting old, he was becoming weary of it. At first it was exciting, then challenging, but now it had become a nuisance.

He put the card in his pocket, checked the Magnum, looked one more time at the kneeling assassin, then he merged with the people heading toward the old city Place Nationale Square.

As he crossed through the tourists at one end of the square, Friedriche was almost across the area on the opposite side walking nervously toward the Rue Sade. He was looking about, checking over his shoulder, bumping into people and objects, as he made his way through a number of umbrella outdoor cafe tables. Patrons looked up at him as he bumped tables and chairs.

Then he spotted Amerigo coming out of the Rue Thuret onto the Place Nationale. Without hesitation, Friedriche pulled up his P38 and fired. People all through the square reacted wildly, knocking each other down, falling, screaming and calling out for companions.

It located Friedriche for Michael, who, after hearing the shot, bent forward and ran along the edge of the square, behind rubbish containers and park benches. Friedriche fired again, this time in the general direction of Michael. The crowd was now more subdued. Those remaining in the area were down on the ground, faces buried with hands over the ears.

Friedriche turned and ran up the Rue Sade toward the open market area. Michael was concerned about someone else using Friedriche as a decoy. There may be others of the Phoenix group about. He bolted forward across the remaining few meters and entered the narrow street on the run. He felt that he now knew Friedriche well enough to know that the man was running fast and hard to save his own life. He was too cowardly to take a stand.

As Michael emerged into the market/cafe area, Friedriche fired again. This time he entered the alley which led to the Chateau Grimaldi. Michael paused only a moment, then he ran between the confused people into the market. No one had been hit, and to some it was as though they thought a car had backfired. The attitude was not as wild as the square had been.

Friedriche made his way through the open gate and on into the courtyard. He stopped only when he reached the stone wall and peered over ramparts at the jagged stones of the Mediterranean below. The drop was over a hundred meters, a plunge that would cause painful death on the rocks in the waves breaking below. He turned with his back to the wall. There was Amerigo standing in the gateway across the courtyard, the outline of his body silhouetted by the lights of the marketplace beyond the narrow alley.

The stone wall hurt as Friedriche pressed backed against it. He slowly brought the P38 up to eye level. Michael was coming toward him slowly with the 44 Magnum in his hand.

"Don't shoot!" Friedriche muttered out. "Please don't shoot!"

Michael stopped face to face with the 110 agent. He reached forward, took the P38, tossed it over the wall and out to sea. Then he pulled the PPK out of the man's front belt. He checked it and placed it in its normal resting place in the belt in the small of his back.

"Please, don't shoot me!"

The 44 Magnum was the next gun out over the wall and on toward the Sea far below. He then reached forward again, this time to Friedriche's pocket and withdrew a green card.

Would this be ironic, Michael was thinking as he turned the card over, if this coward was number three, the last and the leader. It was number 11. He put the card in his pocket, along with the other one.

"They certainly screen their trainees very well." Michael mumbled. "Do you gamble?" he asked.

"Gamble?"

"I just pulled an eleven, which is probably good for me and not so good for you."

"I don't gamble."

"In craps it's called 'shooting an eleven'. Should I shoot this eleven?"

"No!" Friedriche made a gurgling sound as he responded. His arms were straight up as though he was reaching up to hold on to something.

"Put your arms down. You look ridiculous."

Slowly Friedriche brought the arms down. He held his hands cheek high, palms turned out, sort of like school days when the teacher checked for cleanliness.

"You have a few choices, my friend," Michael said casually. "First I can kill you and dump you over the wall." Friedriche shifted. "But I won't do that. Next, I can turn you over to the Antibes police." Friedriche took a deep breath. "But I won't do that. I could turn you in to Germany Central." This time he waited for Friedriche to respond. "But I won't bother to do that, either, because they don't want the embarrassment."

After that comment, Michael took a few steps toward the gate.

"But what I will do is leave you right here."

Friedriche suddenly appeared very relieved. His whole body seemed to settle slightly.

"Don't feel too good about it." Michael continued with a smile. "If I leave you here, then I'll put the word out to the Baader-Meinhof. Not the new Phoenix recruits, but the old line terrorists. Have you read in your files what they do to people who fail?"

Friedriche stiffened. His body was pressed even harder against the stone wall.

As Michael spoke, a few curiosity seekers wandered into the courtyard. They had heard the shots and seen the men running. After a few moments of quiet, they were beginning to slowly venture down the alley and enter the courtyard.

"They could already be here." Michael gestured. "Someone in this group of people could be your exterminator."

"No!" Friedriche mumbled, looking around at the shadowy figures as they entered the gardens.

"Before they finish, you will wish that I had killed you. They will torture you to find out what happened. They'll want to know what you told me. And I'll put a full report in the Central files for one of your associates to find. You told me everything about the organization."

Michael glanced at the stone wall as he continued.

"If I were you," and he smiled a little, "I would jump. You have no identification on you. No embarrassment to your family. The rocks will probably destroy your identifiable features. In less than a couple of seconds all of your problems will be over. There will be no pain, I assure you. A quick jump, a moment in the fall, and instant peace of mind. It will end all the years of your pain and anger. And maybe Germany Central will decorate a hero."

That was it. That was all Michael was going to do. He knew that he had left the coward with two cowardly choices. Either Friedriche could run and try to hide, or jump and have it over with. It really would not matter. If he did run, the Baader-Meinhof would find him and kill him.

Michael turned, walked past the people gathering in the yard, and without even a final glance back, he passed through the gateway out into the narrow alley.

But before he had walked a few meters toward the market place, he stopped at the sound of the crowd in the courtyard as a loud, spontaneous scream went up, echoing off the walls of the buildings lining the alleyway.

Michael took a deep breath, and again without looking back, he continued on his way.

CHAPTER NINE
Interpol Europe

In a very remote section of the mountainous terrain outside of Zurich, is what appears to be a rather inconspicuous chalet fronting on a narrow winding hillside road. The chalet gives the impression of being a resort with restaurant and all amenities available to tourists and travellers. The road to the chalet front has less than a medium amount of traffic for that part of the country, but enough to suffice as the innocent appearance of a place to stop, have lunch and perhaps even spend the night. It does provide, so as to maintain some appearance of commercial enterprise, a certain amount of those accommodations, but on a very limited basis. There is even a souvenir shop.

On another road, just below yet running in opposite compass direction, is what appears to be a school for electronic technicians and machine mechanics. There are signs of automobiles being worked on and machines being analyzed in the front paved area near the road. There is even activity of coveralled personnel making much of efforts in and about the school front. In the evening, certain rooms remain lit as though there may be evening classes. Various rooms are lit on various different nights. All is dark by midnight.

On yet another level some thirty meters below the second road, and in still a different compass direction, is the appearance of a neat little office building, two stories high and some twenty-five meters across. It seems to be about thirty meters in depth, but that is hard to tell because it backs into the mountain with a wall of additional mountainous terrain on one side and vegetation or snow on the other.

All three locations have automobiles parked in parking areas in front of various registrations, mostly representing Switzerland. People occasionally arrive and leave. Travellers with cameras and luggage come and go at the resort level, mechanics and technicians in coveralls scurry about the school building, and people with professional appearances arrive and leave at the office building level.

All of this is intricately interconnected from one level to the other, throughout the mountainside. When inside one feels and sees the workings of a huge central office of what might be a major corporation. All are dressed comfortably but in various strange forms of attire, depending upon which level of entrance and exit each has been assigned.

This is Interpol Europe Central. Michael has never visited here. He has never even been contacted directly from IEC. His communication has always been through the 'voice' at Interpol France Cote d'Azur. On rare occasion he has talked with Raspail, the Director for Interpol France Central. Every location and every bit of information is on a 'need to know', and Michael has no reason to be in direct contact with IEC. The IFC has always been sufficient for his work, and no one has ever challenged the system to make an exception for him.

Inside, in the center of this corporate-like building built within the mountainside, is a large office next to what would appear to be a international war room. In the war room, representatives from each of the member nations of IEC are present, communicating with their respective national central headquarters, exchanging and recording facts and information, and displaying on an enormous world map, the instantaneous actions and reactions of terrorist activities. Years ago the world map was dedicated to international thieves, embezzlers and criminals mostly of civil matters. However, although those problems still exist, the efforts are now dedicated to international terrorism and drug trafficking.

Occasionally, even Michael warrants a spot on the map, pinpointing some activity in which he is involved. Large symbols indicate the locations of terrorist camps, drug distribution centers, training facilities, headquarters and real time activities in progress. Besides the symbols is an array of numbers and letters providing all those represented with computer access codes to locate and interrogate detailed information about each display resident in the central computer system. Contrary to the flurry of a military war room, the atmosphere here is professional and calm, giving the appearance of each person knowing what job must be done, and doing it in a timely and efficient manner. There is an overall plan, and the plan is being worked very effectively.

Next to this international display and information center is the office of the European commander. This office gives more the appearance of a Command Post, with racks of televideo displays, each containing tone alerts for interruptions as situations change. The office, also as in the information room, has computer access and telephone priority communications throughout the world. The Commander's main desk is made into a crescent, with switches and controls to monitor and direct actions, not only in the headquarters, but worldwide. It is of the utmost importance that all information be received in a timely and orderly sequence. It must then be acted upon with equal timeliness and proficiency.

The Commander, who often spends sleepless days and nights acting to direct IEC, sits at the crescent shaped desk monitoring, reviewing, and issuing orders. Sometimes the world is fairly quiet, so then his attention is focused on agent training and mock drills, drills repeatedly staged for situations which might occur. There is a phrase duplicated on plaques throughout the building which states, 'the plan can be easily executed provided that the plan is well thoughtout and thoroughly rehearsed'. If so, then even exceptions to the plan can be dealt with quickly and effectively.

The present Commander represents the country of Denmark, and his code name is Polonius. A Commander has a term of three years, and not only can a Commander not succeed to another term, but the country represented may not have the IEC Commander again for three subsequent terms.

There has only been one female Commander, and she was in the position during the Yom Kippur War in Israel. She represented the country of Greece. It was a very undesirable time for any Commander. The representatives of the member nations, and many of the field operatives, were concerned about her command abilities, to think clearly and execute orders quickly and objectively. Although Europe was not directly involved in the Middle East confrontation, operatives were actively participating in information transfers in the event the war expanded. There is still a strong male chauvinistic attitude throughout the European community. Female agents are mostly used as decoys and couriers. The war was contained and nothing of significance affected the Continent. Although the period was very tense, and many long gruelling hours were spent in the Command Post, nothing truly tested her Command mettles. So no superior male or female position of competitive command ability had yet been made.

During his tenure with IFC, Michael has served under a number of Commanders. Mostly, he never knew who the Commander was or even what nation was being represented. All member nations reviewed the candidates of the next representative nation for the position, analyzing lengthy supplies of information about each. A final three were subjected to rigorous psychological testing as well as weeks of questions by the board of member nations. The whole process took almost six months.

Once, during the early years in the establishment of Interpol, there was a case of dual Commandership. That was before Michael. The European democracies are somewhat accustomed to coalitions, so that did not seem so unlikely. However it was almost the undoing of the young international police organization. The member nations polarized into two factions, each faction supporting only one of the dual Commanders, and obstinately rejecting the other. What progress that had been achieved in the prior few terms was almost destroyed. One Commander represented Spain and the other was from Italy. Many speculated that it was perhaps the conflict of the romantic Mediterranean blood which caused the two to oppose each other. Finally after seven months of a very volatile period, the previous Commander rallied the board of members to put a halt to the destruction and to consider another selection as soon as possible. In a record five weeks a new Commander was chosen. Progress made an upward turn, although slow during the remaining period of the term, at least it was positive. By the next selection, the organization had regained its lost position. It never lost ground again, and has grown to be the only cooperative international police force in the world. Today, agents come from all of the 'free world' countries.

In the beginning, certain countries agreed only to share information about syndicated crime organizations where national borders were being used as refuge. Each country then used its own police force. As the international crime groups grew, the police force had to follow. These crime groups recognized no boundaries, and threatened all countries. So national police members were formed and manpower and technological resources were exchanged. Soon additional nations were encouraged to cooperate. The international organization came into full force during the worldwide concerns of the Viet Nam War and reached its present day level of participation during the Seven Day War in Israel. The organization grew stronger in the 70's in an effort to combat the early stages of international drug cartels. Finally in the 80's member nations began to show concern for international terrorism and all financial and human resources were doubled with the organization being committed to two lines of action. One line is almost exclusively dedicated to the research and elimination of syndicated drug trafficking, whereas the other is committed with the same energy toward the battle against international terrorism.

On the national level, each country selects its own Director, representatives, Central board member by its own various methods. IEC forces no conditions on any nation, only that it must contribute a certain number of representatives, pledge a certain amount of funds, and have a certain number of field agents, all based upon a formula which considers the nation's geographical location, its population, and the monetary value of its gross national product. It must follow the rules and regulations adopted in the IEC Charter written and ratified by all member nations.

There is no international central, only a duplication of the Interpol Europe Central in certain regions of the world. In Asia, the Central is active but not quite as strong as Europe. In the Middle East the emphasis on terrorism outweighs the concern about drugs, whereas in the Americas, where there is not yet an organized Central, the concern is more about syndicated drugs than about terrorism. One of the IEC objectives is to establish an Interpol America Central by the year 1992. The Communist Block nations do not officially recognize Interpol, but do cooperate when it suits their needs. Certain other nations, especially some Arab States, resist any form of recognition or acceptance. In Africa, the nations, although some showing interest have not yet matured in their democracies to fully participate. Their problems are still more of internal economics rather than international crime which crosses their borders.

Commander Polonius had been reviewing a series of incidents in Europe, either as those which directly involve certain countries, or which affect European countries from outside. In a number of these cases, a certain I5 agent of France appeared to have some involvement. It was because of this that the Commander finally reached for the direct French line and called the Chief of Interpol in France.

"Director Raspail, this is the Commander speaking."

Raspail was in his Central Headquarters, similarly disguised as the Europe Central is, in a small village outside of the town of Samur in the Loire Valley in France. He already knew that it was the Commander calling. The call was on the IEC direct command line when it came in. Although calls from the Commander were not unusual, they did always cause some concern for the recipients.

"I want to speak about the German agent found in the Mediterranean on the Cap Antibes coast."

"Yessir," Raspail responded, each speaking in his native tongue, "it was actually on the east side on the rocks below the Grimaldi Chateau." He wanted to properly inform the Commander, but not to appear to be correcting him.

"Harumph," mumbled the Commander. "Why was he exterminated by your agent, and why this ridiculous cover-up about an accident causing his death?"

"It was not an extermination, Sir. The cover-up was only for the sake of his family. We know his double role in the agency, but felt nothing would be served by revealing these outside affiliations." There was a deliberate pause. "Also, it threw the Baader-Meinhof off track a bit. As far as we can tell, they are still trying to piece together the events which happened."

The Commander seemed to ignore the response and go on to other subjects. It always made Raspail uncomfortable. He had served as Chief in France for almost ten years. Each Commander had a different method of leadership, and it always took at least six months to figure out the best method for dealing with a new Commander. This Commander was even more complex.

"There seems to be a number of dead Meinhofs because of your man. What is afoot?"

"The Phoenix training recruits chose him to seek and destroy. He plays the game well." Raspail paused a moment, then with some pride continued. "He will do better than the agents in other countries when they have been chosen by terrorist training groups."

"Why waste him?" Polonius mumbled, again seeming to ignore Raspail's prideful remarks. "He appears more important than the recruits game. He might be killed."

"True," Raspail stated, "but he refuses our assistance, and actually there is little to be done until an occurrence."

"What does the Supervisor you have on the Cote d'Azur have to say about all of this?"

"Actually," answered Raspail, "he is quite pleased with our 15..."

"Friedriche," commented Polonius without waiting for Raspail to complete his statement, "was completely under our control. He had information planted on him. We knew his involvement with the other side." There was a long pause. All Raspail could hear was the Commander breathing heavily and evenly. "When we allowed him to uncover some information from Central, we tracked it through the terrorist organizations." The pause again. "He was a matter for Germany Central. He was very valuable to the service. Your man should not have killed him."

"My man did not kill him!" Raspail responded with a warm flush of anger. "The agent killed himself."

"Well, you know what I mean. Your man drove him to it."

"What about the Baader-Meinhof." Raspail was speaking forcefully now, defending his French organization and his 15 agent. "His history is excellent. Sir, with all due respect, you could have stopped the Baader-Meinhof at the Europe level."

"Maybe we could," the Commander commented, "and maybe we couldn't. But, at that point in our plans, Friedriche was more important."

"More important!" Raspail's voice was louder now. "How soon you forget our man and his dedication to Interpol." Now it was Raspail who paused. He was catching his thoughts, and he was not about to let Commander Polonius make another comment. "You could have taken the Phoenix group out and left him alone. Instead you tell me that what he did was wrong. There is nothing that he did wrong! If he had let Friedriche live, then the Meinhof would have finished him."

"Only, I say," said Polonius, "that at this point in his tenure with us, I feel that Friedriche was more important and he gave us the conduit we needed. So now we have fewer eyes into terrorism."

Raspail was beginning to feel stronger. His subservience was leaving him. He did not want to be angry, instead he wanted to be firm and think clearly.

"What action did the German Central take with all this information? What did Europe Central do about it?"

"Nothing. We didn't want to disrupt our contact with the organization."

"Then what use was it? What real use was Friedriche? He was a weasel. You could never depend on him. From what I know about him, he was totally undependable. It could be that even with the leaks German Central fed him, he was scared and he was till not predictable. German Central," Raspail was careful not to say 'you' to the Commander at this point, "probably did not know what they had. They only thought they had an inside contact." There was that long pause again after Raspail stopped talking.

"Harumph," came the sound from Polonius. "Your man might be a bit too over-reactive at times. I expect you to defend your agents. But don't forget, he is an American."

Now the pause was from Raspail. He was a little disgusted and still a little angry. The anger was because the comments were about his French organization, and the disgust was for the last statement. It was what he had heard many times over the years, but always from the French agents and some of the French administrators. But, he thought the Commander should be above that.

"Tell me about the thing in Beirut." The Commander spoke as though he had either forgotten about Friedriche, or that he accepted what Raspail had said. "He was into something in Marseilles, and then that thing in Beirut. What is he into?"

Raspail waited a moment, wondering what IEC already knew and what it was that they wanted to know.

"I don't actually know. We have tried to help him. His contact has something to do with Abba Dabbus. It's his own project. So far it has led nowhere."

"Harumph!" was the sound Raspail heard. "His history has been good..."

"Commander," Raspail interrupted, "it is about some major terrorist program. The Baader-Meinhof must be involved. German Central should know, if Friedriche served them as their conduit. If German Central is so smart about their network of agents, then have them tell us who is involved."

"That is enough Raspail," the Commander said with finality. "You keep me apprised of his progress. Now I have other pressing needs. Thank you so much."

There was silence, as Raspail's lips parted to respond, but he said nothing. Then there was the sound of the hum on the Interpol line. Raspail held the receiver for a moment longer, again wondering about the conversation. As he put the phone back in the cradle, he looked up and smiled, thinking about how he felt. 'He might be an American,' Raspail was thinking, 'but he's certainly one of the best I5's in the entire organization.'

CHAPTER TEN

Convent d'Alziprato

As the sounds of early morning in Juan les Pins were beginning, Michael was already making coffee and cutting fresh fruit. He liked his coffee very strong, with chicory, and with the coffee he liked a large bowl of fresh fruit, the 'fruit de la saison'. In the market in old Antibes he usually picked the freshest of what fruits were available, enough for a few days, but not so much it would spoil. Also, he liked his fruit before the ripe stage, a little on the green side yet. It gave, he felt, added freshness and taste, plus a few extra days before spoiling. Bananas in the apartment were sometimes so green, they were still bitter. Often they would go from green to brown, almost overnight. He likes apples, peaches and especially pears, to still crack with firmness as he bites into one. The coffee was so strong it was almost like a big cup of espresso. One extravagance he allowed was ample portions of freshly ground coffee. Beans were purchased at a special shop, where also was provided a supply of a chicory-like root which added to the thick pungent consistency of the beverage. 'If you can't stand the spoon up in the coffee,' he would often say, 'then it's too weak.' Usually he drank it black, but occasionally he would boil milk and make a half and half mixture, cafe au lait. Sort of a cappuccino. Once in a while, if his stomach needed something more to absorb the previous night's consumption, then he would add a plain bagel.

"Good morning," he said as Monica came sleepily into the kitchen area. "You look great. Just so... sexy."

She frowned at the thought of her appearance. Disheveled hair, still rubbing her eyes a little to adjust to the light, and wearing a very thin short nightgown. One side of the neckline was down off of her left shoulder.

85

To him, she did look very attractive, very comfortable and inviting. He thought for a moment of abandoning the cutting of fresh fruit. He could scoop her up in his arms and take her back to the bedroom.

"Sometimes," she said as she poured a cup of black coffee, "when I awaken, it takes the first few moments to orient myself to my environment." She sipped the coffee and grimaced, an expression which always followed the first taste. Later, if her taste buds adjusted, the expression would wane. "For a few moments I don't know what room I'm in. I don't even know what city."

"Big talk." Michael said, his back to her as he finished preparing two bowls of mixed fruit. "You gals have the greatest parttime job in the world. And not only that," he continued, "look at the places you visit and the travel benefits you have."

"Sure we have plenty of time off," she said with a slight frown, "but when we work, we really work." She looked directly at him. "What about all those international passengers, stinky, nasty, and some of them don't speak any language I know."

"And some are rich, good looking and speak very clearly about their intentions." He was smiling. "The romance can't be all bad. Look at us."

"...and those damn terrorists," she continued, trying to ignore the fact that he was making light of her mood. "Those bastards could come out of nowhere. They could kill us all trying to kill themselves. All for the sake of Allah!"

She paused for a moment as though reflecting on her thoughts while eating the fruit. Michael was watching her. She had had these moods before. Inside there was a quiet smile, but outwardly he would show her a placid expression so as not to annoy her.

"Let's go to Milano," she mumbled without looking up. "I hate summer in the south of France. Too damn many people."

"That's August," he responded. "It's still June."

"You know what I mean." Then she looked up. "It'll be a nice drive. We can shop in Milano. On the way back we can stay in Genoa for the night."

"I have a better idea. The weather is beautiful and I have somewhere to take you, something to show you."

"...and where's that?" she asked with a mouth full of peach slices.

"It is time for me to take you to Corsica."

"Corsica!"

"Corsica," he said nodding as he gulped back a second cup of thick black coffee. "Corsica. It's a short Hydro Jet ride from Nice. And such a beautiful island." He put the cup down. "Good, that's what we'll do."

"But..." she muttered. She was thinking about shopping in Milano. However, she knew that tone of finality when she heard it. They were going to Corsica.

As they finished the coffee and fruit, Michael suggested packing for a day or two. Enough light things, but then maybe something dressy in case they encountered the occasion. Monica looked at him askance. He is up to something, she thought, but if it was Corsica instead of Milano, then she knew he had a reason. In spite of her disappointment, she would probably enjoy the trip. So, instead of grumbling anymore, she went ahead and packed.

When they arrived at the docks in Nice, there was a chartered business-size Hydro Jet standing by to take them out to Corsica. Monica was enamored by the craft and the entire Jet crew. The terms that were used were from the airline dictionary. When the engines started and the cushion of air lifted the craft above the ground, the Jet prepared for "takeoff". They "took off" down the concrete runway on to the top of the water. Across the Sea they were 'airborne, flying' to Corsica. The Mediterranean was not smooth, but it was not too rough. The Hydro Jet moved smoothly on top of the water at eighty kilometers per hour. The attendants on board were called "flight attendants". There were briefings about ditching, flotation seats and how to exit the aircraft in an emergency. All attention was directed at the two of them. The entire craft was chartered for Michael. Monica liked that. The service was excellent. Chilled vodka was served with a light snack of caviar, chopped boiled eggs, chopped onions, sour cream and crackers. She looked out across the Sea with a vodka in one hand, and a cracker of caviar in the other.

'It's not the way to Milano,'she thought to herself, 'but not so bloody bad afterall.'

Some two hours later they arrived in the Golfe de Calvi and 'landed' by floating up on the air cushion onto a concrete ramp. The engines were shutdown and the craft landed.

Monica was still asking questions as they deplaned. She looked back at the Hydro Jet, almost ready for the experience again. But before them was a new Citroen with driver, waiting for them. What else, Michael, she was thinking. As the driver opened the rear door, there on a small mahogany pull down table was a bottle of Dom Perinon and two glasses, chilling in a bucket of ice.

"It is good to see Monsieur Acadian," the driver said in broken French and English.

"Dishon," Michael addressed the man, "this is Mademoiselle Monica."

She looked wide-eyed, and nodded cordially.

"She is my friend." He smiled. "She is a Brit, but we won't hold that against her, will we!" He continued to smile as he put his hand on Dishon's shoulder.

"No sir. We have long ago learned to tolerate the Brits, even the good Lord Wellington."

"What the hell is going on?" Monica asked as the automobile began a long ascent out of the town of Cabri.

"He thinks that I am French from south Louisiana. Everyone is French in south Louisiana according to what he has read." Michael looked at Monica as he reached for the champagne. "He calls me the 'Acadian'."

"How does he know you? Who is he?"

Michael was pouring the champagne as he replied. "I have a place here in Corsica. A place for someday when I finally convince the service that I am 'retired'. It was part of the arrangement I made in the beginning."

He handed Monica a glass. "Dishon and his wife are the caretakers. We have a staff and few workers in the small vineyard."

She turned and looked out toward the Gulf which was appearing farther below as they drove upward. The view out into the Sea caught her thoughts, but only momentarily. It was late morning and the sun was rising beyond the crest of the hills before them. The Citroen was climbing upward toward the highest peaks.

"Where is this place?"

"We are driving up through the village of Calenzana. At the top, the view of the Gulf and the Sea is beautiful. A little beyond is the little village of Montemaggiore on a high spur overlooking northern Corsica." He sipped purposely for a moment. She waited, sipping and looking. "Perched high above Montemaggiore," he continued, "is the Convent d'Alziprato."

Now she turned her head away from the panoramic view below and looked directly at him.

"The Convent," he continued, sitting back in the leather seat, "is a beautiful 16th Century monastery with thirty-two acres surrounding it on the plateau of the mountain. It has fountains, terraced gardens, ornamental ponds, five acres of excellent grapes, and a solar heated swimming pool." He gestured slightly with his right hand. "The grounds of the Convent border the Forest de Tartagine.

His voice trailed off as he gazed straight forward, envisioning the scenes yet for her to see. He seemed quite pleased with himself.

"There is fresh drinking water from the natural cisterns, and the entire estate is heated by solar panels." He was speaking softly and still looking ahead. "I have had the solar panels hidden from view on the main roof.

Only electricity has to be furnished from generators at the base of Mount Cinto".

As they cruised through Montemaggiore and climbed upward toward the Monastery, Monica reached over and poured herself another glass of champagne. The vodkas on the 'aircraft' had made her feel warm and relaxed. The earlier mood was gone. She even tried to remember why she had felt tense early in the morning. And she couldn't remember. Now she needed a little extra fortitude for what she was hearing, the sights she was seeing, and for what she was anticipating.

Finally as the automobile turned a bend very close to a shear drop below, there before her was a gigantic stone monastery. It was a huge castle-like structure off in the distance. It looked like a giant granite mountain out of which the building had been carved. There were turrets and long high narrow windows. It was like some artist's rendering she had seen in history books. Pictures of what the old castles probably looked like. Michael was watching her reactions to the estate before her.

As they entered the grounds, still some distance from the Monastery, they passed through large wrought iron gates which opened on signal from Dishon. The gateway was framed in iron and steel, and the fence in both directions was of long, high iron rods, fifteen feet in height topped with sharp arrowheads. It was a fence that had stood the ravages of time for centuries.

As they drove up the cobble stoned pathway toward the main entrance, passing the chapel, the caretaker's home, and other small buildings of the same granite stone, Michael continued his travelogue.

"It is said that Napoleon was to be sheltered and protected here upon his escape. Just before his defeat by Wellington at Waterloo, it is said that he was tired of his campaigns and that he mentioned the Monastery as the place of his final retirement. As a boy he had travelled here from Ajaccio, the village where he was born." He paused to sip as the Citroen pulled to stop at the main entrance to the Monastery. "He was a Corsican, but I doubt if any of that is true. Ajaccio is far south of here, and travels in that time, when he was a child, would have been less probable. He may have heard of the Convent d'Alziprato, but I doubt that he knew anything of it."

Next was the time for greeting the small staff. Monica met Madame Dishon, a gentle woman of medium stature and with a very warm, honest smile. The Monastery was her domain and she ran the staff with authority. She was indeed gentle in nature, but Monica could tell by the eyes that she had strength within. As they met, she smiled, took Monica's hand and promised to make her very comfortable.

Next, they meandered through the many large cool rooms, some of which were mostly empty, but in some were still furnishings of centuries before. The weapons room is still intact, almost in its original state. There were swords, axes and weapons of many forms. It was almost a museum of the historic generations of the Corsican monks who had occupied the estate.

In the late seventeen hundreds, after the Monastery was no longer maintained by the Church, Michael explained, the estate was bought from the Bishop of the Holy Sea in southern France by the Bonifacio family. This ancestry had its roots in both France and Italy, and had its ambitions set as pirateers. Although they mostly sailed the Mediterranean, sometimes it was necessary to run down the Spaniards returning from the New World with ships laden in gold and precious jewels. They sailed from the southern tip of Corsica, from a place now named for the family. It was decided in the late seventeen hundreds that perhaps one day they would need a fortress to defend the family. Pirateering was becoming more dangerous and less profitable. It was then they moved their main headquarters to the Monastery. In earlier generations they had family in both Italy and France to hide and protect certain members as needed. But the families grew apart, and it was only the Bonifacios of southern Corsica who kept the traditions alive. Even as recent as World War I they supported both sides of the war and attacked ships of all nations, wherever profits dictated. Their existence had become embarrassing for all countries, especially the French.

The Monastery seemed so vast that Monica wandered at times if she would be able to see it all. Throughout the afternoon they walked and talked. At the north end, on the highest level of the granite structure, were the modern living quarters. Here was a large complex of small apartments sharing a long common balcony overlooking the Mediterranean. Also in this complex within the building was a huge, more recently outfitted kitchen. Next to the kitchen was a large comfortable dining room. Some fifteen bedrooms occupied the top floor, some with private baths and some with shared baths. It was on the balcony of Michael's bedroom, the largest which he had chosen as the master room, where he continued the story.

"From here one can see the sunrise, watch it through its zenith and then have full a view of the sunset. The weather is fairly clear up here. We're above the haze, and in the morning you can see the fog roll in down below along the coast."

It was obvious to Monica that Michael was excited to have her there. She leaned on the stone balcony railing, with a glass in one hand and another bottle of Dom Perinon in the other hand.

The Bonifacio family came to an abrupt end, as tradition continues, sometime around the end of World War I. Weapons and writing in the Monastery substantiate some form of organized life on the estate until then. The disappearance is still discussed in the villages. Each village has its version of what happened. Some say they returned to original roots in either France or Italy. Some say they took their vast wealth and shipped out for America. Others say that the family dispersed by design, but still lives throughout Corsica with guarded wealth. The most popular is that a group of Corsican villagers sneaked up one night while all below as fogged in and massacred the entire Bonifacio family, dragging the bodies down to the inner caverns on the far side of the estate. The superstitious Corsicans buried with them, whatever gold and jewelry they found. No one ever heard from the family again, and finally both the French and Italian governments were relieved. When the decision was made that they no longer existed, the estate was quickly put under the control of the French government. The original plan was to go to auction.

In the meantime, like any bureaucratic control, the estate fell into disrepair. In World War II the French, and then the Germans, used it as headquarters for various Mediterranean activities. When the Allies returned, they rebuilt and restored as much of the rooms and furnishings as possible. Then the bureaucratic French government took it over again with plans to make it a providence headquarters. That did not work. Next they decided that it should be a regional museum. Everything stored in the dungeons was brought up and reestablished in its original form. But that did not work as there was no interest to go so far up a mountain to see so little of history. The country finally began to recognize it as a drain on the treasury.

"About the time I got involved," Michael continued, "they were ready to try it as a regional control for Interpol France. It was then completely modernized with present amenities. That proved inconvenient and impractical. I offered to buy it for a combination fee and services. I had been given a great deal of money when I left Viet Nam. So, with the money and the services which they wanted to hire, it seemed like a good idea. A plan was drawn and by mutual agreement, the estate was transferred to my ownership." He looked up with a smile. "Very reasonable from the dollar value, but very demanding from the commitment value. They have gotten their pounds of flesh. The Dishons have helped to make the place selfsufficient. We sell an ample supply of fresh fruit in the markets, and our vineyards are now producing wines sold in the mainland of France."

"Michael, I still don't understand all of this." Monica was still leaning against the stone railing. "This place is absolutely magnificent." she said, gesturing with a sweeping arm. "I can't believe that all of this is yours." There was a long pause as though she was trying to reflect on the Michael she knew. "Your apartment in Antibes is beautiful. But this," she was making the sweeping gesture again, "...this is unbelievable."

There was no response. He was watching her as the sun was beginning to set over her right shoulder. He ran his tongue around the rim of the tall thin champagne glass, head turned down slightly, but eyes turned up watching her.

"It's too much for just one person." She looked directly at him. "You know what I think!" He shook his head. "I think you should turn this into an jet setter mountain retreat. You could make a helicopter pad and have guests flown in from Nice." She was grinning, pleased with herself and at the thought of what she was saying.

"You're absolutely right. I can't use all of this. I need to do something with it." He gulped down the contents of his glass and poured more from a fresh cold bottle. "I've considered an idea like that. There are two flight attendants from the U.S. who own a place in Nice. It's the Deux Belles en Vert, open from May 15th to September 15th..."

"What!" Monica said, turning to face him. "What about two flight attendants! I don't want to hear about your flight attendants from the bloody United States."

The mood of the morning was flashing back into her eyes. She looked away. The sun was now closer to the Sea. It was that twilight moment between daylight and darkness.

"Now listen," Michael said, "I have no romantic involvement. I'm talking about business." He was saying the words, but he wasn't sure how convincing he sounded. "They opened their restaurant three years ago. They are doing very well. From May to September they take leaves of absence and come over to open the business." He was watching her as he spoke. She was firm, looking away. "They figured this thing out. They have a very unique concept for the French. They have one entree a night and one seating only. The French love it."

"So!" she said looking at him. "So what else?"

"Relax Monica," he said with firmness. "They toured Corsica looking for a way to expand their plans. They heard about the Monastery. What they want is a expensive private location with excellent services and very good food." He reached over and poured some champagne into Monica's glass. "I've been thinking about it. I can control the estate and keep the activity to a small exclusive group. But..." and he looked at the back of her head, "I would want my privacy here. So how can I have both!"

"You sound like one of those Bonifacio pirateers. Supporting both sides and attacking all the ships. You can't have it all."

"Monica." She would not respond. "Monica, it's the same as your idea." She still would not respond. "Hey dummy," he said as he turned her around and kissed her hard on the mouth. He lifted her arms up and put them around his neck. He looked at her, close to her face, he smiled and she looked at him, and she smiled.

"You dated flight attendants before me, and you'll date flight attendants after me," she said, trying to soften the tone, "...and now you might have two of them living with you. Sort of the beginning of a flight attendants harem."

His expression remained almost blank, only the corners of his mouth turned down. There was no way to respond to such a comment. If he denied it, she would balk, and if he agreed with her, he thought, he would live the sex life of a monk in the Monastery for the next couple of nights.

"Excuse me, sir."

It was Dishon standing in the arch of the french doors. His silhouette in the frame was created by the dimly lighted master bedroom behind him.

"Dinner is served!" he announced in his best broken English. It was in such a manner that it was obvious he was trying to impress the lady from Britain.

As they entered the dining hall, following the lead of Dishon, he then announced to the waiting staff in an otherwise empty room.

"His Master of the Estates of d'Alziprato and his guest the Lady of the British Isles of the United Kingdom, Lady Brit."

Monica was amused, but only up to that point. She squeezed Michael's hand and shot him a wide-eyed, tight lipped frown.

Michael smiled and shrugged as though he had no idea what Dishon had meant.

"How many others?" Monica whispered. "How many Lady Swiss, Lady France, Lady Americas?"

Michael walked her to one end of the long dining table. A place was set at each end. Obviously it would be impractical for two people, one at each end of the table to have conversation. Without hesitation he sort of flopped into the chair next to Monica at the end. He could not understand why they always set both ends of the table. He always sat with his guests, especially when they were dates. The dining room attendant was obliged to take up the setting at the far end and carefully place it before Michael.

"The meal is one that Victoria uses in the Deux Belles. She plans to do a Corsican improvisation it if they open a restaurant here."

"Victoria?"

"Victoria and Kathleen. The Deux Belles." It was said as though he had to complete the subject. Somewhere along the way he had the feeling that he had not yet finished talking about the Deux Belles. His tone made it sound like she should have already known their names.

Monica sat back, taking up the Dom Perignon and looking about as though viewing the room but also sending signals to Michael that if he had plans for later in the evening, he had better change his present plan. It would seem that Michael got the message.

The preparation for the meal was excellent, with great care and patience, the two were attended to carefully. M. Dishon was everywhere, overseeing the diningroom. She was prompt and meticulous, and that too began to annoy Monica. For some reason with all the talk about how the estate is being run and about the two flight attendants from America, she was beginning to feel very inadequate.

Then, at that moment to make her self-esteem feel even worse, the meal which Victoria had created, was served.

First, there were the gravlax rosettes, stuffed with salmon mousse and garnished with capers and lemon slices. This was served with a cold bottle of Veuve Cliquot champagne. Next came the moules farci and a bottle of poully fume' from the cellars of the Monastery.

They paused and talked some as the meal progressed. But Monica shifted uncomfortably again when the main course arrived.

Before them was placed a crown roast of lamb with apple calvados stuffing, served with steamed buttered carrots and another bottle of wine from the cellars. This time it was the Beaujolais Bonifacio. The salad was mixed greens with a walnut vinaigrette dressing, and topped with a sprinkling of roquefort cheese and fresh cracked pepper.

It was probably the wine that had mellowed her through the meal, because when the final presentation arrived, she was looking forward to whatever the surprise might be. It was in keeping with the perfection of the entire dinner.

The dessert was creme brulee', a cup of espresso and two glasses of slightly warmed Napoleon VSOP brandy.

As she tasted the brandy, looking over the rim of the glass at Michael, Monica hoped that the evening would have been a little more intimate. But, as the thoughts of the earlier conversation faded and the warmth of the brandy relaxed her, she began to feel heavy lids, and all she wanted to do now was crawl into bed and snuggle with Michael. He offered no resistance.

In the morning, after a hike about the estate, a refreshing shower and then another hearty meal, this time a huge Corsican breakfast of fresh French bread, thick slices of homemade sausages and a huge bowl of estate grown fruits, Monica decided that she wanted to see the island. Michael was pleased to oblige. He loved the island, and he wanted to share it with her. They took the Citroen without Dishon so that they could have a tour on their own. They could both do without the overpowering assistance of either of the Dishons to direct the way.

The first stop was Corte, high up on the center road of the island. There is not much remaining of the 15th century fortress, but it was one of Michael's favorite spots. He could feel the centuries of history as he walked through the ruins.

"Do you bring all your dates up here?" Monica asked when she suddenly remembered the Deux Belles from the night before. She had to make her position perfectly clear. Afterall, she thought, after being so overwhelmed by all of this, she certainly had a right to make her position clear.

"Most of the time..." he said casually, trying to ignore her comment, "...I come up here alone. It's a place I enjoy. In fact, this whole island is something that I enjoy." He stopped and picked up some dust from the stones. "Maybe in some past life I was a Bonifacio."

"And were your dates all sex objects of your Bonifacio harem?"

"Monica, cut this bloody-ass talk out." he said, turning and looking at her full in the face. Both pairs of eyes connected. It was an 'if you don't stop this Monica, Dishon will put you on the next Hydro Jet for Nice.'

They stood for a moment. His expression, though without a frown or scowl, was firm and direct. The subject was now complete for both of them. She felt a little foolish about pushing the subject quite so far. But maybe she wanted a reaction.

"I'm sorry," she replied quietly, "sometimes I just feel so inadequate. I don't feel like I do anything constructive. I feel like a I have a mindless job." She looked up and away from him. "Then I see all the things you do, and now you talk about two other flight attendants from the U.S. who come all the way over here to France and open a restaurant." Her eyes met his. "That really makes me feel bloody dumb."

"Monica," he said, taking her into a hug. "you're not 'bloody dumb', now cut all this talk out and let's have a good time. It's such a beautiful day, and there's so much to see."

She nodded in agreement. It was something she had always felt. Corsica was not the subject, she thought, it was something she just had to deal with.

From that point on, the conversation and the relationship lightened considerably, and soon they were relaxed and gibbering about general topics.

The next stop was Lake Melo. They reached the lake by late morning and Michael was again ready for the moment. He pulled out a small picnic basket which had been contained french bread, cheese and red wine. There were even a few tasty leftovers from the evening meal. Monica almost commented about the leftovers as she examined the basket, but then she decided against it.

"Nope," he said, "no picnic yet. We have to hike up to Monte Rontondo." As he spoke he pointed to a higher peak above the lake. "There you can see almost the entire island and we'll have our late morning snack."

It was not a long nor steep climb, it was just that it was difficult over and around huge boulders and stoneworks. Once they reached the top of Monte Rontondo, the setting and the view of Corsica was worth the effort.

Michael opened a bottle of Bordeaux and set it on a stone to breathe. He broke a loaf of bread in half, making two long sections from each toe. Next he hollowed out as much of the inner dough as possible. He paused a moment to look at Monica. She was watching him. Then he broke sections from the cheese wheel and began to stuff the hollow french bread. Finally when both sections were stuffed full of cheese, he again looked up at Monica. She was still watching, but with more interest now. He handed her one of the bread sections and the bottle of wine. She took one in each hand. He sat back against a large boulder and bit into the cheese and bread, all in one bite.

Monica smiled, she bit into the offering, chewing the cheese and bread together, and then with a long gulp she washed it down with the wine.

'It couldn't be all bad' she was thinking as she handed him the wine bottle, 'he's always there when I come back to Antibes. And there is never any sign of another woman.' She turned, taking another bite and looking out toward the Mediterranean. One could almost see the entire island.

After the late morning snack, which included not one, but almost two bottles of wine, they drove downward on the eastside to Alexia. There they turned southward, finishing the second bottle as they went. They were now heading for the southern tip of the island and the town of Bonifacio.

Once in Bonifacio they checked into the Hotel Grande Bonifacio. The early afternoon was spent wandering through the village, in and out of shops. When the shops began to close for the afternoon, they took the long stroll to the Grotto du Saragonato. It was such a comfortable respite when they finally returned to the terrace of the Ristorante Bonifacio for a delightful snack of fruit de mer and some local Corsican wine. Without revealing his identity, Michael asked for wine from the Convent d'Alziprato, the Monastery on the north end of the island. There was none. He showed some displeasure in his expression. But then he shrugged and smiled at Monica.

Late in the afternoon shops began to open again. This quiet early afternoon philosophy of Europe, especially in Corsica, gave everyone a chance to relax and recharge for the rest of the day. As shades raised and doors opened again, Monica expressed her desire to head out alone and catch up on some local Corsican shopping. She wanted to enjoy a bit of bartering without masculine impatience.

"Why don't we meet back here on the terrace at eight!" she said. "You can seek out your Bonifacio digs by yourself without worrying about me, and I can do my shopping without worrying about you."

Michael looked at her for a moment with a smile on his face. He could not decide whether she wanted to be alone for a while or whether she was giving him some consideration. They agreed, and each left in opposite directions.

It was a passion he had in walking. Something that seemed to cleanse his feelings and give him renewed life when he walked briskly along a pathway or an avenue, purging his mind of conscious concerns. Sort of a 'therapeutic catharsis' is what he would tell others. It made him feel very energetic and relaxed, a phenomenon which he could not explain, but enjoyed.

CHAPTER ELEVEN

DEA Invitation

Out along the coastal road Michael stepped off to a brisk pace heading for the Grotto Saragonato. The Grotto was on a ledge above the Sea. This location, in cool recesses of the hilltop, commanded an excellent view of open water to one side and the straits to Sardinia on the other.

Something was disturbing the tranquil state which he anticipated. Along the walk, he had the feeling that something was out of order. Something was causing unrest instead of the 'high' he usually experienced from such a brisk walk. It was that extra sense he had developed for survival. He concentrated on the hairs on the back of his neck. Were they bristling or was it just the cool breeze?

Michael sat on the edge of the stone wall leading into the main Grotto. He looked out across the open sea, paying close attention to all the movements around him. Something was definitely out of order, he felt, and he was beginning to focus on a point over his right shoulder.

Without telegraphing any sign of suspicion, he rose from his sitting position and began to casually walk along the walkway, acting as though sightseeing and heading for the Grotto. He worked his way over behind a huge scrub tree. It looked like a gigantic bonsai tree. Then he spotted a man in cutoffs and teeshirt sort of walking along and gazing about. Michael smiled to himself. This man was obviously an American. It was his haircut, his facial features, and even though the clothes were from the south of France, his gait and physical gestures were all American.

Michael watched him for awhile, particularly to confirm the feeling that this person was following him. From behind the huge scrub tree,

Michael continued his walk along the pathway. Occasionally he would glance over just to make eye contact. The man quickly looked away, as though interested in some uninteresting piece of the environment. When the man looked away one more time, Michael moved.

"Who the hell are you!" he stated, grabbing him in the tender flesh of his upper arm.

"Uh..." the startled man replied. "Uh..."

"What do you want!" Michael continued. "Who the hell are you!", squeezing the flesh tighter.

"Dammit," he muttered, jerking his arm out of Michael's grasp. "Who are you? Why are you asking?"

"Asshole," Michael said, turning his head away in disgust. "That's an American word I can use on you. Don't keep this up! What do you want?"

The stranger looked away a little, the intensity in Michael's eyes distracted him. He stood very still and took a deep breath. Then with a reflexive glance in one direction then the other, he spoke.

"I'm Charles Alexander." There was a long pause while Michael stared. "I'm here to talk to you." Michael began to relax a little. "I talked to the European Command." Michael backed away and looked for a place on the wall in the shade to sit down. He followed. "They sent me to Raspail."

That was enough. Michael was thinking 'is that supposed to be the key word, is he supposed to get excited because the name Raspail was mentioned. What did this Charles Alexander want?'

"I spent a week with Raspail." He was still watching Michael as he spoke. "Euro Command told me that you were the person I needed. They sent me to France. Raspail agrees, but he doesn't think that you'll volunteer."

"Volunteer!" Michael threw his arms up. "I never volunteered for anything. That Raspail is some kind of sick son-of-a-bitch!" He frowned. He realized that he was using Americanized words for the first time in a long while. "Are you CIA?"

"No! I'm DEA..."

His response was toned to mean something else. Michael thought about it for a moment. It sounded like envy.

"...but we work closely with the CIA."

That sounded like admiration and a little bit of confusion about how he was supposed to answer. Michael watched the man's face.

"We went to the CIA for help. They deny any knowledge of our problem. They claimed that their concerns are more 'global' than our South American drug trafficking."

Michael frowned and backed up a step to sit down again on the wall.

"Charles Alexander, what the hell are you talking about?"

"Law enforcement in the U.S. knows about you. Your Interpol work is in the textbooks!"

"Bullshit!" There was that American talk again.

"True. Besides service information between countries, there are articles about you."

Michael sat up. His brow was knitted, not in a frown this time, but in interest and pride. Articles in the U.S. about him. How much, he was wondering, and how often, he thought. No matter how long he lived away, no matter how much resentment he might have, America was what he was all about. He even reflected a moment on the Lost Generation of the Twenties, the expatriates of the Thirties and Forties, and yet, they all eventually went home.

"I'm an Assistant Chief of Staff for Operations for the DEA!" He said it trying to sound important and authoritative. "I know what we need in the theater of action when it comes to agents." He looked away. "I wanted the CIA to help in our covert activities. They were patronizing and demeaning." He turned to look at Michael. "But, when I went to them to ask for help to locate you," he paused, Michael looked up, "they were suddenly not so patronizing or demeaning. They must know all about you."

Michael got up from the wall and walked a few yards away. Charles followed him.

"What is it with you and military security?" Charles asked. There was no response. "That's when I knew I had to talk to you." He stepped boldly in front of Michael. "I had no idea where to find you. You were in the French Interpol, but where? I could only make inquiries from the top down."

Michael shifted uneasily. "What is it you want?"

"Carlos!" Charles said. The sound was a puncture. "Carlos, the South American drug king and terrorist."

"So, what do you want?"

"Obviously you are American," Charles said, "the Viet Fox." He watched Michael as he spoke, but got no reaction. "I want you to come home and help us cut the throat of Carlos. Cut the South American connection."

Michael stood, looking out across the open water. "No! I won't go back!" He turned to Charles. "Do you know how long I have tried to forget about all my memories of America, to forget those bastards who tried to get rid of me." He walked farther away. "You have no goddamn right to come all the way over here and ask me to go back." There was a trace of tears in Michael's eyes. "Dammit, get away from me. I don't want to hear about it." He turned and walked briskly away, as though dismissing the subject.

Charles stood for a moment, looking blankly at Michael. He did not know the background. He did not know all the history of the Viet Fox. The Viet Fox had happened years earlier. Yet there were still glowing reports about the Viet Fox in Nam, archived in all the service organizations. All he knew was what he had compiled from articles about Interpol, and references to the Viet Fox. There was more from the confidential exchange of government files of international police information, but nothing about Michael the person. Before coming to Europe he thought that this French I5 is an American and would probably like the idea of going home for an assignment.

"...besides," Michael continued, looking away as he felt Charles come up alongside of him, "I am retired. I pick my own assignments."

"I just thought that you would like a trip to the U.S. And the fact that the target," he was still reaching to play his cards, again trying to find a trump, "is Carlos. He is in the Americas what Abu Nidal is in the Far East."

Michael stopped. He looked at Charles. "I know who Carlos is." His tone was disgust. Charles' lack of maturity was showing and it made Michael uncomfortable. If they sent a man like this for me, he was thinking, then what must the rest of the DEA be like. How many Assistant Chiefs of Staff Operations were there?

Both men stiffened momentarily. They looked at each other, then around the pathways. From behind the ridge over the Grotto, shots could be heard. Without an exchange of words, they took off together, running for the ridge. For Michael it was reactive, for Charles it was curiosity.

On the ridge, they looked down into the ruins of the original Church of Saragonato. Behind ancient columns on the left were three men engaged in shooting at a single man off to the right, who in turn was shooting back from behind other fallen columns.

The two watched from the ridge for a few moments. There was no progress. Shooting, reloading, shooting. Finally the three began to spread out a little. It looked like the beginning of a flanking maneuver.

"You take the single guy." Michael said while concentrating on the three to the left. "Take him alive. He might be the good guy. Don't use your piece unless you absolutely have to."

Charles hesitated a moment as Michael dropped down over the ridge wall and began making his way between boulders and ancient structures. Then Charles moved out to the right. As he reached for his gun, he glanced back over to Michael who was now halfway down and positioning himself behind the rear man. Michael had empty hands and appeared not to have any intention of using a weapon. Then as Michael disappeared behind a razed column, Charles set his jaw firmly and again started making his way through the boulders.

After what seemed a very long time, Charles, hot from the Mediterranean sun and nervous about entering into such an engagement, especially on foreign soil, positioned himself a few yards behind the single man. He was not noticed because of the man's interest was in the opposite direction. However, Charles was thinking, he could be hit with bullets from the other side.

While he planned his move, he realized that the sounds of shooting from the other side lessened, then the shots seemed to come from only one location, and then the shots stopped completely. Charles was straining to see over to the other side, when he noticed his target was now standing and trying to see also.

"Hold still," Charles said into the man's ear as he grabbed him around the neck with his left arm and jerked the man's pistol away with his right hand.

"Move!" Charles commanded.

The man looked at him with wide eyes, struggling as if not to understand. Charles shoved the pistol into the man's ribs and gestured for him to head over to the other side. The man was obviously frightened. He was confused about Charles' role in the shootout.

"Move!" Charles said again, louder and deeper, shoving the pistol harder. The man moved.

As they turned past the large column where Charles knew Michael had gone, both the man and Charles were startled by the scene before them. Michael was leaning back against a low stone wall, three pistols laying on the wall next to him, and there on the ground were the three men, face down with arms stretched as far in front of their heads as possible. All three were stripped naked from the waist down, trousers down around their ankles, bare butts exposed to the Mediterranean sun.

Michael reached up and grabbed the single man standing in front of Charles.

"What is this all about?" Michael asked.

The man struggled again, still looking down at the three men on the ground.

Michael reached over and began to unbuckle the man's belt.

The man dropped his raised arms and grabbed his pants. "No!" he shouted. "I can tell you!"

Michael smiled, and then he shrugged while Charles just stood watching, still holding the man's gun.

"I am Bonifacio." His English was broken with Italian sounds. "These men are Mafioso, Black Hand." He paused and looked down at them. "They are Sicilian. They are Mafioso."

Michael took the man's shirt front in his fist and looked into his eyes. The man, still wide-eyed, blinked frequently.

"Drop your pants!"

"No, I won't!"

Michael reached over to the stone wall and picked up one of the large old revolvers. Then he pointed it at the man's testicles and cocked the hammer.

The Bonifacio stood still for a moment. He glanced at Charles, who was intently watching the situation unfold, and he looked back at Michael. Another moment passed, then he began to unbuckle his belt and lower his pants.

"See," Michael said to Charles, "no underwear. They must not believe in underwear on this islands. If they do, you could probably throw them in a nuclear waste dump when they finally take them off."

"I am Bonifacio." The man was standing naked in front of Michael. His pants were down on his ankles. "I am having a few fishing boats. They try to take my boats!"

"Why your boats?"

"They are very fast!"

"Fishing boats?" Michael continued. "Very fast fishing boats?"

"Si! Very fast. I have to get very far to fish and come back very fast."

"Lie down over there. Face down, like your friends."

Michael gestured for the man to lie opposite the others with his feet against the middle man's feet.

"What now?" Charles asked.

"Well," Michael replied, nodding his head upward, "we have witnesses all along the ridge."

Charles looked up. There were some twenty or thirty people, he thought, looking down, watching them. Some even had cameras out and were taking pictures. On the hills around the ancient ruins were some shepherds, other Corsican natives and what appeared to be a few more tourists.

"The rest is up to you," Michael continued. "I don't believe any of this story. Look at these guns." He held the revolver in his hand forward for Charles to examine. "This is an old Russian piece, and those two are an old Italian automatic and probably a French or Italian revolver from the Great War." He took the gun Charles had taken from the single man. "This one is a little nicer. Not as old, but probably dates back to WW-Two days."

Charles looked at Michael with a questioning expression.

"If these guys are mafioso, they would have newer hardware. And he's no fisherman. Look at his soft palms."

Michael emptied the guns as he spoke, laying them out side by side on the wall. "My guess is that this guy is running something with his boats between Corsica, Sardinia and Sicily, with maybe a run to Malta on occasion. He could be bringing something up from north Africa." He turned and leaned back against the wall. "Anyway, they need to sort it out between themselves and the police."

"What do we do now?"

"I don't do anything." He made the comment and pointed up into the hills. Charles looked up and saw uniformed men climbing down through the boulders.

"That's the Corsican police, and over there," he pointed to another area of the hills, "are the Bonifacio regional police. If we are here when they all arrive, we will be held for hours, maybe overnight." He stepped past Charles and started to climb toward the ridge wall. "Their biggest problem will be to decide in who's jurisdiction all this happened."

Charles hesitated a moment, looking first at one group of uniformed men climbing down, then over at the other men in different uniforms climbing down also as quickly as they could. It looked like a race to the site to claim first victory.

"I think..." Charles turned to speak, but Michael was gone. He looked up to see Michael disappear over the ridge wall, absorbed into the large crowd that had gathered.

Quickly Charles started his climb, but by the time he reached the wall, Michael was nowhere to be seen. He stood for a moment, checking in both directions, but even if Michael was near, the viewers were still arriving and blocking any surveillance. Charles looked back down at the scene below. There were the two groups of police, merged and arguing with arms raised in active gestulations. The gunmen were still face down on the ground, pants at their ankle and bare buttocks exposed for all. Cameras were clicking all around.

Finally, after one more glance about, Charles started on his walk at a slow steady pace. Not toward Bonifacio, but instead he headed down the ridge road in the opposite direction.

'What is it about this man,' he was thinking, 'if only I could convince him to come home.' Charles was walking almost with his head down. He was not about to continue in his push for Michael. There was something about the way all that happened. There was a message somewhere in there. Charles continued to walk along the pathway. Raspail said that Michael was the man, and from his history, Charles knew that he was the man, but Michael had made it clear that there would be no more pursuit. He was not interested in going home.

CHAPTER TWELVE

Viet Fox

I t was obvious to Michael that Monica was aware of the afternoon disturbances at the Grotto Saragonato. They overheard conversations about it that evening at dinner, and the receptionist even mentioned it as they checked out the following morning. But she asked no questions, and Michael volunteered no information. Each thought it strange that the other did not comment on the subject. Monica was suspicious of Michael's lack of interest. Surely, she thought, he must have heard something about the shootings at the grotto, or was he part of it?

After breakfast, they drove up along the west coast of the island. Some time was spent at Ajaccio, where Michael showed Monica the museum, statues,and general memorabilia of Napoleon. This was the birthplace of the Emperor, and it was a place to which he had returned more than once. As Emperor, it was rumored that he had risked a visit in a cloak of secrecy. Even at this modern date, on could stir up heated arguments in the streetside taverns about the greatness and prowess of their native son. Most arguments stemmed from opposing views of how he should have rallied his supporters after escaping from the island of Elbe, and how he should have campaigned his troops at Waterloo. Was Wellington a brilliant commander or was he an opportunist who took advantage of Napoleon's weakened health from Elbe?

The weather throughout the day was cool with a light breeze, and actually quite comfortable either in the valley villages or on the mountain tops. Michael decided that the disturbances of the Saragonato Grotto must not have reached Monica, other than hotel gossip. So he dismissed it somewhere along the drive back up the mountain to the Monastery. They talked of many things, of crops of cabbages and of Napoleonic kings. But at some point in the evening he was to find out that he was wrong!

After dinner they went out on the terrace for brandies and a breath of fresh air as they looked out over the Mediterranean, northward toward France. Dinner was a kalamari appetizer, squab stuffed with wild herb rice, glazed carrots, fresh garden peas, and a Caesar salad which M. Dishon called "salate Napoleon". She said it was full of garlic to be eaten in hearty quantities so that the consumer could conquer all. 'With his breath', Monica had assumed. And there was the vintage wine from the cellars. Dry and full with just an extremely slight hint of yeast mold, exactly the way Michael liked it. The brandy on the terrace was naturally of the Napoleon label, and had been set up in the 100th year of the anniversary of his death.

"So what happened at the grotto yesterday?"

Michael looked at her in the dimming light of the sunset. He could see her face as the setting sun shown directly on it. Her expression was blank, her words were direct.

"Nothing important," he responded. He was disappointed, not sure if at himself for having dismissed the subject, or at Monica for bringing it up.

"It bloody well is important." Now her face matched her tone. "Before you met me back at the hotel, news had come into Bonifacio. It was you they were talking about. I know it." Michael was quiet. "Who was the other man?" she continued.

Now he looked at her again.

"The news was about two men. I know you had to be one of them."

"Monica, it's not important."

"Did you drag me to Corsica to meet somebody?"

"No!" Michael stood up and turned to lean against the stone railing. He sipped the Napoleon brandy. "It just happened. There was a confrontation between two parties at the grotto. All I did was neutralize the odds for the police."

"Who was the other man?"

"He came out of the crowd." Michael sipped again. He was poised, exuding relaxation. "Whoever he was, he tried to help. But then he got involved."

"So you uninvolved everybody!"

The two were silent for sometime. Monica was gazing off toward the northwest, wondering why she couldn't leave well enough along. It seemed that she spoiled romantic settings by demanding explanations. 'Perhaps', she thought, 'he would be more vulnerable then'. But what would it accomplish? If silence about his work was part of his strength, why try to weaken it.

"Michael, I don't want to sound like the fishmonger wife..." she said as she looked at him, "...but I get caught up in all of this. I've been involved in relationships before. I never seem to be able to make it work." She sat back and looked straight ahead. "Maybe it's confession time for me. I need to know about you. I care about you, and I seem to always be screwing it up!"

There was a long quiet pause. It would taken a Heinkle knife to cut the silence. They both knew it. Finally, after what seemed to be a very long time, Michael spoke.

"I was a noncombatant in 'Nam'," he said as he sat back down next to her and poured them both more brandy. "I carried a side piece with a couple of extra clips. But that was all. I had a natural shooting ability. In college I was captain of the shooting team." He looked at her. "Targets, not people. Moving targets, but only targets."

Monica did not speak. Instead, she sat very still swirling her brandy. What is he talking about, she was wondering. But whatever, it sounded important and he did mention Viet Nam.

"I was a forward weather observer for air strikes. Most of the time nobody knew where the targets were. The Minh moved about a lot. So, from time to time some of the pilots would come out to where I was. They wanted a closeup view of the terrain and the hills to the northwest."

"From where I was setup, we really couldn't see much of anything. We had a nice little operation on top of a hill with a short landing strip. We put together a bar and eatery, served by the Vietnamese. We had to stay loose because the Minh might overrun us at any time. This one particular day, when some of the pilots came out to see me, they had a gooniebird." He looked at Monica. "A DC-3." But then he realized that she would not know what either was. "An old two engine propeller military plane. Used mostly for cargo." He turned away again, looking out toward the sea.

"The pilot of the gooniebird was a very young Second Lieutenant. One of the guys I knew was Russ McGowan from South Carolina. He was a Captain, I was a First Lieutenant. There were six of them, plus the gooniebird pilot and me. The highest rank was Major Diedre."

Michael was making short, staccato-like statements about his past. And Monica was listening carefully, but the sound of his voice, she was thinking, and the way he was delivering the story, was not like the Michael she knew. He always projected a casual air, but right now he seemed sort of uptight, and even a little anxious. The memories of Nam must be dredging up old angry wounds.

"After an afternoon of boozing at the Officer's Club," Michael continued, "The Major decided that we should all take a flight into Minh Cong territory and check it out." There was a long pause. Again he reflected for a moment and took a deep breath. "Russ insisted against it, and so did I. The pilot didn't say a word, but I could see that he had paled. Diedre told him he would fly the goonie if there was any resistance. It was not an order, but the pilot knew that he had to take us. He was only a cargo pilot."

Monica was not saying a word. She kept herself very still. There was nothing she would do to disrupt his story.

"One of the interesting things about Viet Nam," and he made a grunting sound, "was that no one ever knew where the battle lines really were. Neither side really knew. They were mostly in front of us to the north, but sometimes they came out of Laos, sometimes out of Cambodia, depending on how far our troops advanced, and sometimes they just flat-ass out-flanked us. It was like the jungle growing up behind you once you've cleared a path. Our guys would press deep into the north country, turn around and find communist troops around behind them. The real trick was always to flush out the Viet Minh. This was the hardcore center of the Cong. The Minh dated back to before the French. And they were more elusive then any of the others."

"So," he continued, "you never knew where they were. The gooniebird has a fairly long range, low altitude profile. Good lift and a long glide path. A real stable, well made sitting duck for any enemy arms. It couldn't get out of its own way. Somebody with a 22. could take out an old DC-3. But, with all that booze in us, the Major decided that we would go find the Minh concentration. So we went. My commanding officer made an attempt to talk him out of it. But he was reminded that his role, as the Weather Commander, was only to support the airborne combat units and nothing else. It sounded like a good idea at first. So we went. A Second Lieutenant at the controls, an airplane of World War II vintage long overdue for retirement, a group of fighter pilots, a loud mouthed Major Diedre, and me.

The DC-3 groaned and lurched as the young pilot tried to bank and turn sharply to avoid small arms ground fire. It was like Columbus' men sailing farther out on the flat earth, wondering how they would ever get back." Michael paused long enough to look at Monica. "As we flew through the enemy corridors, they began unveiling heavier weapons. Someone was radioing ahead that the ole bird was coming their way. The Major sat in the right seat, barking commands at the pilot. The rest of the group was at windows looking, not for target information, but for an aircraft or gun emplacements. It wouldn't take much to focus on the goonie and blow it out of the sky.

And then, it became obvious that as the Major got more frightened by the stupid venture, the louder he yelled, and finally he was back with the rest of us screaming at everyone. The airplane was bobbing and weaving. Russ bolted for the cockpit and got the pilot calmed enough to turn the DC-3 in a wide, long circle to the east with the hopes of heading back south over new lands, or even out over water. It was a good tact, but everyone knew that no matter which direction the plane took, word had spread all over the northern zone that a tired, old American airplane was lumbering along at some forty-five hundred feet."

Michael stopped. He sat for a moment, looking out across the Sea.

"Michael," Monica said softly, "are you alright?"

"I'm fine." he said. Then he continued. "The gooniebird was already a couple hundred miles into the northern territory when it was finally turning southward again.

Russ pushed the flight controls forward, using a fighter tactic. It brought the aircraft down and he settled out at about twelve hundred feet. There were hilltops that looked higher. But at least at that altitude he could fool most radar. And even though the speed was slow, he could pass through gun emplacements with surprise. By now the alert was out that a U.S. plane was in the area.

The Major was yelling that his purpose had not been accomplished. He had to come locate targets. It was hard to tell whether it was fear or alcohol doing the shouting. He kept yelling that he wanted to turn the plane around and head north again. If nobody else did anything, I decided that in a few minutes I was going to do something to shut him up. He jumped out of his seat and went forward again. Just as he reached the cockpit, the gooniebird jolted to the left. The right wing had been hit. There was only the stub of struts remaining. Russ brought the aircraft upright momentarily. Everyone struggled for seat belts."

Once again Michael stopped in his story. This time he sat silently, and Monica decided not to prompt him.

"The first thing I remembered, is that I woke up with a gentle drizzle coming down on my face. Without moving, I stayed still trying to reconstruct what had happened. The seat cushion was still strapped to me, and I was somewhere in woods, in a huge clump of underbrush. Slowly I felt around me, moving my body and checking for broken bones and lacerations. Other than stiffness everything seemed in order. I had no idea how long I had been that way. The forty-five was still in the holster on my hip. As the drizzle continued to fall, I checked the piece in the dim dawning light. The forty-five had a full clip and I had two full spare clips. There was no sound except for the drizzling rain.

As I sat up, taking off the seat cushion, I could see the plowed woods in front of me, heading off into a darker area of trees. Everything was very quiet. I strained to hear. There were no voices, there was no movement. Nothing.

So as to keep very low, I crawled along the plowed path to where the wreckage of the DC-3 had come to rest. It was about a hundred yards ahead of me.

What remained of the airplane was deserted. There was no one in or near the wreckage. At first it was a relief to find no bodies, killed in the crash. Then another feeling came over me. Where the hell were they? Had they survived and gone off without me? Were they captured?

The morning light was getting brighter. In checking around the fuselage, I found a few footprints and a trampled area leading off in the direction the nose of the airplane was pointing. The body of the airplane was broken completely open on the right side. I tried to remember where I had grabbed the cushion and strapped the seatbelt on. It must have been right where the fuselage split open when the airplane crashed along the hilltop. All I could figure was that I went out through the side, landing in the brush while the plane skidded on without me.

Suddenly I heard voices from the direction in which the trampled footprints led. They were Vietnamese voices. It sounded like more than just a couple. I dropped down to my hands and knees and crawled through the wet ground to nearby underbrush and boulders. Even with the overcast sky, the daylight was bright and I could see the Viet Cong soldiers checking through the airplane. They were in no hurry. They more curious about the gooniebird than concerned. There were six of them, and they looked like kids.

After a long lapse of time, one of the group called them together and they trooped off back down the trail."

Michael looked at Monica. "Are you sure you want to hear about this? I mean, it's really boring to anybody else."

She just looked at him. The sun was almost completely set, but they could still see each other's face. When Monica did not respond, Michael frowned a little, then continued.

"There was no sign of the crew, so I decided that they must have been taken away during the night, probably right after the crash. The soldiers would lead the way to camp. If the crew was captured, they should be in that camp. If they had gotten away, the Viet Cong soldiers would have been more excited. So, since I had no other plan, I decided to follow the soldiers. That was the first time I took out the forty-five. It gave me a kind of comfort.

After almost three hours of trailing behind, the soldiers crested over a hilltop and in the clearing below was a Viet Minh camp. That was where I stopped, and they continued on down the recently formed path to the camp. The day was very bright by now. As we trekked through the woods from the airplane, I kept looking back for landmarks for a return trip. It would be a long way back, but I felt I could find my way. Why I would go back was unknown, but to memorize the trail seemed like the right thing to do.

The camp was not very large, certainly not big by U.S. standards. That was part of the Viet Minh plan. They had many small, highly mobile camps. The Vietnamese regulars were more stable, somewhat permanent in their camps. And while the Viet Cong was mobile, they were still not as quick to move as the Minh. The Minh held the distinction of being the elite corp, guerilla leaders for both the Cong and the regulars. U.S. fighters came over frequently bombing and strafing, trying to hit Minh camps. The lines of combat shifted frequently, and with a highly mobile camp, they could attack and run. Farther north, as I found out later, the camps were more formidable and more of a permanent structure. They were manned mostly by the regulars.

Throughout the Minh camp below were a dozen bamboo buildings, spread around amongst the foliage for camouflage, haphazardly erected only for convenience. A broad roadlike trail ran right through the middle of the camp. Their entire design was that they went where existing trails led them. They did not like to cut new trails. Old trails weaving through the jungle, even broad enough for vehicles, would be harder to detect than a long straight road. There were a few land rover jeep-type vehicles parked about, some with machine guns mounted. Soldiers meandered around, going from one bamboo building to another. The drizzle had stopped and the sky was clearing.

In the hiding place where I nestled, I felt secure. I had backed against a rock wall under an overhanging bluff with a good view of the camp. Other than being wet, I tried to relax and think about a plan to get back to the southside of Viet Nam. It would probably be easier to head out southward by myself. But, if anyone else was alive and if they were captured in the camp, then I should at least know that.

My body ached and I realized that somewhere on the back of my head, there was a huge lump. I sat there awhile, feeling my limbs and joints to find something broken. Then my stomach growled. It was like I would wake up any minute, sitting in the Officer's Club at happy hour, having a few toddies. How the hell did this happen?

Survival training came back to me. When I went through it, I couldn't imagine why a Weather Officer had to go through survival. I had not done it in the beginning, but when the tour for Nam came up, everyone had to survive. I sat against the rock looking down at the camp, and now I began to force myself to remember.

Nearby were young bamboo shoots and some early palms. I used my Swiss knife and cut the bottoms. Not as tasty as I remembered. Chewy and filling. The palm bottoms were better. My stomach rebelled momentarily. But a picky eater I have never been. I cut some extra bottoms and stuffed then inside my shirt. It could be a long walk back to Saigon.

The day dragged on and the activity level stayed about the same. Rover jeeps came and left. Minh soldiers and farmers mingled about, walking from one place to the other. There was no pattern and no focus on any special event. I was beginning to wonder about my missing buddies. Maybe they had survived and escaped. Maybe they couldn't find me and they beat a path back to the south. I hurt, and I was scared of the thought of them leaving me help. If nothing happened by dark, I decided, then I would head south.

It was sometime in the late afternoon when suddenly there they were. The rest of the DC-3 crew. They were being ushered out of one of the buildings and across the main road. My adrenalin began pumping. I leaned forward, knelt up and watched. I even touched the forty-five on my belt. An act of reassurance. One of the group was missing. Again I counted, but there was still someone missing. It was too far to tell if I could determine which one. Russ was there. He had a sort of cocky attitude and cocky walk, swinging his arms and looking around. And the Major was there. He was walking straight up and looking directly ahead. It was the young pilot I couldn't find. But it was too far to tell. They were forced into one of the bamboo buildings. Should I stay and try to help them, or should I try to make my way back with the information about their location. The location, I knew, was temporary. By the time I got back again, the Minh camp would have been moved. Nobody would know where they were.

So I had to stay with them. It was a resolve well within myself which I think I already knew.

After a few hours of darkness and the activities in camp settled down, I left my hiding place and began to sneak toward the bamboo buildings where the crew was. There were no fences or guards. Everything was calm. A number of Minh fires were burning. Some soldiers were sitting around, and some were sleeping. On the side of the hut where I had seen the crew put, I tapped on the bamboo.

'Russ!'

'Russ,' a voice inside said. 'It's your buddy out there. He's on the outside.'

There was shuffling inside. Then Russ was against the inside at the same spot.

'Here's my Swiss knife.' I said as I pushed it through the opening.

'You bastard,' Russ said. 'I thought you were dead. You alright?'

'I'm fine.' I flexed a little and felt the aches. 'Cut the ropes and come out on this side. You're covered on this side.'

Russ was direct, my kind of guy. He spoke not a word but started cutting through the bamboo rope. I stepped around to check both sides of the hut, even pulling the forty-five. It was a feeling of having to protect them. They were about to be released into my custody.

Every now and then I could hear the Major mumble, but it seemed that Russ stayed directly with his action. Soon, enough of the bamboo poles could be pushed away so the men squeezed out. Russ grabbed me.

'You bastard. You did it!'

'Move it!' said the Major. 'Goddamnit, move it!'

We moved away from the hut and into the jungle. The Major spotted the pistol in my hand. He said he wanted it. As the officer in charge, he had a right to have the weapon. It caused a momentary delay in our escape. Everyone stood still, looking at me and looking at the Major. The light from the camp fires was just enough to give us both enough for facial expressions.

'Major,' I said to him, 'I came back to help. You're a big mouth, pain in the ass. This is my gun.'

I guess I was feeling pretty macho in front of the rest of the crew.

'If I give it to you,' I remember saying, 'it'll be up your ass.'

Suddenly around the corner of the hut, two Minh soldiers appeared. They screamed out and raised their weapons. As the rifles came up, I brought the forty-five into position, heeled by my right hand. One shot dropped one and the second shot dropped the other.

Without hesitation, Russ jumped forward, grabbing both rifles, tossing one to the man closest to him.

'This way!' I bellowed, and we were off into the jungle, heading south back toward the wreckage.

The camp was alive with shouting and running about. Some were dowsing fires and some were lighting fires. In all, there was a great deal of confusion. It seemed that no one really knew where the sound of the shots came from. It gave us the advantage.

Finally, some distance from the camp, we stopped so Russ and I could talk. The Major never said a word.

The plan was for Russ and one more to head for the wreckage while I took the others to lead the soldiers away from the plane. He wanted to get to the ELT, an emergency locator device. Just before they were captured, he set it off, transmitting signals. Search aircraft should pickup the signal and locate the wreckage.

If it worked, an attack of gun helicopters might show up at any time. They could come in low and destroy the camp. It was always a matter of location. By now back at the base they knew the DC-3 was down. If they were getting the signal, it would only be a matter of coming in with force to clear the area and pick up survivors.

'What the hell are you talking about,' huffed the Major. 'I'm going back to the plane.'

'Major,' I said, a surge of strength continued to grow inside of me, 'see this forty-five?' I paused. 'You get your chicken ass with me, and we'll try to save you.'

He stepped forward, raising his hand, but Russ shoved the rifle out as though to separate us.

'Major! Let's get it on. I've got to check the aircraft. By daylight, we can have choppers crawling all over the place.' He lowered the rifle.

Russ and one other took off in the direction I pointed. I took the others, with the reluctant Major, and we followed the plan to circle out and around, and hopefully meet the other two somewhere near the wreckage. The Minh were supposed to follow us, and we were suppose to lose them. I really didn't think we could lose them. Maybe that wouldn't matter because the consensus was that the Minh would not follow until daybreak. If that were true, then we had quite a few hours to get signals back to the base.

We roamed about for awhile, checking back behind just in case. So far there was nothing. Either the Minh had followed Russ, or the consensus was correct. The Major was fairly cooperative along the way. His ego was bruised and he had to make objections to maintain his position. It seemed as though everyone understood and allowed him to make his negative comments. In any case, we proceeded as planned.

Finally, we came in on Russ from the flank. He had moved some distance from the airplane and it took time for both parties to quietly find each other.

'It was a strange feeling,' Russ said as he and I were sitting off to the side, away from the others. 'He had control of the plane as we went in, and we were both together on the controls. I guess we took the rest of the wings off through the trees. Then suddenly the plane seemed to pick up speed.' He paused, looking straight ahead. 'It didn't pick up speed, but I guess without wings against the trees, it didn't keep slowing down as fast. That's what got him. It was like we were prepared for the impact, then the plane's speed changed, and the nose slammed into the hillside.' This time he turned his head toward me. 'When I came to, the soldiers were all over us. I looked over at him. He had smashed his head against the window frame. I lifted my left arm and ripped away his dog tags.'

During this time, I was not sure if Russ was talking to me to get my thoughts away from the situation around us, or whether he was talking to clear his own mind. I kept having flashes of the two soldiers I had killed. People always talk about what they would do in a situation like that. And it seemed so easy for me at that moment. Why was it so easy? It was almost like I had left my own body and had watched it all unfold from some other vantage point.

'...and I guess I didn't realize you were gone until we reached the camp.'

Russ was still talking when I realized that I had drifted away into my own thoughts.

'You know,' I said, 'there are a few first times in one's life that a person never forgets. Losing our virginity, starting high school, getting married, and the first time you kill a human being.'

Russ smashed me hard on the shoulder.

'Hey,' he said, 'do you know how many people I've killed?'

'Sure, you do it from the sky. You drop napalm bombs and machinegun a target. There's no person to person.'

'What about aerial combat. I've got three kills.'

It was obvious that he was trying to help, but he already knew that it was not the same.

'We never saw the pilot's body again.' He was going back to the gooniebird. There was a feeling I had that I wanted to get my story off my chest, and Russ wouldn't let me. 'When I didn't find you, I figured you were dead.'

We looked at each other. Russ and his wife lived below my wife and I when we were stationed in Germany. Russ and I belonged to the gun club and we used to shoot a lot. Although he had an edge with rifles and shot guns, he was no match for me with handguns. I could clean the center out of all the targets, standing, kneeling, and even quick draw. He was a Captain and wanted to make a career, but his future was uncertain because his was not regular Air Force. I was a Lieutenant about to make Captain and had been offered the regular status, but I wanted out as soon as I paid the military for my Masters in Meteorology. I was assigned to the 7th Squadron in the 49th TAC Fighter Wing. And suddenly we were all sent to Nam.

'I couldn't believe it when you were outside the hut.' Russ continued. 'I mean not only were you alive, but you were there outside the hut. Why didn't you just haul ass south?'

Although the sky was fairly light with a bright moon, occasionally clouds darkened the area. At that moment I wanted to see his expression when he made the statement, but it was too dark.

'Hey,' I responded, 'you owe me twenty bucks from the last poker game. I'm not leaving you out here with a debt like that.'

Everyone took turns sitting on the side of the group, facing in the direction of the Minh camp. They were supposed to listen for sounds which might forecast the coming of enemy troops. Even the Major did his time. I dozed for awhile. I don't think that I ever slept. Every now and then the sight of the two soldiers falling to the ground with shots from my forty-five reentered my mind.

Finally, as the first hint of the morning sun's rays began to lighten the area around us, everyone was up and anxious. We had to call the choppers in on the wrecked plane's ELT device. That meant we had to be around the wreckage when they came in or they would not get us. And we all knew that the Minh would first converge on the wreckage. We had figured that out individually without anyone mentioning it. It was a race of the gun ship choppers versus the Minh soldiers. But we had no way of knowing if the aircraft signal was doing any good.

'I hear them!' someone called out.

Everyone was quiet, straining to listen for the sound of helicopter blades. And then we could hear them. It sounded like the 1812 Overture. The sound of the blades was getting louder. There seemed like there must be a dozen choppers coming in.

We all jumped up, waving arms and shouting and running into a clearing. There they were, three Cobras and a 'Huey'. The wreckage was a couple of hundred yards beyond us, between where we were and where the troops of the Minh would be coming. The choppers would have to fly right over us to home in on the wreckage signal.

The lead Cobra pilot spotted us and directed the Huey down while the three gun ships began unloading firepower into the jungle around us. They circled and fired, canons and machine guns were firing into the perimeter in all directions. The Huey touched down and everyone started scurrying on board.

Suddenly, from across the clearing right through the explosions and rain of machine gun bullets the Minh soldiers were running directly at us, firing at us and firing at the circling Cobras. Two of the gun ships dropped down closer and annihilated the first wave of the Minh. We were trying to get in the rescue ship as fast as we could. The onboard crew was grabbing and dragging us up and on. I dropped to one knee and emptied my clip at three of the soldiers running at the chopper. In the excitement, killing was easier for me now.

Over the noise of the helicopter blades, voices were screaming at me. I remember that I turned and jumped up on the landing skid. One of the crew grabbed my arm and started to pull me in. Just as the craft lifted off, a ground shot hit the crewman in the chest. I looked up as he let go of his grip and fell back into the ship. The upward thrust of the helicopter and sudden release of my arm caused me to fall backwards, down to the ground below. A Cobra came in over me, spraying machine gun fire into the oncoming soldiers. They died as they dropped, but some were getting back into the brush for cover.

It was probably seconds that passed, but it seemed so much longer that I lay there watching the Huey climb out of the clearing. The Cobras circled again as I got up, still holding the forty-five in my left hand. It was too late! I was stranded! The instinct of survival overcame me, and I ran for cover from the Minh soldiers.

Again I had no recollection of time. I just kept moving as fast as I could. I couldn't tell whether any of the soldiers were aware that I escaped or whether they all gave up and were heading back to camp. A lot of Minh had been killed, and at least one American had been hit.

Finally, I sat down against a tree stump to reload my pistol. It was my last clip. Somewhere along the run I decided that I had better reload. Behind me all was quiet. I listened for a while, but there were no noises. At that point I had no idea how long I had run, or in which direction I had run. The sun was still in its early rise in the east, so I took a deep breath and started slowly toward the south.

Sometime after a few hours of my southward trek over hills and through heavy brush, I began to feel my stomach acting up. I was hungry, and slowly as I worked my way along, I began to realize that I was alone in enemy territory with no idea how far I would have to go.

Travelling along like this, without caution, could very easily bring me right into Cong troops. At least, in this heading, I felt that if providence smiled I might come across some American squad, or maybe be found by one of the South Vietnamese guerilla groups.

Sometime in the afternoon, after I had again dug up and cut some bamboo shoots, I heard Vietnamese voices nearby to my left. Carefully I made my way to a vantage spot to see them.

Two Minh soldiers were sitting by a campfire having a midday meal. My hunger pangs began to take over. I could move silently away and continue my trek, or kill them both and have their food. My stomach was working on the bamboo shoots, but not very well. The humane side of me was beginning to win out. I would have to survive on bamboo shoots. My shots earlier were in self defense. This would be clearly a case of attacking and killing two men.

Just as I started to back slowly away, out of the bush to my right came a third soldier. He almost passed by, but my movement must have caught his eye. He turned toward me and raised his rifle.

Almost by reaction, my forty-five was up and I fired, hitting the soldier in the center of his chest. Without watching him any further, I stood up to see the two at the campfire grab their weapons and turn toward me. Two more shots rang out and two more Cong troops fell dead.

For a moment I paused to look at all three bodies. And I wanted to make sure that there were no sounds from any others in the area. The soldiers were dead and the area was quiet.

Down at the fire site I found automatic weapons and a can of shells. On the fire was some kind of small animal roasting, and in their knapsacks were packages of foodstuffs. At least for the moment, I felt that all of this was the sign of providence which meant that I would survive and that I would walk out of the northern region. I ate the cooked animal, double stuffed one of the knapsacks, and then with my forty-five in the holster, I picked up an automatic weapon and a can of rounds. My stomach was sufficiently satisfied and now it was time to begin my southward journey again.

The next few days were rather strange, as I remember. I went from anger about the whole damn Viet Nam thing, to being scared about getting back to the U.S. troops, and then I had recurring thoughts about the killings. It was such a big deal when I killed the first time, but now, as I trekked southward it was like a feeling of pride would come over me. Sometimes I was afraid I would turn a tree and be faced with a squad of Cong; other times I hoped for it. My subconscious and my psyche were playing games for odd man out.

During the day I tried to sleep. I thought that it was better to travel at night. I kept remembering the comments about the Minh only searching by day. If I was hidden by day, then I could travel by night. For some reason the thought of Viet Cong or Vietnamese regulars did not bother me. It was the Minh I thought about. At night, when I travelled, there would probably be a light or campfire and I could skirt the area. As each morning approached, I would find a niche under a log or small cave and bury myself in it for the day. It was hard at first - I thought about bugs, snakes, animals and whatever. But within a couple of days I learned how to find a place to hide, and be off to sleep.

It seems like it was about a week had passed since the campfire shootout and nothing else had happened. Then suddenly one night my eyes popped open and there was the sound of machines and men somewhere nearby. I crept out of my hiding place and crawled to the edge of an overlook. There below was one of the Minh mobile camps. They had just arrived, setting up tents for the soldiers and prefab bamboo huts for the officers. I munched on some of my knapsack foodstuffs as I watched.

What I figured then, which was to help me many times later, was that each unit was made up of about a hundred men. That way there were enough of them to be decisive in a guerilla attack and few enough to break, hide, and regroup somewhere else. It was like watching an ant hill being developed. They all seemed to have duties and they went quickly about them. By the first break of the sun they would be off on a skirmish. Ants scurrying about doing their chores.

An hour or so must have passed while I watched. Just as I was getting ready to ease down from my viewing place, I spotted four American prisoners. I froze in my movement, reflecting on the sneak escape attack I had pulled for the gooniebird crew. Two of them were Air Force, but the other two uniforms were too tattered to tell. They worked right along with the soldiers putting up bamboo walls and dishing out food from gallon cans. The four of them were chained together at the ankles.

'What the hell could I do?' I kept asking myself. I couldn't leave them. I probably couldn't rescue them, and if I did, how could we get away? To where?

Suddenly, I turned and ran off farther into the woods. It seemed like an hour of running, but I know it was not that long. I trudged across soft ground, vines, trees and just stumbled along. But when I stopped, I knew that I was far enough away and the best thing that I could do was keep moving.

In all the rest of time that I spent in north Viet Nam, I don't know that I ever found those four guys. Whenever I was back in that area I always tried to locate the camp.

As I dragged on during those days, trying to keep a southward direction, one of the concerns that began to build inside was what I would do when I reached a combat zone. Everything was so scattered. There were no lines of fighting where I could sneak through and be safe. In World War I there had been trenches which stayed occupied with both sides shooting at each other for months. In World War II lines were fairly definitive. Combat lines could shift as much as a hundred miles in a day. But certainly in Europe each side knew its own men. Korea meandered about the peninsula, but pretty much kept a combat zone defined. In Viet Nam, with a sea on the east, attacks out of Cambodia and Laos on the west, and with the thick dense jungle hiding partisan guerrillas, a soldier never knew where he was fighting. Often when the Americans would punch through and take a strategic advantage in the north, suddenly out of Cambodia from the west would come a major attack. Sometimes these attacks were even south of where certain Air Force bases were thought to be extremely secure.

My only hope was to keep moving southward. I was afraid I might stumble onto some South Vietnamese guerrillas and open fire on them before I realized who they were. My best hope was still to sleep by day and move by night. Hopefully I would find myself inside some American zone.

Time has a way of slipping away, so I can never remember actually how long it was that I stumbled through the jungle. But one day in a hiding place, sound asleep, I was suddenly jerked awake to find a half dozen Vietnamese staring down at me.

If I could have pulled the forty-five, I would have started shooting. I was scared. And then almost instantaneously, it was like some kind of relief.

'Ameligo?'

The Vietnamese holding my collar was speaking.

'Amerigo?'

I had no idea what he was saying. But there was that sense of rescue that suddenly covered me.

'American!' I said slowly. I still wasn't sure which side they might be on.

He nodded. 'Ameligo!' He was smiling, obviously pleased with himself.

With that comment, he dragged me out of my cave and sat me up. He was nodding and smiling. He pointed at me and looked at his friends. They were all mumbling 'Ameligo!'

For some reason, the only thing I could think of was Sir Walter Raleigh. So I looked at him, pointed to his chest and said 'Raleigh!'

He smiled even broader. He pointed at himself while looking around at his friends again, and said 'Lareigh!'

'Raleigh!' I tried to correct him. It was the 'r' and the 'l' thing again.

He nodded and pointed to himself and repeated, "Raleigh!"

And so it was with 'Ameligo' and 'Lareigh'. I had been saved by a band of South Vietnamese guerrillas. For the next few days we seemed to roam about in the jungle regions. I was certain that we had back tracked a few times. A few of his men spoke some words of English, and his understanding was not too bad. Overall, I did feel as though we were heading southward. At least that would give me the general direction I wanted.

About the fourth day out, we came across a Cong camp setup in the thick of the woods. There were three American prisoners tied up in the middle of the group. With gestures and hand signs I indicated that I wanted to go in and rescue them. Raleigh did not agree. Instead, they produced a large old WW II hand crank radio and proceeded to contact someone. After a few moments on the radio, he grabbed my collar.

"Ameligo, we go!"

Suddenly all hell broke loose. Raleigh and his team of eight guerrillas, turned, with me holding up the rear, and blasted headlong into the Cong camp. Raleigh's men went in shooting wildly at anything that moved. The Cong returned fire almost as quickly, also shooting back at anything that moved. One of his men went down, and one of the tied up Americans was killed immediately. I went straight to the tree where they were tied and cut them loose. From the dead one, I took his dog tags. We hurried out of the camp with Raleigh and his men covering for us.

As we got into the brush, I stopped and grabbed hand grenades from the guerrillas. The Cong was trying to regroup. As they did, I lobbed a couple of grenades right into them. A few well thrown grenades and the Cong was scattering into the woods without weapons, running away from us.

"Ameligo!" Raleigh yelled as he grabbed me and hugged.

The Americans were navy pilots downed during an air ground assault about two weeks before. They had been captured and moved through different camps with the Cong. Once we were settled, far enough away for Raleigh to feel comfortable, he brought out food for the pilots.

We rested by day, then moved slowly by night. Raleigh felt that if we stayed still in the day, the Cong would not find us, and he too was more concerned about the Minh. When we moved at night, we could see the camps and avoid them. Occasionally Raleigh would crank up the radio and contact someone.

After a few more days of circling around, Raleigh led us into a clearing, and almost as we entered I could hear the sound of helicopters. His timing was perfect. Suddenly over the trees two Cobra gun ships came into view, swinging around and checking the area. Then the Huey ship appeared. I had goose bumps.

It was exactly like the scenario I had lived through before. The gunships circled and fired into the trees while the rescue ship came in and landed. I didn't realize how exactly the same the scenario was about to be.

As we rushed up to the Huey, they started offloading supplies, weapons and munitions. The navy pilots scurried onboard. Just as I started to pull myself up, the aircraft commander jumped out and grabbed my arm.

'Your orders are to stay here with the Vietnamese for two more weeks.'

I stood with my leg cocked up against the landing strut.

'Find the camps with prisoners. Nghia will be in contact with us.' He was gesturing over toward Raleigh. 'We brought him another radio!'

Still I stood with my leg on the strut when the commander climbed back into his seat and the helicopter started to rise off the ground without me. The upward motion and the downward draft knocked me to the ground.

So while Raleigh and his men were cheering as the helicopters flew out of sight, I was trying to understand what the hell was happening to me.

That was the beginning of the Viet Fox. It probably had already happened sometime before, but I didn't realize it. Apparently Raleigh had been sending radio information back, asking for me to stay. From that moment on, I lived behind the lines for about three years, coming out occasionally for rest and recuperation. But mostly I lived in the jungle, working with guerrilla groups to rescue Allied prisoners. I was listed as an MIA in the military annals.

At first the Fox was a great American hero. Then, the mood in the States changed. There were antiwar demonstrations, and Viet Nam became a dirty word. The thought of the Fox was despicable.

So, after Viet Nam was over for me, I was told not to go home. The American government did not want the embarrassment of the Viet Fox, now no longer a hero, to go back to the States. News was that the Fox had died. And I found out that my wife had already remarried! At first I thought the whole thing was a joke. But they told me that for her safety, they had convinced her that I had died in the beginning.

So as soon as I thought my head was back on straight, I went to Israel and the fight in the Yom Kippur War. The U.S. paid me great deal of money to start somewhere else. And the Jews paid me well to fight with them. So, the money was good and the work was exciting. I tried to forget my home. I'm making light of it, but it took years to get over realizing that I was not suppose to go home.

Then I spent time in Lebanon, especially Beirut. The French government contracted me to work for them in Damascus and again in Ankara. After that Interpol enlisted me and the French particularly wanted me to work with their agents."

Michael stopped talking. There was a long, icy silence. Monica was not about to make any sound. Anything she said would be anticlimactic, she felt. So she sat quietly waiting. Michael turned from the railing.

"Come, Monica," he said as his thoughts came back to the setting on the balcony. "It's time for you to get some rest. You've got a trip.

My throat is dry. It hurts. Tomorrow early we'll head back to Nice."

Monica got up from her chair, not speaking, just looking at this strange man. She remembered the heroic stories about the Viet Fox. She was trying to remember what she knew of his disappearance, but nothing would come to mind. This was the man she had come to love. A man, she felt, she could never own, but only be happy to have when she could. At least now she knew who he was. She put her arm around his waist. He held her for that same moment. Then arm and arm they went out of the cool damp night and into the bedroom.

CHAPTER THIRTEEN
Nicosia

Michael was stretched out on the large comfortable sofa in the living room. On the stereo were the sounds of Tchaikovsky, while on the television the steady constant monotone of 24 hour news droned on. He was sipping Glenlivet and studying the latest reports sent to him on current subjects of world unrest.

Written reports were forwarded to him from all over the world, in local languages, but translated into English at Interpol France Control. He had two copies of every written report. One in the local language, and one in English. Depending upon the country, sometimes the reports were literal, in word by word, verb by verb translations. Even though the subjects were sensitive, sometimes he would look up and smile at the structure of a translated sentence. The verb at the end, or a passive verb in the place of an active verb, would cause him to pause. Sometimes he would have to interpret the interpretation. So occasionally he would attempt to read the report in its local language. Sometimes for necessity and sometimes for practice. Video tapes were usually included. Tapes gave him a first view of an insurrection or a terrorist attack, or perhaps only of a surveillance situation. In any case, even though retired, Interpol France wanted to keep him current.

The stereo sounds had just started into Mussorgsky's 'Night on Bald Mountain', a heavy Russian piece, when suddenly a phrase from the television pierced through the music. Like walking through a crowded airport with noise and announcements all through the terminal, and suddenly something familiar penetrates the subconscious and gets the mind's attention. He sat up and looked over at the screen. What he saw was the picture of a girl and what he heard was the name Carlotta Mourenux.

"...the skyjackers have landed in Nicosia," the announcer was saying. "These are the crew members. There are two hundred and fifty-two passengers in addition to these crew members."

Michael spun his body around and put his feet firmly to the floor, leaning forward slightly, peering directly at the screen.

"Carlotta," he thought, remembering then that he had not seen her in over a year. He wondered momentarily, as he had done before, if Carlotta and Monica knew each other. He did not always date flight attendants, but these two both flew for Air France. Carlotta is French and Monica is English. But they both flew for the same airline.

"...and two of the skyjackers are apparently the brothers of George Ibrahim Abdallah, presently in prison in Paris."

The language barrier slowed his comprehension. He had to think about the words, mostly because of the seriousness of the subject. He was missing a lot. Quickly he checked the BBC station, which was too sensational. Next the switched to the Armed Forces Network channel, which was more factual, but seemingly disinterested in the matter. He reflected on the general complacency of the Armed Forces broadcasting station.

As the U.S. Army announcer continued, Michael was able to put the story together. The skyjackers wanted George Ibrahim Abdallah flown to Nicosia where they would exchange the airplane and the passengers for his release. A picture of George was on the screen. Michael studied it carefully. There was something familiar.

Then, leaving the stereo and television still sounding, he freshened his neat Glenlivet and went up to the study off the main bedroom. As he climbed the stairs he thought again of Carlotta, and he remembered the things Monica had told him about terrorist training. He wondered what Carlotta was doing at that moment. Once they were very close. People used to think that they were 'in love', more than just lovers.

In his study he pulled files of terrorists, producing a picture of George. He studied it again. Then he pulled the files of Interpol international agents. There was a face that he was remembering. He was looking for a particular face. A face of one of the agents. Then he found what he wanted. He found Ryad. Although Ryad was of Syrian birth, he was an agent of the Interpol Middle East. Michael had worked with him in Beirut. He held the picture of Ryad for a moment, then he looked at the picture of George Abdallah. A plan was developing. They look a great deal alike, Michael thought.

Michael went out on the veranda, sipping the malt scotch and looking out across the sea. There were some possibilities of a safe rescue. If the Abdallahs got their brother, they just might leave everything alone. They might let everyone live. It would be in their interest, he thought, to show the world that they only wanted their brother, and that they were not irrational terrorist bent on irresponsible destruction. If he could get the brother to them, they just might take him, and scurry back to Syria. Then again, he thought, they might just blowup the airplane anyway. They might want to warn everybody. Don't mess with the Abdallah brothers. His plan, as always, would have to be to rescue the passengers. The lives of the Abdallahs were not important. '...and we never give in to terrorists...' Raspail had stated so often.

"This is the Apartment," he said when the line was opened on the other end.

"What can I do for you?" the Voice asked.

"Are you tracking the hijacking in Cyprus?"

There was a long pause, then the answer sounded somewhat disgusted. "Of course we are!"

"I want you to get Abdallah out of prison and fly him to Nicosia. I want you to locate Ryad el Ahssem, wherever he is, and bring him in." Michael paused a moment. He knew that others were gathering on the other end to hear his demands. "I want an airplane in Nice as soon as possible." He waited again. "And send an automobile now!"

The Voice responded, "Is that it?"

"That's all."

"We have alternatives already in motion." the Voice said. "We will consider your requests."

Michael hung up the receiver, took another sip of scotch and looked across the room at the television screen. Now the AFN was showing pictures of the crew. There again was sweet gentle Carlotta, he thought, a picture of her when she was hired in to Air France. How young she was then!

He changed his clothes and packed lightly for the trip, only the PPK and two extra clips. He checked to make sure one round was already in the chamber, then he inserted a full clip. They would fulfill his request. The car and the airplane would be there. They always fulfilled his 'requests'. The Voice would have followed through as soon as possible.

THe automobile was there, and when he reached the airport in Nice, the airplane waiting. Many times in the past they had gone through the same crisis routine. The Cote d'Azur Voice had come to understand Michael's needs. There was no interference. The disguised French corporate aircraft taxied out onto the runway, engines powered up and it was ready for takeoff. Nice Control cleared the airways. This was an Interpol France clearance, no obstacles, no delays. Michael sat back, alone in the passenger section of the airplane, thinking ahead about Ryad and the scheme he had contrived for the Abdallah brothers.

The flying time to the eastern portion of the Mediterranean was much longer than his usual casual flights from Nice to Paris. He had quite a bit of time for reflection and relaxation. It was the thrill of the chase that made him comfortable and at one with himself. He could not stand to sit idly by and watch such events unfold, bungled by others.

As they approached Nicosia in the hot afternoon, it was obvious that no other air traffic was allowed in the area. The IF aircraft, disguised as a French corporate airplane, was vectored directly in and finally came to rest some one hundred meters from the hijacked jet airliner.

Michael walked casually from the airplane across the parking pad and into the terminal. Those bristles of hair on the back of his head gave him to know that he was being watched and probably aimed at from the jet liner.

People, excited about the hijacking were everywhere, being pushed back as best the Cypriot police could do. In front of him, as he entered the terminal, was a group of serious men, two of whom looked somewhat alike. George Abdallah, who was on the left did not seem to notice the other man standing off to the side. His eyes were on Michael as he walked up. George and Michael stood staring at each other for a moment. From his position, Michael could see Ryad standing nearby, and he was pleased with the closeness of appearance of these two men.

"Get that knit cap," Michael said, gesturing toward the cap on one of the Interpol agents, "and that long black wind breaker," he continued gesturing toward the jacket on another agent. "Put those on Abdallah."

George Abdallah continued to look directly at him as the others pulled the cap down on his head and struggled to get his arms into the long black jacket. He stood very still, jacket collar pulled up and knit cap pulled down, only the middle of the face was showing.

Michael looked at his creation. There was George Ibrahim Abdallah, Marxist terrorist, standing directly in front of him. He reflected on the image before him. The cap was pulled down to the shoulders in the back and down to the eyebrows in the front. The black jacket was big enough to wrap around most of his clothes. With some concentration one could look directly at the face only. A brother could barely recognize him. And that is what Michael planned for. With a little luck, he thought, this just might work.

George never spoke a word and offered no resistance. It was as though he knew better. Perhaps he felt that he would really be exchanged. Somehow he should know better, Michael thought. This was going to be a very delicate maneuver.

They had been standing in front of the huge glass window on the second floor, a point of view which enabled all in the group to have direct visibility of the airfield before them. The skyjacked Air France jet was near enough for walking, but far enough away to have a complete solitary position on the parking pad. Everyone inside The Air France jet was probably watching the terminal, just as those in the terminal were watching the airplane.

As the two men descended the stairs toward the airfield doors, police pushed back crowds of waiting passengers, onlookers and media personnel. There was a quiet that came over the terminal. Some people whispered, explaining to others what they thought was happening. But mostly, unlike when Michael arrived, now the terminal was very quiet.

The two men walked out into the late afternoon sun, and stopped about thirty yards from the Air France aircraft. A figure dressed in black came out of the plane and descended the staircase. He waved an automatic weapon high over his head.

"George," he called out in Arabic as he came down the stairs and approached, "my brother! George is that you? Are you alright?"

"Yes, Emile, I am fine!"

George answered in that big brother tone, like trying to give his younger brother assurance and yet also trying to maintain a superior attitude. It was purely Arabic, but Michael was able to understand the body language and gestures and enough of the words to know what was happening.

"Good," said Emile, "I want you to come with us."

George felt the PPK nudge his ribs. Michael never took his eyes off of Emile, and yet he kept George clearly in his peripheral sight.

"What do you want?" George said in English He wanted Michael to understand. "I mean what is your term for getting me."

Emile began to move closer, casually shifting the automatic weapon from one side to the other.

"Stop," Michael said in Arabic. Then he continued in English. "One more move, one more shift of the gun and George dies." The skyjacking of the airplane was no more than a desperate attempt to get their leader back. "What do you want?"

"We want brother George!" Emile mumbled. "We want him now. If we don't get him, we blow the airplane."

They probably will anyway, Michael was thinking, but not until they get George.

"We want George, and he must have guns, and then we want that fast company jet over there," gesturing toward the plane Michael had come in on, "to take us all home." He held the gun high. "All the brothers united again. George must have a gun. We must have a car and someone to take us to the company airplane. We will not walk in the open to the airplane"

"I will speak with my superiors!" Michael said, turning George around by a strong grip on the upper arm and the PPK painfully lodged in his ribs.

"We're not killers!" Emile called out. "We just want our own lands!
I just want George back with us so we can be a family."

Michael never looked back. He knew better. The history of the Abdallah brothers was written all through the books on terrorism. They kept a low profile of identification, until each time they were safely back in Syria. Then they took credit for bombings, murders, innocent people blown up, all for the sake of their lands. All of Syria, Michael was thinking, as well as Jordan, Lebanon, and Israel. His neck bristled a little. He knew that Emile was considering shooting him and trying to grab George right there on the taxiway. But nothing happened. Emile was not stupid. Expert marksmen were stationed across the rooftops waiting for such an act.

Michael did not speak with his superiors. In fact, he spoke with no one, but he did give orders. He told an agent to get a car, a large one, and what he should do with the car. It was brought around to the Air France plane, and the agent, posing as the driver, left it at the bottom of the stairs with engine running. Michael watched from the terminal windows. He reached over and got an automatic weapon from one of the uniformed guards. The stage was set for the final Act.

When Emile had reboarded the airplane, he pulled his other brother aside. The passengers were huddled in groups throughout. They looked forward at Emile and the other Abdallah brother. Their eyes were frightened and pleading. At any moment any fanatic terrorist group could do whatever entered their minds. They would even blow up the plane killing themselves for some irrational radical purpose. Michael had a saying that 'one cannot deal rationally with an irrational situation'. One must deal equally in such cases, and if only to at least gain the status quo.

"They have brought a car for us," Emile whispered to his brother in his Syrian dialect of Arabic. "We will have the corporate jet to take us home."

"What about George?" the brother asked.

"He will be armed and ready to join us."

"What about the agent?" was the next question.

"He cannot do anything. He is only one against all of us, and he is afraid for all of these people." Emile looked up toward the faces crowded in the rear of the plane. "This is the plan," he continued, "when George returns, we put all the explosives on those seats over the right wing. It will appear as a gesture of good intent to the passengers. It will comfort them. I will explain that we are leaving, and that we apologize for their inconvenience and fear. I will tell them that we are leaving the explosives and taking only our weapons. After we leave, the Captain will immediately radio the tower and everyone will relax."

Emile shifted a little. He noticed one old man close by staring at him. He lit a cigarette then asked his brother about the man.

"He cannot hear us. He is deaf."

Emile looked at him again. The man's gaze was almost fixed upon him, without blinking. He shrugged and continued his plan.

"Then, when we get to George, we take the agent with us. He will be our hostage to get to the corporate jet. At the jet we get the engines started, then we kill the agent. The pilots in the corporate jet will be our next hostages." He paused a moment, drew on the cigarette and looked directly at his brother. "When we are ready to takeoff, we will use the grenade rifle and shoot that area of seats over the right wing. We will explode the airplane." His brother did not show any sign of reaction, so he continued. "When we get to Syria we will kill the pilots and keep the plane. Assad will be proud of us, Abba will be proud of us. We will announce to the world why we have done such a thing. It will be an act to right the injustices heaped upon us." He put the cigarette out against the cabin wall. "And soon Abba will make us all proud to be together when the world truly comes to understand our strength."

"George and the agent are returning!" one of the terrorists called out from the airplane doorway.

So the plan which Emile had conceived was put into motion. They laid their explosives on the seat, made numerous apologies to the passengers and filed out of the doorway one at a time. They spaced themselves for their own safety. As one would reach the bottom of the mobile stairs, then the next would start down. The whole group was never bunched together at any moment. The black Mercedes sedan was parked at the bottom.

Emile stood alone while the others, one at a time got into the car. He watched as the two men approached. It was the agent and his brother with the knit cap pulled way down and the heavy jacket, collar pulled way up, carrying an automatic weapon. Emile thought that the cap and jacket were strange the first time he saw his brother, and now he thought about it again. It was so warm in Nicosia. But he dismissed the thought, being more interested in the automatic weapon he could see. The agent had his hands in his jacket pockets. No doubt with a pistol in each, thought Emile. While they were still separated by some thirty meters, the two approaching men stopped.

"Fire the weapon, my brother!" Emile called out. "I want to see if it is real."

There was a long pause, then Michael pulled out the PPK in his left hand and aimed it at the man next to him. He nodded an affirmative gesture. The man brought the weapon up to his hip and fired a burst of bullets at a nearby tow truck. It was obvious that the weapon was real. The tires on the tow truck flattened with loud hissing sounds. Michael still had his right hand in his jacket pocket.

"Good," said Emile in English, "now you will come along with us as our hostage till we get to the corporate jet. We need someone with us until we takeoff. At the jet, if we need protection, we will have the pilots as our hostages."

"There are no pilots," Michael stated, "I am your pilot."

Emile shifted a little, glancing around the taxi area. "You are the pilot, also?"

"Yes," said Michael. His senses were fully turned-on. He knew exactly where each terrorist was located, who was in the car already, and those who were getting in or standing near. "But that won't matter."

Emile shifted again. Suddenly, he felt that somehow he had lost the edge. He still had all the cards, he thought. George has a weapon, they have a car to get to the jet, and they have the jet to get to Syria. No pilot, he realized. He would have to make the agent fly them to Syria.

"You will fly us to Syria!" Emile screamed.

"No," replied Michael. "No one is leaving here. You will join your brother in prison.

Emile broadened his stance for stability as he started to bring his automatic rifle up to a firing position. He was screaming in Arabic for his comrades to blow up the Air France plane.

Michael and the man next to him both moved at the same moment. Ryad ripped off the knit cap and raised his weapon as did Emile. But Ryad got off the first burst of fire. From where Emile was, the man in the black jacket still looked like George.

Large gaping wounds of blood suddenly burst all across Emile's chest. He reeled backwards dropping his rifle and rolling his head off to look toward the car. The last sight he saw before his eyes closed was his own brother George shooting him. The man was now firing into the automobile at the other Abdallah brother and his companions. The automatic weapon sounds were exploding into a deafening roar.

Michael had withdrawn his right hand, as Ryad raised his weapon at Emile. In his hand was a small electronic detonator. He pushed the button as Ryad turned his fire toward the automobile. The others were trying to scramble back out of the car when the explosion occurred. The black Mercedes with the remaining terrorists, inside and nearby, went up into a ball of blazon red and yellow flames.

A silence fell over the area for a few moments. Nothing moved. There was not a sound. Their nostrils were filled with smell of burning fuel. Michael and Ryad stood side by side watching the dead Emile and burning automobile.

Suddenly cheers and applause rose from the Greek and Turkish crowds who gathered on the terminal roof and walkways around the taxi areas. The crowds were cheering and yelling "Death to Terrorists!" Michael put his hand on Ryad's shoulder. By now the Cypriot police had crossed the tarmac and boarded the Air France airplane. They were now bringing the passengers down the stairway. The passengers and the crowds in the terminal were waving and cheering.

As the two men turned, Michael looked up to the airport director's window. He had had George restrained there to witness the ultimate act of his terrorist brother. George was being held by two guards, and his eyes were staring down at Michael. Michael, with Ryad beside him, looked up at the window. There would not have to be any words. George had seen it all. The justice of the courts would not allow for this man to be executed, so then one must execute his brothers.

As the two men walked through the crowds of people into the terminal, fire trucks were arriving to control the fire of the exploded Mercedes. They ascended to the second floor to meet with the airport investigator. Over the investigator's shoulder, Michael could see George still in the area, being held by the guards. The eyes of the two men met again, and they stared directly at each other.

"They were going to blow up the airliner!"

"What?" Michael responded, looking away from George. "What did you say?"

"The hijackers," the investigator stated again, "they were going to kill you and blow up the airliner." He was speaking in Greek. Michael could not understand him. The investigator realized what the problem was, so he began again in French.

Michael looked at him when he understood. "How do you know that?

I knew that they would. But how did you know!"

"There was an old Arabic man on the plane who is deaf. He read the lips of one of the hijackers. I think it was one of the brothers. As soon as they left the plane everyone moved the explosives to the back in one of the toilets. The Captain radioed the tower. Everyone went forward and got down on the floor and waited."

"What were they going to do?"

"When the corporate jet was ready, they planned to kill you and use the grenade rifles to hit the explosives they left." The investigator smiled. "But the passengers had already moved the explosives. The worse that the Abdallahs would have done, would have been to blow a large hole on the side of the plane."

'And I would have already been dead,' Michael thought to himself. He turned and headed over to George. The two men stood before each other for a moment. For Michael it was something he had to do. He had to stand in front of George Ibrahim Abdallah.

"Someday I will kill you," George said. "I will remember you, and someday I will kill you." He was speaking in French, slowly and deliberately. "It gives me a reason to live."

Michael stood motionless thinking about the terrorist acts George and his brothers had committed. He felt for a moment that he would like to have his moment to defy the courts and to cut the throat of George. He would not like to turn his back on this person. Someday George just might surface somewhere when he least suspected it. For a moment he thought that instead of Ryad, he should have taken George back down with him. He could have executed George along with the others. It would have closed the book on the Abdallah brothers.

"You are an American. I can tell. I can tell by your look, your face, your attitude. Well, Mr. American, in a few days you will remember me. Remember the bombing of Tripoli in the early morning in April."

Michael deliberately turned away. He knew that if he responded with too much interest George would shut up, and probably laugh. But if he responded with little interest, George just might try to impress him and keep on talking.

"Remember, Mr. American, your Statue of Liberty. Mohammed Abba Dabbus is going to make everyone remember the bombing in Tripoli."

Michael gave him a casual look of disinterest.

"You will see!" George continued. The guards started to move him away toward the stairway which was the route to the airplane awaiting George's return to the Paris prison.

"You will see, Mr. American." His voice was louder and more angry. "People in major cities all over the world will see! In London, Rome, Bonn, Madrid, Athens...they will all see!"

Michael shook his head and started to walk away.

"In Paris my people will free me at the same time." George waited for a reaction from Michael as the gap between the two men was widening. There was no reaction.

George screamed out, "I will kill you American! I will get free and I will kill. Remember your Statue of Liberty! Remember your Fourth of July. Remember the bombing of Tripoli! Mohammed Abba Dabbus will explode your Statue of Liberty! He will cause destruction in cities around the world!"

One of the guards twisted George's arm around and up his back. The man grimaced a moment in pain. Then he took one long last look at Michael, who had by this time stopped. Michael turned back around, facing from a distance the guards and George Ibrahim Abdallah.

"Monsieur."

Michael turned back to the present surroundings. An older man in uniform was approaching. This person was speaking French with a Greek accent.

"Interpol Europe is on the telephone for you, Sir."

"Tell them that I will call in later." Michael said. He was still feeling the high of the excitement. It was not time to start giving reports.

Ryad was moving off in another direction, and the two glanced an acknowledgement across the concourse. As best the police could, they had kept back the crowd, especially the news media. But now people were beginning to break through.

"Tell them," he continued in answering the old uniformed men, "that I have plans now. My business is not finished."

He hoped that it would satisfy their curiosity for the moment. If they thought that there was more for Michael to do, then maybe they would leave him alone.

"Can I help?"

It was Ryad. He had come back to where Michael was standing. He had overheard about the call from Interpol Europe, and he wanted to at least offer his assistance. It was obvious that Michael's mind was far off somewhere else.

"If you'd like, I'll talk to them."

"No," Michael replied, looking past Ryad out across the airplane taxiways, "let them stew in their own confusion." His mind was already back to the comments by George. 'Remember the Statue of Liberty - Remember the Fourth of July'. Then he smiled at Ryad. "Thanks, but I think they should know that afterall, I'm not on active duty, and I am retired."

Nearby were some of the Air France crew. They were talking with police detectives and generally trying to relax after their ordeal.

Michael turned to the older uniformed man who had told him of the Interpol European call.

"I need a telephone to call the South of France. Get me maps of North Africa, and especially Libya." He paused. "Ask Air France for any maps of air routes for Tripoli. Get me tourist maps or anything you can that might be of Tripoli." He paused again, this time thinking about Marcel. He had to get to a phone and talk to Marcel. July Fourth was not too many days away.

Michael pulled out the Tripoli pass, turned it over and read the statement on the back. "Remember 1986 April Remember."

"Monsieur?"

Michael looked up. It was the older uniformed man.

"We have a telephone room set up for you. All very private. We are already working to gather maps and information for you. It may take some time. Are you staying tonight in Nicosia?"

Michael nodded.

"Where will you be, Monsieur, so I can get these things to you?"

Michael started to answer, but a voice from behind him spoke out.

"He will be staying at the Amelia Hotel, where the crew is staying."

Michael felt someone's arms around his waist from the rear. There was the slight fragrance of a perfume he had known. She snuggled up close to him. He could feel her body tight against his.

"He will be in my room!" she continued.

Michael squirmed around, his waist still inside the grasp of her arms. It was Carlotta.

CHAPTER FOURTEEN

Raspail

The next day, back in Juan les Pins as he paced anxiously about the Apartment, Michael kept mumbling to himself that Marcel should have the messages by now. He had called and left a number of messages. There was no return call yet. It was obvious that he needed to speak with the Interpol France as soon as possible. But he wanted to leave his phone line open for Marcel. Marcel might not be as persistent as he, he thought. It was Marcel who was originally anxious, now he felt the pressure. Then after Beirut, Marcel wanted to forget the whole thing.

Finally, Michael stopped, stared momentarily at the receiver. He grasped the handset quickly as if to cut off any incoming connection. He punched in the security code to jam any listeners and then he dialed the number for the Voice.

"This is the Apartment."

"Yes, good morning."

"I want to speak to Raspail, immediately!"

Even though Michael had secured the line, it was that the Central Command must initiate the call from the country Command Post to assure further security. One must call on the local level to request a contact on the higher level.

"Excellent job in Cyprus. We all pulled for you, you know. We felt..."

"I must get through to Raspail immediately." He shifted in his stance. "Abdallah told me what is happening!"

Sounding a little annoyed at being cut short, the Voice questioned. "What is happening?"

"Don't delay me." Michael's voice made no attempt to pacify the person on the other end. In fact, it was meant to emphasize displeasure. "Get me through to Raspail."

"I may have to screen this need," was the reply. The Voice was exercising his authority.

"Listen carefully," Michael said, "you get me through to Raspail immediately or I hang up this goddamn phone and go on my own."

As soon as the Voice attempted to respond with authority again, he slammed down the receiver. The Voice listened to the sound of the dial tone on his end.

Michael went straight to his bar and poured two fingers of Glenlivet, neat. He drank back part of it, clenched his teeth, knitted his brow and finished it. The warmth of the scotch caused a slight, rumbling sensation in his empty stomach. He looked up at the crystal and brass clock on the side table. Only moments had passed since slamming down the receiver.

Suddenly it rang that strange European telephone ring. A sound that he never got used to. It always startled him. Marcel or Raspail flashed through his mind, or even Monica he thought, as he lifted the handset.

"Yes?"

"Amerigo?"

"Yes!"

"Raspail here. It is urgent! Is that true?"

"Yes it is!"

In all of the strength of accomplishments, and for all of his conquests, he always felt subordinated by people of powerful authority. Not as adversaries, but only as associates for a common objective, yet it made him feel a twinge of nervousness. Raspail was the Commander Interpol France. Only a few times over the years had they spoken. It was understood that the Commander Cote d'Azur, the Voice, was his direct connection. That chain of authority should never be violated. He had now summoned Raspail with demand. As he began to speak there were quick thoughts of Marcel trying to call in and questions of what the 'Voice' had told Raspail.

"It's Abba Dabbus," he said. "George Abdallah has revealed to me a plan of Abba's for the Fourth of July."

"Yes?" was the response.

"Abba has sent agents to certain major cities. At the Fourth of July ceremonies in New York harbor, it sounds like he plans to destroy the Statue of Liberty..." he wasn't sure of some of this, but it fit, and he had to make Raspail listen, "...and other international cities are targeted. It is as though..."

"That was an excellent job that you did in Cyprus, Amerigo."

"Thank you, sir." This time he was comfortable waiting for a response. Besides, having Raspail make such a statement pleased him. Occasionally he appreciated the approval of those whom he held in high regard.

"Obviously we are somewhat aware of your doings. During this recent period, your activities seem to have accelerated." Raspail spoke in fluent Queen's English, having attended, in addition to his French education, certain schools in England, Italy and Yugoslavia.

"What you're now saying begins to make some sense." Raspail continued. "It will, perhaps, put together some missing pieces. We have permanent surveillance on certain Arab individuals..." there was a pause, "...and only recently did some of them, all at the same time, leave their usual places of hiding and head for major cities. Athens, Rome, and London are a few that I recall having been mentioned."

The pause was longer this time. Michael waited, without interrupting. Raspail was assimilating what information he presently had.

"You mention Colonel Mohammed Abba Dabbus. Do you think maybe someone else is behind this?"

"It sounds like an Abba Dabbus plan." Michael replied. He started to continue, but Raspail continued instead.

"...but what about Abu Nidal? Or maybe Habash or Salim el-Khoury! Maybe the madman himself, Abu Akram!"

"No, I don't think so." Michael said. "The pieces are beginning to fit on my side as well. What George Abdallah said fits into my puzzle. I've been met by a person who is originally North African. Marcel Akmed. He took me with him to Beirut..."

"This Marcel Akmed," Raspail interrupted, "has provided you with certain useful information. Understandably, you have hesitated to believe it. We have attempted to make a connection with this Akmed."

Michael wondered at how much knowledge Interpol France really had. If Raspail had any, then Michael would want to make sure that they had it all correct.

"What abut Syria? Could it be Assad!" Raspail had dropped the thought of Akmed, and was continuing down the roster possible terrorist choices. "He wants to rally Lebanon and Jordan to his cause. This could make him a hero!"

"No," Michael said again. "I'm sure it's Abba. I'm trying to get in touch with Akmed at this moment. There may also be something he doesn't realize he knows that will help me."

"I am going to ring off now," Raspail said, "but I will be back with you shortly. Do not leave the Apartment until we have talked again. I will exert some pressure in certain areas for more information."

With no further conversation, the telephone line between the two was disconnected. Michael, who did not like to wait when there was action to address, began his pacing again. His stomach was still empty, and it made strange sounds. Another Glenlivet was not the answer, but trying to fix some food at that moment did not seem like the right solution either.

While he waited, knowing that it would be at least a few minutes, he tried to locate Marcel again. This time, along with the statement that it was urgent for them to speak, he told the answering service to tell Marcel to come immediately to the Apartment, prepared to leave the country to complete his original mission.

Finally Michael pulled out some salami and cheese, and made a sandwich on french bread, lathering the salami with hot, dark mustard. This time, instead of scotch, he washed it down with a Stella Artois beer. Beer has nutrition and food value, he always told himself.

In the middle of the last bite, the telephone ran. He picked up the receiver, swallowing and trying to clear his throat.

"Yes!"

"His father," Raspail said, continuing as though they had not disconnected earlier, "was the Minister of the Treasury for Libya, or actually, Treasurer for Abba. Abba had indicated that he had to be removed from office for reasons of mishandling funds. We suspect that is not true. He was not the kind of person to mishandle funds. He was framed and sent to his death."

"Framed," Michael mumbled. "By whom?"

"Unknown," was Raspail's reply. "But before he died we do know that he tried to contact Marcel with certain information. Information that appears to be coming together in the form of the Fourth of July celebration."

"Would Abba have told him of his plan?"

"It would not be so much that Abba told him, but more that Abba boasts a lot. He has a big mouth. Perhaps old Akmed only overheard the plan. However, we now think that he knew of it, and he wanted Marcel to contact someone to prevent the bloodshed."

"Me?"

"No, I don't think he really knew of you. But there are others who do know you. It would seem that information has been purposely fed to Marcel with the idea of getting certain specifics to you."

It was a long pause. Michael took advantage of it by washing down that last bite with the beer.

"There seems to be some reason to get directly to you, Amerigo."

"Me?"

"Yes, you! Don't be modest, Amerigo. You are one of Interpol's best agents."

There was a pause and Michael thought he should acknowledge the compliment. But then at the same time, if Raspail truly felt that, then leave it and don't act subordinated at this moment.

"Your trip to Marseille was monitored. The Baader-Meinhof thing seems to be a nuisance. But," and there was an air of lightness in Raspail's voice, "you have certainly handled that situation very well."

Again he almost reacted to acknowledge the compliment, but he held his tongue.

"We have problems with agents dealing with the Red Brigade, the Sign of the 13, the Lisbon Liberation, and so on. Some have not fared so well. Some of the agents of Interpol Europe, I am not pleased to say, have been recruited into the terrorist groups. That also you have recognized and dealt with. Friedriche was an example of just that problem."

Again Michael was feeling a little prideful and personally very good about himself.

"But about the Fourth of July..."

"Yes," Raspail said. "In Marseille when you met the French officers, it was obvious to us then that they were mere pawns. Someone set them up for you to use. They would get you into Beirut. They would get you to Girod Said. We did know who was there to help you." Raspail cleared his throat. "Said was a good man for us. On more than one occasion he helped our agents."

"So why didn't someone tell me!"

"My dear Amerigo, to tell you would have put you off, and you would not have had any further interest. Besides, we were not sure, and until almost this very moment, too many parts have been laying around carelessly. A messy way to run any business. It was too early for us to think someone wanted you. At first it looked like this Akmed was on a fishing expedition."

Michael thought about that for a few moments, but could not be sure what his reaction really would have been. He should have been told.

"Sometimes we are lucky to assist our agents. Sometimes we don't find out until too late. It was actually the Baader-Meinhof that caused us to keep an extra eye on you." There was a pause again. "Do you understand?"

"Yes!" Michael's tone was firm, but a little resentful.

"We were not sneaking about keeping an eye on you. But with the Phoenix training group about, it was my idea to maintain a distant surveillance in case it got out of sorts!"

"About the Fourth of July...!" he interjected, accepting the explanation and waiting to proceed with the subject.

"Yes," in his tone, Raspail seemed to come back the subject. "In Beirut we were prepared to assist, but it all came together. And especially with those Abba passes you have for access to Libya."

Michael started to comment on the passes, but thought better and passed on to the main subject. After all these years he still wondered how they knew so much. But, he had learned a long time ago to cooperate and do his own job. Somehow they always knew, and somehow, that thought could be both comforting and discomforting. Anytime they thought that he had become expendable, then he could easily be expended.

"I am trying to reach Marcel to leave as soon as possible! I want him to go with me. If I need to get inside Bab Azizya, he will be of great help."

"It appears to us that the plan is to be put in motion on the Fourth of July. It is to be in concert with the U.S. celebration. The Middle East agents discounted the information which they had received. It was thought to be once again the ravings of Abba. But now, what they have gleaned is that there are ten prime world cities where terrorist attacks will take place. The first is to be the destruction of the statue on Liberty Island in New York."

There was a long pause. Raspail stopped to speak with someone on his end of the line. Michael could hear the voices, but not the words. Soon he returned to continue.

"An historical monument is to be destroyed in each city. Abba has reserved the right to command the attack from his Command Post inside Bab Azizya." Raspail's delivery was stilted, almost like he was reading the information. "As each location is readied, a transmission will be sent to Tripoli. The groups will standby and await the command from Abba. This is to be a verbal command so that Abba has the personal pleasure of directing this worldwide destruction."

"He is to be in the Command Post during all of this?" Michael said it, but ended with a question. "Abba will be in the Command Post!"

"That's the way it's coming in to us. We do not know all of the cities yet, nor which monuments. Reports are that we will have all of this shortly. When the transmissions take place, we should be able to pinpoint the location of each group."

"Are you saying that regardless of what I can do in the Command Post, you will be able to move quickly on the groups."

"...if necessary." Raspail added. "Once we have the transmission frequencies, we will monitor all the activity and act accordingly. Some of these individuals will not be allowed to return to protective hiding."

"What am I suppose to do with Mohammed Abba Dabbus if I find him in the Command Post?"

"The ultimate objective is to prevent the destruction and to discredit Abba. If that can be done, then the task will be a complete success. We would allow certain individuals to get back to protection only because they would reek havoc within the Abba terrorist organization."

"What do I do with Abba?"

"That depends upon how it goes for you. I have no idea what he expects to accomplish by this tactic."

"You are thinking rationally," Michael interjected, "about an irrational situation."

"You don't have much time," Raspail continued, "you can only be there on the night of the Fourth. If you arrive too soon, then you will find nothing. Someone has been feeding information to you for a purpose. Follow that lead!"

"Am I suppose to think that this someone is a neutral person?"

"Not necessarily. It could be Assad, trying to make sure that Abba gets caught. Then Assad will try to be the undisputed terrorist leader." There was a pause again. "So to destroy the Command Post too soon will only alert the agents around the world to proceed." He paused to emphasize a point, "...and with added vengeance. In reviewing the reports which we are receiving, it is becoming more evident that perhaps we should all be on alert."

"You want me inside Bab Azizya as an agent or consulting?"

Michael knew that the first would implicate Interpol France if he failed, whereas the second would give him free rein to do as he pleased. *Maybe that's why I'm supposed to be retired*, he thought. *They get more out of me now than before.*

"Whichever you prefer. However, I would like to see you go in as a 'consultant'."

Michael was quiet for a few moments and Raspail respected the silence. He was thinking quickly back through the events which had lead to this telephone conversation.

"We might have an ally in a person very close to Abba," Raspail said, pausing to make certain that he had Michael's attention. "Have you ever heard of Colonel Mahkmuud?"

"Not really. I think Akmed has mentioned him as a friend of his father. Mostly what I know of him is through the papers."

"We will not contact him, but if you find him in Tripoli, he might be useful. Ask Akmed more about him. He has always acted as a very rational and sane person, gathering a number of strong supporters to follow him. He is probably as close to Abba as anyone. He professes to want to lead Libya in peaceful negotiations with the rest of the world." There was that

Raspail pause again. "Reports that we have, indicate that Assad does not trust him."

"I want an Air France clearance into Tripoli for Marcel and me, with no questions. I want clearance to get out as soon as we're finished."

"Of course!" Raspail responded. "We will have the aircraft equipment for you, but you must pass through Libyan security in both directions.

I need not remind you of the Abba passes you have."

"If the passes work, then we'll be back through Tripoli security and onto the aircraft. I want extra Air France equipment ready to roll, no later than midnight. Put on extra service."

"Extra airplane!"

"A small commercial jet, announced as an extra flight to handle the load out of its next stop in Tunisia. Understand!"

Excitement was beginning to well up inside of Michael. He wanted to continue to be respectful of Raspail, but he had to move, and he could no longer think about his 'game plan'. It was now time to put the plan in motion. As he was listing his needs, the thought of going without Marcel crossed his mind. If the time got too dangerously close, he would have to go without his guide.

"Yes, Amerigo," the Interpol France Commander said. "We will proceed to close in on those who have taken positions for additional destruction. As soon as your work is done, we will take them. They have come out of hiding, and therefore they belong to us."

Raspail's voice was calm and almost too patronizing. Michael was intently listening to tone and inflection. It could be his 'swan song' of the Interpol, he thought. They could be sacrificing him in this mission. Afterall, he was already retired and he had refused certain missions in the past year. Perhaps this was their excuse to 'unsupport' him at the last moment.

"Raspail," and he paused. "I have done my work well!"

"Yes, you have."

"I want to be able to report to you on the Fifth of July from here in the Apartment."

"Yes, Amerigo. I understand. But do keep in mind, that if you fail, then our effort of capturing the others before they can complete their tasks becomes gargantuan."

"Marcel can get us inside and we can do the job. But," and his voice grew stronger, "we will need to be out of there immediately. Nothing unusual! Air France routinely changes schedules and equipment. We cannot wait for the sunrise."

"I will say that I expect the best! We have not interfered with you in the past, and I do not intend to change that course of action. Obviously, I have other pressing matters, as well." Raspail paused. "At this moment, yours is the most important. If you fail, there will be a long period of revenge and antirevenge, etc, etc. If you are successful, but fail to escape, then your identity will also cause a long period of turmoil."

"Yes!"

"If you do not succeed, and are not on the Air France aircraft, which will not depart before half after midnight..." That long Raspail pause again. "...then we'll send in additional agents to bomb Bab Azizya. If you are out and on the flight, we'll do nothing. Rounding up the others will be an easy procedure."

"Yes!" Michael almost nodded affirmative.

"In their confusion and anger, they will reveal anything that we don't already know." The authoritative pause. "The rest of the world will not know anything of this incident. Do you understand? You will have set it so that we are not involved, and there will be no recourse."

"Sir," Michael interjected, again feeling that sensation of superior to subordinate. Raspail's direct, firm, outspoken attitude gave Michael a confident feeling. "I will find Marcel, ...and we will arrive late in the afternoon flight in Tripoli."

"Very good, Amerigo." Raspail seemed lighter and pleased. "God's speed and good hunting."

As the phone was hung up on the other end, the dial tone droned in, and Michael thought about old black and white World War II movies where the Brit's used such cliche's to send men into battle.

"...or into bottle," he mused as he picked up the Glenlivet and poured another neat shot. Now he felt much better about Raspail's conversation. It was comforting to know, that although he first resented the idea of Interpol agents watching him, it was very nice to have a backup.

As he poured a second 'two fingers' he thought about the Baader-Meinhof and the possibilities of their interference in this mission.

Perhaps he should have asked Raspail to proceed to intercept them if they attempted to interfere. But then, he thought again, better not to ask. Raspail will handle it. This time he will handle Abba as best he sees fit.

Just as he raised the glass to sip his drink, the phone rang. Finally, it was Marcel. He spoke briefly and to the point, explaining his plan. Marcel was being caught up in the excitement, and offered no resistance.

As he hung up the phone, Michael thought about Abba again. He would like an encounter with Abba. Tomorrow they head for Libya, and this time in Tripoli, the choice would be his.

CHAPTER FIFTEEN
Liberte'

A s the two men crouched across the wide street from the Compound, Michael looked up at it with deep interest. It had been sometime since he had seen Bab Azizya. For some reason it seemed smaller to him this time. Perhaps because the last time he was here it was his first view of the awesome stone works which housed Mohammed Abba Dabbus, his family, and the elite personal corps for the dictator.

So far so good, Michael was thinking. His adrenalin was pumping. The Abba passes had worked perfectly for them when they arrived at the airport on Air France. Security was laxed as the guards were talking and laughing about girls and fly traps. Some Captain in charge was called, but he found nothing out of the ordinary. The Abba passes appeared to be legitimate. He shrugged and waved them through. The two were allowed free access into the city of Tripoli.

As trucks passed in front of them, heading into the Bab Azizya Compound, the two hid back to avoid headlights. There was some bombing destruction around the Compound, but not as much as Michael had thought there would be.

"How long ago since you were inside?" Michael sort of mumbled and whispered to Marcel.

"It was almost ten years ago, but I still know the way." Michael looked at him and he continued. "I went to the Compound almost every night. My father worked so long and so late. That was the only way I could see him."

Without looking from studying the Compound again, Michael asked another question. "What about Colonel Mahkmuud? What do you know about him?"

"My father's dearest friend," he replied shifting from one foot to the other. Marcel was a little annoyed. The tone of the question was deeper than just a curious question. "My father was always pleased to see me. He would laugh when I snuck down the air vent into the Command Post."

Michael turned to face Marcel. He wanted to see the expression. "... and what about Colonel Mahkmuud? Did he laugh?"

"Sometimes he was not there. It was better then. Father and I could share those moments, man to man. But when Mahkmuud was there, he would frown sometimes, but usually he did not seem to mind."

"Usually?"

"Occasionally he got upset about my appearances." Marcel was looking toward the Compound, past Michael's inquisitive face. "Mostly he was upset about security. Especially coming down the air vent directly into the Command Post. If I could do it, he felt anyone could find their way in." Then he looked at Michael. "The air vent is supposed to be their secret escape in case of an attack at the entrance to the shelter."

"Why didn't he forbid you to come down.? Why didn't he close the escape hatch and build another way out?"

Marcel only shrugged. "I don't know. He just didn't."

"That was ten years ago." Michael continued. "What do you think he might be like now?"

"I don't know." Marcel looked at Michael. "What I mean is, he was always tolerant of me then. But I never did really know him. He never came to the house for visits. He knew that I came down the air shaft to visit my father. It was a long time ago! The last few times I visited, I came in through the front entrance. I was older then. By invitation, I could visit my father in the evenings. Then I was sent to prep school, and I never came back to Tripoli. That was ten years ago."

The two men turned their attention back to the street and to the Compound. Seventeen trucks had passed, turning slowly into the main gate of the Compound. It was obvious that this was a night of great importance. The people of Tripoli, Marcel had learned from posted handbills, were warned to stay off the streets and in their homes. From above the walls of the Compound lights shown brightly, filling the night in the immediate area. Occasionally a truck horn or engine could be heard. It was too far away, and the walls were too high to hear voices.

Years before, Michael remembered, when he visited Tripoli and he had met Abba Dabbus. Abba was a loud mouthed dictator then, threatening Egypt with invasion and flexing muscles at his southern neighbor Chad. But he had not reduced himself to these new levels of inhuman terrorism. Now it was death without reason, only for his own glory.

Michael reached back and touched the PPK as he thought of Abba. His visit then was also a short visit. But he had had the opportunity to take out Abba. Interpol instructed him not to do so. The timing was bad and Abba would probably have been martyred. A replacement might have been worse.

"Let's go!" he said tugging on Marcel's arm. "We don't have much time."

The frequency of trucks passing was much less now. At the next break the two men bent low to the ground and hurried across the street to the base of the compound walls.

For the next few minutes Michael followed, checking about them, as Marcel led the way. He found the area which although not designed for that purpose had acted as the drain for heavy waters from rain. The rain was not too often, yet when it did come, the hard surfaces of the Compound could not absorb the water. At first, when the Compound was built, it filled with water like a wading pool. The Libyan engineers then picked away at the base of the inside wall near the lowest point in the courtyard. Water would then flow downward and onto the streets surrounding. But that would be someone else's problem. Over the years, the rain water washed away the poor construction soil, and the picked drainage area developed into a tunnel large enough to allow a person to crawl up amongst the jagged rocks and enter the courtyard. This was to be their entrance through the broad outer walls of the Abba Dabbus fortress.

As they crawled up into the courtyard, Michael wondered if it was Libyan mentality or just human negligence that would build this massive impenetrable fortress and yet overlook the drain tunnel.

It was good to have Marcel along.

Inside were trucks and soldiers everywhere in the courtyard. The main interest was near what appeared to be the main living quarters. Soldiers were carrying out boxes, not large in size but what seemed very heavy. It took two men to carry each box. The boxes were loaded into the trucks. From the arrangement of vehicles, certain trucks were being loaded and aligned to leave. Other trucks waited in queues to pull up and receive their loads.

Even with all of the soldiers and the bright lights, the buildings and walkways were mostly in shadows. Marcel led the way along one row of outer buildings. Certain buildings were part of the massive structure, where supplies and soldiers were actually quartered inside the walls. The Compound was built high above the surrounding streets of Tripoli. Walls, very thick and very high, extended still upward from within the Compound. The open area inside the fortress was the size of a football field. Certain buildings were built away from the walls, one such being where most of the activities flourished.

Michael knew that the main headquarters, the Command Post, was located below the courtyard with only one entrance. The entrance was situated down a staircase where one would first enter a fortified stone room on the courtyard level, then descend to the main room. It was because of Marcel that they could avoid any such confrontation with soldiers. They would descend somewhere else, through the air vent.

As they silently moved their way along the dark shadows, two soldiers coming from the building with their heavy load stumbled and the box fell to the ground. The wooden slats of the box gave under the impact. Gold bars tumbled into the dust. Michael immediately took a firm strong grip on the fleshy part of Marcel's upper arm. The two soldiers dropped to the ground trying desperately to gather the bars back into the broken box. Another soldier, apparently of authority, appeared. He looked about, then ordered them to stack the bars against the side of the building, in the darkness. From their hiding place, the two men could see that there were six gold bars. By the way the two soldiers carried each bar, Michael estimated twenty to twenty-five pounds per bar. That would be a hundred and twenty to a hundred and fifty pounds of gold, Michael thought. Each soldier made three trips to the dark side of the building while the other soldier-of-authority watched, occasionally looking around. There was so much confusion, none of the other Libyan military noticed the gold or the three soldiers.

When the trips were complete, the three stood close together, talking, and then they disappeared into the darkness where the gold was hidden. Marcel and Michael were close enough to hear the muffled report of a gun fire twice. They watched the soldier-of-authority reappear in the light, alone.

Michael still had the fleshy part of Marcel's upper arm when he spoke softly.

"Easy my friend. That was about a million dollars in gold." He gave a little extra squeeze of the arm. "You just can't trust anyone these days."

As he felt the tension in Marcel relax, he then relaxed his grip. After pausing a moment longer to make certain their direction was clear, they proceeded along the way, working themselves toward where Marcel remembered the air vent.

Then it was Marcel who reached for the fleshy part of Michael's upper arm. Abba Dabbus appeared near one of the trucks, talking with one of the officers. Michael's eyes narrowed and muscles from his jaw to his ankles tightened.

"Easy my friend," Marcel whispered in his ear.

They watched soldiers bow and nod and move aside as Mohammed Abba Dabbus walked between the trucks, inspecting the work and shouting out orders of corrective action. He ruled by fear. Marcel tugged on the arm of his comrade and they began their movement toward the Command Post again. Michael glanced back thinking that still the timing to kill that bastard was not right. It had to be done from within. The Arab terrorist hot spots would have to self destruct from within their own leadership. Death to Abba Dabbus would only strengthen their commitment.

His memory was still good, and Marcel located the air shaft. Michael went first. As they descended the narrow shaft to the lower vent grill, they could hear the voice of one man obviously angry and talking at some other person. The grill at the bottom was hinged, providing an easy entrance into the back of the Command Post. One voice was predominant but occasionally another voice could be heard, responding to the first voice. The language was Arabic and the voices spoke quickly. Michael crouched behind one of the equipment racks and tried to understand the conversation.

"One of them is upset. He was supposed to sit at the console," Marcel whispered to Michael, "and he's angry because the other person was sent down by Abba himself."

Slowly and quietly they moved around to one side, very low behind the rack to get a view. The one talking person was pacing back and forth waving his hand. His uniform was khaki with no rank, while the other person was seated at a large console. He had the rank of Sergeant with additional ribbons and the insignias of Abba's elite corp.

Before them was a huge backlit plexiglass map of the world. Ten cities were identified, and each had dual light bulbs, green and red. Some of the green were already lit. The soldier at the console sat with a microphone. As they listened, he watched the map, and another green light came on.

"You take the one at the console," Michael whispered. "I want the anxious one. He'll help us!"

Before Marcel could digest what Michael had said, his companion was out from behind the rack. He grabbed the pacing man, spun him around and held him between himself and the Sergeant.

"Don't move!" he said in his elementary Arabic. It was then that Marcel saw the blade of the knife held tightly against the soldier's throat.

Marcel came out from behind the rack, approaching the Sergeant slowly. Both men eyed each other as the gap between them closed. The Sergeant sat still, both hands on the arms of the swivel chair.

"Ask him how the command is given!" Michael said to Marcel. He pulled the sharp side of the blade across the soldier's throat. A trickle of blood appeared and rolled slowly down the neck. Marcel was fascinated. He thought he might see a person have their throat slit.

"Ask him about the command!" Michael said softly again. "Tell him to speak slowly." The man squirmed, but Michael held him across the chest with one arm and the knife blade tightly pulled against the throat.

Marcel looked from the Sergeant and followed Michael's instructions. He began his dialogue with the soldier.

"Each green light comes on when reception is made from that city," the frightened soldier mumbled.

"Shut your foul mouth!" the Sergeant said, acting as though he might rise up out of the sitting position.

Michael looked at the Sergeant a moment. He wasn't sure what all the words were, but he knew what had been said. Then after a pause, he looked past the Sergeant at the lights of the cities on the plexiglass map. The cities had names taped above them. There were the ten. Marcel looked over also, while the Sergeant sat still again, staring at Michael and the soldier.

"Then what?" Marcel asked.

"Then," the soldier continued, "when all are received...Abba is suppose to come down and give the command."

"How are they received? How can you transmit?" Michael asked. He was understanding enough of the Arabic to get the general idea of the plan.

"Russian freighters are in the Sea. They have open channels to receive and send for us."

"What do you send?" Michael asked. He squeezed the throat. "...and speak slower." He was having some difficulty understanding all of it, yet he knew Marcel was getting it all.

"Abba himself will come down and send the final command."

Michael pulled the soldier a little tighter and raked the blade across his throat again.

The soldier made a gurgling sound.

"Why do they need a command from Abba?"

"It is Abba's idea. Abba wants to make the command. Or in case Abba Dabbus changes his mind," the soldier responded, trying to shift in his position.

Suddenly there was the loud sound of a gun firing. The sound reverberated throughout the room. The soldier in Michael's arms lurched backwards as a bloody mass appeared on his chest. Marcel hesitated only momentarily before he leapt forward and grabbed the large Russian revolver from the Sergeant.

Michael stood for a moment holding the dead soldier upright in front of him. Then he let the man slide slowly to the floor. Marcel had the Russian revolver and was looking back and forth from Michael to the Sergeant. He had no idea what to do next. He had no idea what Michael would do.

"What if we prevent Abba from giving the command? Can you send a command?" he asked Marcel. "The answer to quit and come home?"

"I could send the message, but," and he looked directly at Michael, "my Arabic is long out of use. Someone might detect the French accent."

Michael looked at Marcel a moment, then over at the Sergeant. He knew that what Marcel said was probably true. Even if the transmission was weak and no French accent detected, there might be cause for doubt. The Russian freighters would get a strong signal. Someone there might get suspicious. Acts of terrorism would still be carried out. It had to be someone authentic, like a Sergeant of the Abba Elite Corp.

"It looks like it's going to be you and me," Michael said in English, looking directly into the stare of the Sergeant. There before him, looking over the seated man was the plexiglass map. Michael glanced at the clock. The Sergeant held his hands tightly on the chair arms, staring at the large Russian revolver which Marcel had laid on the console, almost within his grasp. So as to ease such thoughts, Michael reached over and removed the revolver off to the side.

"Explain to him what I want him to do," Michael said to Marcel, who by this time was standing next to the man looking at the map. "He understands English, but I want to make sure he knows what I want him to do! I want him to abort the mission. I want him to tell them that Abba has quit the cause and has left for Jofrah!"

Marcel explained in his native Arabic exactly what Michael had said. When all the signals were received he was to open the master microphone switch, and then instead of waiting for Abba, he was to give the command to abort the mission.

The Sergeant's eyes widened even further. He looked at Marcel and shook his head in a negative response. Marcel repeated the instructions.

"Abort! Abort! Mission cancelled!" Michael said loudly. "Abba Dabbus denies us all! He escapes with the gold! Abort mission!"

"No!" the Sergeant yelled.

Michael grabbed the man's hair and shoved the PPK barrel against the tender back of his neck.

"I knew you understood what I said!"

"No!" the Sergeant yelled again, trying to pull away toward the Russian revolver.

Michael smacked him on the side of the head with the PPK, jerked his head back and shoved the barrel into the his mouth.

"Say Yes!" Michael said, looking straight into the Sergeant's eyes. "Say Yes or I blow your fucking head off!"

Marcel had backed away a step. He was not sure what would happen next. If the PPK did go off he did not want blood and gore spewing all over him. A glance at the map showed that there were only minutes remaining. Almost all of the green lights were lit.

The Sergeant sat upright and rigid. His hands still gripped the chair arms. His eyes were wide as he stared up into Michael's face. The PPK was shoved in his mouth up to the trigger guard.

"Say Yes!" Michael said softly again. As he spoke he pushed the PPK a little harder and pulled the man's hair. The man's head, though it could not move much, again indicated negative.

"I'll do it," Marcel said. "I can pull it off!"

"No," Michael responded. "There are too many relays listening. Even the freighters will interrupt if anything sounds wrong." He looked at the Sergeant a moment. "Get down on the floor!" he said, jerking the man straight out of the chair and down on his knees on the floor. "Pull your goddamn pants down!" The Sergeant hesitated. Michael hit him again on the side of the head. The man began pulling his pants down.

There was electrical wiring laying about the room. Michael grabbed up a couple of long sections and went to work. In a moment the Sergeant lay on the floor trussed up like a holiday turkey. His hands were wrapped and bound behind him, while his legs and knees were pulled up tightly under his chin. He was on his side with his pants pulled down, exposing his dirty brown buttocks. Michael put the microphone down next to the Sergeant's mouth.

"Tell him again, in Arabic, what to say!" he told Marcel.

Marcel stepped over him, and again explained what was to be said. Bound securely in a fetal position, he was beginning to sweat. His heart was pounding and he breathed deeply. But again he shook his head in the negative.

Michael reached over and picked up the Russian revolver. He stooped down next to the man's face. His smile was very relaxed with a confident grin. He ejected one shell from one chamber of the cylinder. There was a deliberate pause.

Marcel nervously looked up at the green lights on the map, and then looked back at Michael, afraid that he might miss something.

Michael carefully rotated the cylinder of the revolver until he had the empty chamber where he wanted it. The sergeant stared at the gun.

"Tokyo light is on!" Marcel said in a nervous voice. "There goes Madrid!"

"Respond!" Michael said calmly and deliberately. He kept his eyes on the Sergeant's face.

Marcel was leaning over the console, trying to keep his eyes on the lights and still trying to watch Michael. His attention left the map momentarily as he watched Michael make his next move. What he saw was Michael grab the Sergeant's buttocks, and with as much force as he could muster, shove the barrel of the Russian revolver into the man's asshole. The Sergeant screamed! Marcel looked away, then back again. The Sergeant was stiff against his wire bonding, still screaming. Tears rolled down his cheeks.

"Say Yes!" Michael said again. This time he spoke louder and with more intensity. He shoved the revolver deeper into the man's anus.

The Sergeant clinched his teeth tightly, grimacing as he did. Again he shook his head negatively.

Michael pulled back the hammer on the revolver. There was a long deliberate pause, then he squeezed the trigger. As the hammer fell on the empty chamber, the startling sound of the 'click' was so loud it reverberated off the walls of the room. Marcel felt the pain in his own anus.

The Sergeant wept openly now. He was sobbing and shaking. His arms were still tightly bound behind him, with knees wired up and around his neck. Blood was oozing from the wire cuts as he pulled against the bonds. Deep between the cheeks of his buttocks was the barrel of the Russian revolver. Michael calmly pulled back the hammer once again.

"One city to go!" Marcel stated emphatically, wanting to watch but not wanting to actually see what would happen.

The Sergeant was almost to hysterics. His body convulsed as he sobbed and cried. More blood began to flow from the wire cuts.

"That's it!" Marcel called out. "All signals are in! All lights are green!" As he spoke he moved slowly away from the console and away from the two men on the floor.

"Now speak slowly," Michael said. The man looked up at him through his tears. Michael wiggled the revolver, causing the barrel to penetrate deeper.

Suddenly a voice, in Arabic, spoke from speakers in the room. The voice was strong and it sounded authoritative. The Sergeant stopped whimpering and listened, wide-eyed.

Then without hesitation, the Sergeant spoke into the microphone. Michael did not understand the first voice, and trying to do so, missed what the Sergeant was saying.

Michael reached for the revolver handle. Marcel raised his hand and spoke.

"It's alright. The Sergeant aborted the mission. He said what you wanted. He said that Abba Dabbus has deserted everyone and escaped with the gold to his Jofrah Headquarters."

Michael stayed down next to the Sergeant with a finger still on the trigger. He would not back off until the transmission was complete. The Sergeant was repeating the message. The tears and crying, Michael was thinking, would only add to the authenticity of the transmission. The sender was grieving over the abandonment by his almighty leader Mohammed Abba Dabbus. The Russians would be listening and since an abort could mean disaster, they would be quick to disengage themselves and proceed with innocent freighter activities. Michael was picturing the reactions throughout the world. All further transmissions and receptions would be cancelled. Somewhere out there, he thought, Raspail would be in control now.

At the last word from the Sergeant's mouth, Michael switched off the microphone and stood up. The muscles throughout his body had been tense and now he ached a little, especially in the knees.

"What was that voice?"

"I don't know! He told the Sergeant to abort the mission. He told the Sergeant to do what you said."

Michael looked around the room. He stared momentarily at the speakers. Why would someone in the Compound have helped them? Why would someone who must be the Sergeant's superior have helped them?

"What now?" Marcel asked, as though all after this was anticlimactic. All that they had planned for suddenly left him. He had really never thought past this most important moment.

"You go up the entrance." Michael answered. "Abba might still be coming in. Check the yard above. If you see Abba let me know. We'll wait a bit...then we go home." He was still thinking about the voice.

"They'll destroy Abba Dabbus," Marcel said confidently. "I'll bet they're already contacting each other. I know these people. They're trying to get to Libya as fast as possible."

"That may be true," Michael said as he returned the PPK to its resting place in the small of his back.

"What do you mean that it may be true?" Marcel asked, a puzzled look on his face. "We did it! Just like we planned!"

"Well," Michael said as he stepped over the trussed up Sergeant and sat back in the console chair, "I learned a long time ago that when everything goes this smoothly, something is yet to happen. Take your friend Mahkmuud for instance. What's his role in all of this? Was that his voice on the speakers? Why haven't we seen him? ...even in the courtyard."

Marcel shook his head toward Michael. He felt they were heroes having just done the impossible. They had actually prevented worldwide terrorist destruction. He looked down at the man on the floor. That poor soul was still bound up in wire, wrists and ankles bleeding, and that Russian revolver, with the hammer cocked, was still shoved up his butt.

Finally Marcel agreed. He would go out and have a look around. He wanted to find the 'voice' if possible, but more important, he wanted to see what was happening up top. Certainly, he felt, that if Abba Dabbus was still there, word must be arriving about the aborted mission. If so, what confusion there would be now!

Michael suggested that he take the dead soldier's side arm just in case. Marcel was not a violent person, but at least he thought, he could defend himself if needed.

In the quiet of the room, with only the continued sobbing of the man on the floor, Michael looked a little closer at the plexiglass map and the panel. Electronics had always fascinated him. His father wanted him to be an electrical engineer. 'Electronics is the way of the future'.

After sometime of looking over the equipment, suddenly something in the room changed. Michael continued to look at the panels of switches and knobs, but now his senses were strained to the rest of the room. The sobbing had stopped.

"Well done, Amerigo!" spoke a voice in English with a French-like accent.

As he recognized the 'voice', he realized that it was the same that he had heard from the speakers. Also he felt the hardness of a gun barrel being placed against the back of his neck.

"Mahkmuud?" Michael asked, not attempting to turn around.

"Yes, Amerigo," was the reply. "I have come to complete my task." He moved to the left side of Michael, still holding the pistol on Michael's neck. "I have brought us some cognac to celebrate the excellent job you have accomplished." He put a snifter of cognac on the console before Michael, keeping another for himself. "And now ease out the gun you have in your back belt. Do it with your right hand."

Michael followed the instructions carefully. It was obvious that this person knew a great deal about him. Why does everybody know so much about me? Possibly, Michael thought, he could take this man with a sudden lunge directly at the pistol. 'He who moves first, wins'. But he was sitting and Mahkmuud was standing with a pistol in his neck.

Mahkmuud took the PPK and backed away, stepping over the trussed up Sergeant on the floor. From the floor the Sergeant looked up wide-eyed, not crying, but looking quickly from one to the other and back again. A strange sight it was. One man sitting at the console, another backed away holding a pistol, and a third wired in a fetal position with the barrel of a revolver stuffed up his butt.

Colonel Mahkmuud released the clip of the PPK. He slowly ejected each shell, every round making a resounding metallic sound as it dropped to the stone floor. Michael sat half turned watching the bullets bounce on the floor. When the clip was empty, Mahkmuud reinserted the it into the PPK and laid the gun on the console.

"A toast to our success." The Colonel lifted his snifter. "First to the excellent execution of your effort, as I knew you would, ...and then to mine which will take some time for me to complete, but for which you have helped me prepare the foundation."

As Michael lifted his cognac it was apparent that the Colonel was moving far enough away to avoid a sudden attack. But, in spite of that, Michael knew that there would be time to foment a plan. It sounded as though the Colonel wanted to talk.

"There are extremes in our world of terrorism," he began slowly. "There is the Syrian strong man Hafez Assad. He is a sophisticated professional, and he plans his moves very carefully with no suspicion toward him." He deliberately sipped his cognac for a moment. "There is the loud mouthed Mohammed Abba Dabbus. He wears his actions on his sleeve, bragging about his murders and killings. He is an embarrassment to the Arabic community. But then," he continued, "consider the second in command in both cases. Hafez has Abu Nidal." He looked at Michael, but got no reaction. Michael knew Abu Nidal, but he wanted to hear Mahkmuud's story.

"So," he continued after a long pause, "Abu trains the killers and carries out the plans for Hafez. He acts like the front man. He is the fanatic! But he only carries out the plans made for him. So there! We have one seemingly sophisticated world leader with a fanatic madman as his puppet. And here in Libya we have a wild fanatic world leader who has a seemingly sophisticated man as his second in command. Abba rants and raves, and authorizes acts of murder while I try to keep his image as clean as possible."

There was silence for a while. Michael watched as Colonel Mahkmuud seemed to be thinking of specific instances.

"Hafez calls the Syrian acts cases of Arab revolution, and he can blame Abba when something goes wrong. Actually he plans a new nation for himself, one which would include not only Syria, but also Jordan, Israel and Lebanon. Khomeni, who is as irrational and destructive as any of them, does it all for the sake of religion." He paused again. "Any may by his own stupidity make it possible for Assad to occupy Lebanon in the name of peace. It will be the beginning of the Assad empire."

Mahkmuud raised his glass toward Michael as he continued.

"However, now with the confusion which you have just created, all eyes will be focused on Libya. It is the beginning of my finest hour!" While Michael eyed the Colonel and sipped on the cognac, the story began to slowly unfold. No doubt Abba Dabbus was a crazy madman with no regard for human life. Abba planned the terrorist attacks to render death and destruction throughout the world. During this murderous confusion his plan was to move to a new secret headquarters in the Jofrah region, until he would once again be summoned to lead the terrorist offense. Abba knew that he would have to hide because of his fear of world retaliation on Tripoli. However, the more destruction he caused, he felt, eventually the more the West would fear him and beg to pay homage to him. The gold was his greedy possession, and it would finance his plans everywhere.

"But now," Mahkmuud continued his story, "with the aborted missions, the terrorists will be after Abba and when they catch up to him, they will kill him. Unless..."

"Unless you intervene and prevent his death," Michael interjected. "At that moment it makes you a curious unrecognized leader. You could gain the confidence from everyone. And you could save Abba in case you needed him later."

"Very good, Amerigo," Mahkmuud marveled. "But I suppose that is why I chose you to carry out my plan."

Mahkmuud explained how he had been working on the plan for some years. He never knew how it would come together, but he knew that he could make it happen.

After the April bombing, Abba decided to attack the U.S. at the unveiling of the Statue of Liberty. He ranted and raved about warplanes and ships and a full scale war on the United States. Abba had lost face, and he had to recover it someway, regardless of lives and people. That was Mahkmuud's opportunity to begin to make his play. With Abba screaming and shouting, preoccupied with anger, Mahkmuud moved in even closer in the role of advisor and leader of the troubled Arab groups. He calmed Abba and developed the Fourth of July plan, telling all, much to Abba's pleasure, that the plan was brilliantly devised by Abba.

"I allowed the information to leak to Marcel's father. I knew Marcel was living in the south of France, and I knew that his father would get the information to him."

"Why Marcel?" Michael asked as he warmed the cognac glass in the palms of his hands. "What could Marcel do to help you?" Michael was asking the questions but already anticipating the answers.

"Because, Amerigo," and Mahkmuud grinned at that point, "the best of the Interpol European Corp lives in the south of France. I left nothing to chance. I even prompted Marcel's father with enough clues to simplify Marcel's search for you, my good friend. I paid contacts in the south of France to point you out."

Michael looked up at him. The cognac was warming, in contrast to the cold atmosphere in the room.

"Then, armed with the facts, you, my good friend, would simply come to Tripoli and save the world from such a madman, and prepare the way for my entrance."

It was essential, Mahkmuud continued, that someone outside prevent the attacks from occurring. In the event that Abba himself might survive the terrorist leaders, then there could be no suspicion on Mahkmuud. The plan stalled when Abba became concerned about Marcel's father. The long time advisor to Abba was showing signs of mystery. He was late to meetings, quick to leave, and then he was caught trying to contact Marcel. Abba was furious that anyone would contact a Westerner, which is what Abba had grown to feel about Marcel. Marcel was never pure Arab in heart and soul, according to Abba. Marcel's mother was an American.

"So then I quickly engineered a meeting between Marcel's father and Girod Said. The journalist was free to travel as he pleased, and he had known Marcel as a child. I realized that Abba might kill old Akmed before he could fully connect with his son. And Abba did."

But, he continued in his story, Girod was kidnapped in Beirut before he could get to Marcel. So, Mahkmuud provided information about the French officers in Marseille to leak to Marcel. They could get him to Girod, even if Michael did not accompany him. Mahkmuud would protect Marcel on his Beirut trip. The French officers were to be eliminated to maintain silence. They were paid well. They were so greedy they had no idea what was happening.

There was one major obstacle which was out of Mahkmuud's control. The Baader-Meinhof training group selected Michael as their kill. That interfered with the plan, Mahkmuud explained. Only once did the Colonel have to intervene. In Beirut he had Girod killed after the information was transferred so that he would not break under further interrogation.

"At the precise moment a person completes his task, he is expendable." Mahkmuud said, firmly. "Either he will think too much, or be tortured too much. But he might say something damaging." Mahkmuud was pacing as he continued through his story.

The problem of intervention, Mahkmuud pointed out, was when the Lebanese police grabbed Marcel and Michael. That set them up for the Baader-Meinhof who had been tracking Michael all along. It was Mahkmuud who designed the plan for them to escape from Beirut. Once they had recovered the Abba passes, he had cleared the way for them to leave Beirut. Then he felt the plan was ready.

"I have come to learn how good you are at your craft," Mahkmuud said, looking at Michael. "But a little assistance at the right moment was my insurance to get you out of there. It also helped to convince you of the seriousness of the story. In case you could not abort the mission, I decided it was too close, so I commanded the Sergeant to cooperate."

Michael held up his cognac, nodding in the form of a toast.

"In Nicosia I knew I had the right man. I was anxious for a bit, but then I knew you could pull this off. The Abdallah brothers got too excited and acted too soon. They wanted their brother out before it all started on the Fourth of July." Mahkmuud lifted his glass again. "And George Abdallah helped by explaining the plan to you. I had him filled with information, and he was bursting to tell you, just to get revenge. An excellent plan. Just in case you didn't understand the plan, it was best to have George tell you in a burst of anger and hate."

"Have you killed Marcel?"

"Marcel will soon be in his father's bosom." He paused to look at Michael, who in turn gave no expression. "It was essential to my plan to endear myself to all that I catch Marcel and turn him over to Abba."

"Dead?"

"Foolish Libyan patriot that he is. I watched him come out. As we do all such traitors in part of the world, I will have his tongue cut out." Mahkmuud sipped his cognac.

Mahkmuud went on to explain that to complete his plan, Marcel, who is weak, will be the convincing factor for Abba and his staff that he and Michael broke the code, and got into the Compound through ways known only by him. Marcel will be very sincere, and it will convince the terrorist squads that Abba is truly the danger to the Arab nations. If Marcel hesitates, he will be killed instantly.

"Abba is already getting messages back. I told him I would personally come down here and investigate." As he spoke he gestured to a large leather satchel near the door. "I will explode the entire Command Post. I have a transmitter to send the signal to detonate the trigger device. The destruction of Bab Azizya will also act as a gesture to the outside world. To the Arabs, and especially Abba, it will do well that I found, inside the Command Post of Bab Azizya, an American expatriate turned French Interpol agent. So you see, you are also very helpful to me because of your American heritage."

"With Abba and his elite corp immobilized, then the terrorist groups will turn to Mahkmuud for leadership and direction. I have always acted as a subtle connection between all the Arab factions and Abba. They will follow without hesitation. If Abba should survive, then he too would eagerly give control to his friend and confidant of many years. Abba is really a frightened coward." Mahkmuud was smiling as he spoke.

"I like the acronym the Western newspaper use for Abba. Mohammed Abba Dabbus, the MAD leader of Libya."

"What about your man on the floor?" Michael asked, gesturing loosely with his cognac glass. "Certainly you knew he would resist pain, and that he might not give in."

Mahkmuud laughed and looked down at the trussed up man on the floor. Then he looked over at the dead soldier near the equipment rack.

"The dead soldier is my man," he said. "I picked him because he would not have resisted. I picked him for his cowardice." He turned back to the trussed up sergeant. "I got a little concerned when I found out that Abba had sent one of his own Elite Corp to the Post to help my man."

Without hesitation he kicked the handle of the Russian revolver, sending the hammer forward against the firing pin. Michael flinched slightly as he heard the muffled sound of the shell go off and saw the top of the man's head explode outward, splattering blood against the wall under the console.

Michael shifted slightly and stood up to face the Colonel.

"So what's next?"

Mahkmuud continued with his story, toasting himself as the new peaceful world leader. He would rather lead civilized western nations than live in the deserts of Libya. And now he would have such an opportunity. A report had already been sent out that Mahkmuud has come to the rescue and he has his old friend Abba under control. While he expounds of love and peace throughout the world, he will secretly build a strong and well disciplined terrorist organization which will eventually bring the world to its knees. In the final hour, he will rule over a world of confusion and destruction.

"It is written that a world saviour will come from this part of the world, in this time of history. I am only making certain that the scripture is somewhat helped along. This is my destiny."

Everyone will have listened to him and believed him peaceful, and that he too was fighting terrorism, he was continuing to explain. His world popularity will grow, and leaders of all nations will follow his advice and leadership.

"The western world is ready. It is the prophecy, especially of the western world. They will be ready for the survival of the world by one man!" he said, grinning at his own pleasure. "I am that saviour. It is my destiny!"

Suddenly the main door burst open and Marcel came hurriedly into the room.

"Michael!" he was saying loudly. "Michael..."

Mahkmuud was startled. He swung around toward the doorway and fired point-blank into Marcel's chest. Marcel reeled backwards against the doorframe, clutching his chest, looking wide-eyed at Mahkmuud. The eyes were pleading and confused.

In that moment, Michael made his move. He bolted forward and grabbed up his PPK, turning as he did to face Mahkmuud. The Colonel was confused. His plan for Marcel was disintegrating right before his eyes, and Michael was making a move for the empty PPK. Mahkmuud turned to face Michael.

Michael's motion was controlled and very smooth, knowing that he would have only one chance. He released the brandy snifter as he picked up the PPK in his left hand. Moving his right hand over under the heel of his left, he brought up the PPK, cocking the hammer as it came up to eye level.

Mahkmuud was quickly trying to recover. Now he was wide-eyed, bringing up his U.S. 45 toward an angle to get a shot at Michael. He knew that he had emptied the clip, and he knew that he had to kill Michael now!

But his reaction was too late. The PPK was leveled directly in his face and the trigger was squeezed ever so smoothly. Mahkmuud heard the hammer click into place, but he never heard the sound of the gun firing, as the small hole suddenly appeared right above the bridge of his nose, in the center of his forehead. A much larger hole opened out of the back of his skull as he staggered backwards, moving only on nerve reactions. Silence! Then there was the sound of Michael's snifter glass finally hitting the stone floor and shattering.

Michael stood for a moment, looking down at Mahkmuud. He released the empty clip and replaced it with a full one from his belt. He was satisfied that the Colonel was dead. His next thought was of Marcel.

"Marcel," he said softly as he stooped down next to his friend. "Marcel."

Marcel opened his eyes slowly. There was blood all across his chest. The breathing was very slow and very weak.

"Michael, my friend. We did it! Are you all right?"

Michael nodded. Marcel is worrying about him at this moment, he thought.

"I'm sorry to leave you here. You can find your way home."

Michael nodded again. He was looking down into Marcel's eyes. So many times he had had this moment with friends before. So many times he had been the focus of disaster, yet it was always those around him who suffered the most.

"The Beast is dead, Marcel. We got him," he muttered, saluting Marcel with the barrel of the PPK to his forehead.

Marcel never spoke again. He had probably not heard the last few words which Michael said. But whatever his final thoughts, Michael thought, he was at peace with himself.

As he looked around the room, he reflected on Marcel, and the brief friendship. It was always the excitement of the chase which brought people together with him.

He lifted Marcel into the chair at the console. Then he took the soldier's side arm from Marcel's dead fist. Carefully he aimed the gun and fired, making another larger hole in the same place as the PPK hole in Mahkmuud's forehead. Then he placed the pistol back in Marcel's hand.

"Today, my friend, you are the only world hero. You have killed the madman Mahkmuud, who has planned terroristic destruction all over the world. I will leave the gates of Bab Azizya open for the people of Libya. They will come to find you." He stepped back from the console. "There are those in the Arab world who are sensible, and they will revere what you have done. There are a few who are radical and they will despise you. No one will know that I was even here. We will leak the story of what has happened. The day is yours, my friend!"

Michael carefully mounted the explosives from the satchel up under the back panel of the radio receiver. The explosives were well hidden. He looked at the detonator transmitter, then returned it to the satchel. Today he would not explode the Command Post, but someday he might want to come back and have the option. Then the transmitter would be his means. Abba will return, he was thinking, and someday the 'timing' will be right.

As he picked up the satchel and reached the doorway to leave, he looked about the room one last time. The soldier was dead near the console, a huge gaping hole in his chest, Marcel was slumped over the console controls, the Sergeant's body was shredded from the lower back of his neck upward, leaving no head on the uniformed shoulders. And there was Colonel Mahkmuud, lying backwards across the floor with a hole in his forehead, just above the bridge of his nose.

Michael saluted Marcel again, muttering, "You acted alone, my friend, God bless you!"

By now he knew the trucks and soldiers in the courtyard earlier would be well on their way to Jofrah. He mused, Abba would be much more concerned than originally planned. Let the newsmen, politicians, and military sort this out, with a little help from Interpol.

Upstairs in the cool of the evening he looked around the silent courtyard, so filled with activity earlier. Now there was not a sound. There were a few vehicles parked about, probably those that would not start, and there were lights from certain buildings, but there were no people, not even guards on the walls.

Michael had plans for the gold bars as he walked openly across the courtyard to where he had seen them hidden. The leather satchel would come in handy. Certainly he should not leave such treasure about.

That soldier would probably come back later to collect his hidden cache. No one could be trusted these days.

Stepping over the two dead bodies, he managed two bars into the satchel with the transmitter and the satchel onto the back of a jeep. The remaining four bars were stacked in an empty machine gun box and placed on the floor of a jeep. He shorted the ignition wires and started the engine. With his Abba Libyan pass, he thought, worse case he could check all the bars right through to Nice. On his way out, he made certain to leave the gates to Bab Azizya wide open. It would be good for the people of Tripoli.

Part way through the backstreets of the city, he again thought of Marcel. It seemed at least a fitting burial ground for him. The place where he had played and now the place where he died.

In spite of the posted warnings by Abba Dabbus for the people to stay indoors all night, they were beginning to venture out into the quiet night. No soldiers and no speeding jeeps. They were curious and they were concerned. Michael watched as people came milling about him and the jeep, passing on both sides, moving slowly toward the Compound in the central section of town. Word was spreading that Abba had left and Bab Azizya was open and deserted. He turned his attention back to his mission. It was time for him to continue toward the airport. It was time to leave Tripoli.

CHAPTER SIXTEEN

Laissez Les Bons Temps Roules

A s he sat quietly reading the Herald and sipping on the Campari, which Misser Joe kept fresh and replenished, he wondered whether he was actually reading the newspaper. His mind wandered about thinking of the last few days, of the last week. It had been good for his rusty bones, but then again, and he grinned a little as he thought about it, the beaches of Juan les Pins were much more attractive and certainly more appealing. As he looked up, across the tables, he remembered the day Marcel came to the cafe. He remembered how embarrassed Misser Joe was to introduce them.

There was nothing much in the newspapers about Libya. Some news had gotten out about Abba spending time in Jofrah with his Elite Corp. News about Bab Azizya had apparently been suppressed. He wanted to read about the attempted worldwide terrorist attack, and maybe find Marcel Akmed's name mentioned. It must be Interpol, he was thinking as he scanned the pages. His talk with Raspail was brief. Everything at Interpol France was busy and hectic. Raspail was pleased, and promised to be back with him soon. In thinking back through the activities in the Command Post, he was trying to picture what could be happening in Tripoli.

Very slowly, a shadow passed over him. There was the presence of someone before him, and he looked up from the newsprint. A tall, well tanned blonde stood before him with an unlit cigarette in her hand.

"Bon Soir," she said.

Her blonde hair was long, below her shoulders. She wore a cutoff strappy T-shirt, and was obviously not wearing a bra. Her breasts were large and firm, the nipples made perfect cylindrical obtrusions. The T-shirt was cut so short, that looking up he could see the lower orbs of her breasts, almost to her nipples.

"Bon Soir," she said again.

It was not a French voice, he thought. A foreign languaged person saying French words in a perfectly articulated speech. But whatever the language, this attractive body stood before him. A small leather bag hung from her shoulder, pulling one of the straps of her shirt to the side. Below the well tanned mid section she wore a micro khaki skirt, halting just below the curves of her buttocks, at the top of her sun-browned bare thighs. Right above the belt of her skirt, looking out directly at him like a one-eyed cyclops, was her navel. But all of that was just in a glance, and he would have to look down to see if she had sandals or bare feet. He looked up into her blue eyes. She must be six feet tall, he thought.

"Do you have a light?" she asked in English, holding the unlit cigarette in an awkward manner. Now she cocked her head slightly and let the long blonde hair fall off to one side.

"No," he said, still gazing into her eyes. "I don't smoke." Maybe for just that fleeting moment, at least, he wanted to have a light.

The eyes he saw were crystal blue and penetrating. Even in the setting sun behind her, glistening off of her blonde hair, he could see into the eyes.

"Vhat a pity," she responded with the heavy accent, "I had hoped to share a light with you," and she leaned forward, "for the evening."

Misser Joe, in his ever attentive way was there, lighting her cigarette, nodding at her and smiling at him, hopeful to have provided some quick and responsive service.

"I am Claudia," she said, seating herself next to him and flicking no ash into the ashtray.

"That's nice," he said.

Her voice was speaking English now, but it formed and pronounced the words as meticulously as it had in French. This person was not French or English.

"I am on holiday, and I have been looking for an interesting man." She was looking at his face. "Only now have I found such a man. Not a young boy! Only now have I found vhat I have looked for."

That peripheral training worked very well for him. Without gawking, he looked at her eyes and viewed her entire body. Great tits, he thought, and the blonde hair on that well exposed tan body. The Herald was put down slowly, folded as it went, and he sat back picking up the Campari.

"What do you want? His comments were said with almost a sneer. "Nobody just walks up, asks for a light and sits down like this."

"I vant to fuck you!" she said, leaning closer and again flicking no ash into the ashtray.

Now he looked at her for a moment, then away and around the cafe. This must certainly be a setup, he was thinking. This tall goodlooking gal comes up to him, makes moves on him, and now wants his body. He glanced around. The sun was almost set and lights were coming on. Enough for awhile, he thought. Not another setup.

"You vant to fuck me!" he said, sort of mimicking her sounds. She nodded. "Good, I vant to fuck you. But that's all. Just for the holiday. Nothing else!" His expression was blank and deadpan.

She nodded again, and sat back rounding her shoulders, thrusting her breasts upward toward him. Her face was filled with a smile.

"Nothing else!" she said. "I just go home, after my holiday, with the memory of an interesting man."

It had to be a setup. He was just sitting there, minding his business. No one would come over to him and tell him that he is interesting. He sat for too many years at the Juantibes Cafe without anyone ever doing this. The girls glanced, nodded and flirted, but they never came on to him like this. She couldn't even have seen him behind the newspaper.

"I've been vatching you all afternoon. For two days I've valked the beaches of Juan les Pins looking for you."

He looked at her again.

"This afternoon, vhen I vent to use the toilet here, I saw you! You had your face at the newspaper, but your mind and eyes were somewhere else. I vatched you. There was something deep inside, maybe vandering all over the world. And even as you turned pages, you didn't read the print."

He looked away. She's right, he thought. Maybe he did look interesting. Afterall he did take care of his body. He tried to look trim and fit. Maybe, under these circumstances he did look interesting. He relaxed a little and looked back at her. Great tits!

The conversation started slowly, mostly guarded by him and with occasional glances around the cafe. Their talk was trite, of trips and holidays, the South of France, sights to see, and some talk of other areas of the world. She was visiting on a holiday, and her time, she said, was getting near to return home to New England. A town in Maine was her home, ...and her ancestry was grandparents from Austria. As she talked about her family, he reflected on the sound of her voice, and the perfect words. The strong 'v' was replacing the 'w'. It seemed to make sense that her grandparents were from Austria. Maybe, he was thinking, it was convenient for him to believe that all this was true. Afterall, people are not always out killing other people. Sometimes people just meet, have a good sexual fling, and go on about their business. He was almost nodding the affirmative, convincing himself that what he was thinking was true.

Misser Joe was as attentive as ever. Every time a drink was near empty, he was there. After awhile, the Campari surrendered to Remy. She stayed with her drink. She drank chilled Jaeger Meister.

The sun was set, the sky was dark and the lights of the avenue were on, illuminating cafes and sidewalks. The lights served her well, Michael thought, brightening the blonde hair, twinkling the eyes, and causing the tanned body to glow.

"If we don't get up and walk a bit," he said, "I might fall off the chair." Their conversation and the Remy had helped him to relax. "Why don't we meander along the avenue to the Casino? We could do a few hands of Baccarat and see how our luck is."

"I know how my luck is," she said. "Tonight is my last night in France." His hand was on the table, and as she leaned forward, her left breast came to rest on the back of it. "Vhy don't we meander along the avenue to your place."

"My place!" He sobered momentarily. How could she know about his place.

"I mean, you must be staying here somewhere. Let's go to your place. I have roommates in my room." She leaned her body against his. "I told you vhat I vanted."

A moment of long hesitation and silence lasted between them. He glanced around the Cafe once again. Then it was time for them to leave and to walk along the avenue to 'his place'.

As he turned into the walkway, through the garden, holding her hand she was wide-eyed, smiling, and looking everywhere.

"I don't believe this place," she said once they were inside. "I really don't believe that you stay in a place like this."

She turned in the middle of the room. Her blonde hair tussled out behind her head as she spun around. The well tanned arms were straight out, her chin was up, head back, hair spinning outward, breasts thrust upward and legs spread as she turned and turned. Her micro skirt had inched up, and there were no panties. He sat on the bottom step of the wide stairway leading to the bedroom, watching her turn dizzily about.

"One more for the road," he said, crossing over to the bar. At this moment he felt a little more secure in the confines of his house. The memories of the last few days were behind him. He flipped a switch on the stereo and into the room came the sounds of Stan Kenton. Another Remy for him and a tall chilled Jaeger Meister from the bar fridge for her.

"Come on!" she said, grabbing his hand and pulling him up the stairway to the bedroom. "I vant to fuck you."

It was the way she said 'fuck you' that kept penetrating his lustful thoughts. It didn't sound right. All the other pronunciations were perfect, too perfect, even the 'v', but when she said 'fuck', it had a harsh different sound, as though it came from somewhere else.

"Oh my God," she said as she pulled him out onto the bedroom balcony. "Vhat a fantastic view!"

The lights along the boulevards of Cannes were bright. She could see all the way across the Golfe of Juan to the coastline of Cannes. A light breeze felt cool and refreshing as he stood on the balcony behind her. He took a deep breath. With all the Remy he had had, he hoped to himself that he would be able to perform. There was no conversation for quite sometime as she stood looking out across the water.

She turned toward him, pulling the strappy T-shirt up over her head. There was certainly no bra as her breasts stood out, erect and firm, no strap marks and no swimsuit marks.

He bent forward and kissed her left nipple, fondling it with his tongue. Then, so as not to deprive the other, he moved his mouth to the right nipple and kissed it.

"Just a holiday!" she said.

They moved back into the bedroom, dimly lit by the small bedside lamp. She unbuckled her belt and dropped the khaki skirt. Lighter bikini marks outlined the triangle patch of blonde hair between her legs. He looked at her a moment, then did likewise. First, he pulled his shirt off, being careful to conceal the PPK as he did. No need to alarm her. The gun, wrapped in the shirt, was carefully laid on the night stand. Next he unsnapped his shorts and stepped out of them. He stood in briefs, but now due to his anticipation, the briefs hid very little. It was obvious, he thought as he went through the checklist, that he was excited about the blonde hair, blue eyes, tan body, long legs, great tits and curly blonde patch. He pulled off his briefs and climbed into the huge master bed.

She reached back for another sip of Jaeger Meister. As she did, she picked up her purse from the foot of the bed. He watched and relaxed. She sipped the Jaeger Meister, and he watched her naked body. Her right hand slipped into the purse. He watched, arms propped up under his head against the brass headboard, giving him a better view.

"Ich bin Nummer Drei!" she said as she pulled the 9MM German sidearm out of her purse.

He sat up slowly, bringing his arms down as he did, controlled and even, so as not to make a sudden move.

"Ich bin der Fuhrer. Ich bin Baader-Meinhof."

In her right hand, she lifted the gun slowly up to an eye level position, bracing it in the cup of her left hand. Well trained, and well disciplined.

Michael was reflecting on how stupid he was. All of his training, and all the years of self-preservation. Once again he had let his penis get in the way. But even as he admonished himself, he trying to take charge of the situation.

'Bling! Bling!' startled the silent moment.

"Vas ist das?" she asked.

"I don't know," he responded, shaking his head, trying to act casual.

Here he sat, naked, facing the leader of the Phoenix Gang from the Baader-Meinhof. The one remaining number, number three. Always, he thought, that was his lucky number. He had forgotten what the 'Voice' told him. How could he? He tried to think how he had forgotten. What a stupid way to die! Anyway is a stupid way to die! The PPK was too far away, and it was wrapped in his shirt. The old Army 45 was wedged up under the frame and mattress, too far away. His excitement for the tall, tanned, naked body was past.

"Why me?" he asked, playing for time.

"You are an I5. We picked you a long time ago."

"But you don't have cameras..."

"I vill take a picture of you and show you dead!"

"Oh," he moaned loudly, "don't shoot me. Torture me," and he was almost yelling, "but don't shoot me. I'll do anything. Don't shoot me!" This time he did yell.

She backed a step, confused by his actions.

"I did vant to fuck you. You are an interesting man," she said. "I thought about fucking you first, then killing you." She smiled. "But I vanted you to vant me, and vithout having me, I vould kill you."

BALAM!

Her head lurched to the side, as blood burst out on the blonde hair.

BALAM! BALAM!

Again and again a gun sounded in the doorway at the top of the stairs. She reeled to the right, reaching upward and looking toward the doorway. Blood ran down the well tanned shoulders and across the upright firm nipples of her breasts as she landed backwards on the carpeted floor. She fell spread eagle, the curly blonde triangular patch of pubic hair was now covered by rivulets of blood.

"Hey kid," he said, leaning back against the brass headboard, "of all the gin joints in all the towns in all the world, you gotta pick my gin joint to come into on a night like this."

Monica stood in the doorway, in uniform, with arms lowered, but still the gun in her right hand in the cup of the left hand. She looked up from the body on the floor to him on the bed. He was grinning widely.

"You bloody bastard! I ought to take you out right now." She still had her arms down, as though they ached. "You would have gone to bed with her, wouldn't you?"

"Monica, my luv!" mimicking her accent. "I knew who she was all along. I had to lure her up here to get her in the open." He was still grinning. "You had to help me get her."

"You bloody lying bastard! You didn't know I was coming in tonight!" She dropped the gun and came over to him. "I don't believe a bloody word you're saying."

He pulled her toward him and kissed her mouth full and deeply, but still grinning. She pulled away. They sat a moment, and she looked over across the foot of the bed at the body.

Michael got up from the pillows, still naked, and went over to the body. He looked at markings on her arm. Then, while still stooping, he looked back at Monica.

"If you hadn't arrived when you did," he said "I may have had to go all the way. I was stalling." He looked at her and shook his head. "It would have been a tough duty, but I guess I would have had to do it." The grin was back. "Somebody has to do it!"

"You bastard!" she said loudly. "You bloody, bloody bastard!"

He picked up the phone from the night stand. "This is the Apartment." There was a pause. "I got number three. She has a name tattooed on her wrist. It looks like Eva Osric." He looked at Monica.

Michael waited for the pause and the reaction. And it came.

"Eva Osric!" the Voice said. "You bagged a big number three. Eva Osric, hmmm!"

"She's on the floor upstairs." Michael then continued. "I'm going to check into the Eden Roc. When I get back, have the place spotless."

Michael put the phone back into the cradle. Still naked, he took Monica in his arms and held her tightly. A moment passed, then he pushed her back slightly to see her face, and with a smile said, "Laissez les bons temps roules!"